HAP AND HAZARD
AND THE END OF THE WORLD

HAP AND HAZARD
AND THE END OF THE WORLD

Diane DeSanders

Bellevue Literary Press
NEW YORK

First published in the United States in 2018
by Bellevue Literary Press, New York.

For information, contact:
Bellevue Literary Press
NYU School of Medicine
550 First Avenue
OBV A612
New York, NY 10016

Library of Congress Cataloging-in-Publication Data

Names: DeSanders, Diane, author.
Title: Hap and hazard and the end of the world / Diane DeSanders.
Description: First edition. | New York : Bellevue Literary Press, 2018.
Identifiers: LCCN 2017005067 (print) | LCCN 2017021016 (ebook) | ISBN
9781942658375 (e-book) | ISBN 9781942658368 (softcover)
Subjects: LCSH: Dysfunctional families—Fiction. | Domestic fiction. |
BISAC: FICTION / Literary. | FICTION / Coming of Age. | FICTION /
Historical. | FICTION / Family Life. | GSAFD: Bildungsromans.
Classification: LCC PS3604.E75485 (ebook) | LCC PS3604.E75485 H37 2018
(print) | DDC 813/.6—dc23
LC record available at https://lccn.loc.gov/2017005067

Bellevue Literary Press would like to thank all its generous donors—
individuals and foundations—for their support.

This publication is made possible by the New York
State Council on the Arts with the support of Governor
Andrew Cuomo and the New York State Legislature.

This project is supported in part
by an award from the National
Endowment for the Arts.

Book design and composition by Mulberry Tree Press, Inc.

Manufactured in the United States of America.
First Edition

1   3   5   7   9   8   6   4   2

paperback ISBN: 978-1-942658-36-8
ebook ISBN: 978-1-942658-37-5

To Dick and Jane
and for Molly, Kris, Nora, and Ieuan

Author's Note

This is a work of fiction. Names, characters, places, and incidents, while based on fact, are partially products of the author's imagination and are used fictitiously. Therefore, resemblances to persons living or dead, to events or locales, while not coincidental, have resulted in this: a work of fiction.

As Edward Albee once said, "fiction is fact distilled into truth."

—Diane DeSanders

*How much more they might accomplish
if only they could talk to each other.*

—Jane Goodall

CONTENTS

HAP AND HAZARD
AND THE END OF THE WORLD

Lone Star Oldsmobile and Cadillac

"That's the ugliest thing I've ever seen," Daddy shouts, glaring across to the other car as if to pick a fight. "Just look at that piece of junk!"

We rotate our gazes to the maroon Lincoln beside us at the traffic light to the tune of Daddy's ongoing "What a pile of horseshit! The streamlining is all wrong! Just look at that line! Look at it, Jane, look at it!"

Streamlining. Stream-lining. What is that?

The three people in the Lincoln look over at us round-eyed, as if to say, What?

It's the end of summer now and car windows are down. Mama looks straight ahead out the front window.

"Please, Dick . . ." she says.

Daddy lets the Lincoln pull away first, urging us all to consider the car's rear end.

"Look at that!" He's yelling to Mama now. "They just don't get it! The whole thing is out of balance, no sense of proportion, absolutely no grace!"

I'm leaning out into the wind, looking, trying to figure out what *balance*, *proportion*, and *grace* might mean.

"The fittings are trash! They say you can't get one that doesn't have a right front door rattle! And you should see the dashboard! The glove box door doesn't fit! Parts are not flush! How could they let a thing like that leave the factory? It wouldn't happen at General Motors, I can tell you that! And what kind of an idiot would be seen in something like that?

Daddy believes in General Motors.

Mama glances back at me. "Please, Dick . . ." she starts weakly. But there's no stopping him now. Daddy hits the gas.

"And that color! Pretentious! And murky at the same time! It has no class at all! It doesn't know the meaning of class!"

A Studebaker glides by, and then he really starts to yell.

We power-roar past the Lincoln and the Studebaker in our shiny sea-green Cadillac, me still leaning out the window, pigtails slapping my cheeks, squinting back at the Lincoln and the Studebaker, trying my best to detect their inferior qualities. And what is the meaning of *class*?

I turn around and lay my elbow out the window, my face into the wind, the same as Daddy's, listening to everything said between the two of them, me in the back with Annie, our legs sticking to the warm leather seats.

Annie sits frozen, staring wide-eyed at Daddy like a small animal in danger. The baby, up front with the two of them, starts to fuss and cry. Mama's keeping what she has to say to herself.

Daddy keeps looking over at Mama, his chin thrust forward over the steering wheel, as if he's saying and doing all this for her reaction. But Mama keeps her face blank.

We've been at Brook Hollow Country Club for an early

dinner. Daddy's still talking as we pull into the A&W Root Beer stand near Love Field on the way home.

"But we just ate, Dick," says Mama.

"Well, I'm thirsty, Jane, do you mind?"

"No, okay, let's all have root beer." She opens her door. "Besides, it's hot!"

He's still talking as we all get out. We always get out to eat or drink, as our cars are always for sale. Mama says everything we have is for sale, and she's lucky she's not for sale, as well.

We drink our root beers standing up, the creamy foam running down the heavy cold mugs. Annie spills hers down her dress and cries, and Mama cleans her up. No matter how hot it gets, Mama looks cool. We hold the frosty mugs to our faces and arms. It's September but still almost as hot as summer now, when everything both cold and hot is sticky and dripping into drive-in dust.

Daddy's still talking about how General Motors management is so sharp, so forward-looking, so ahead of the pack, how the new Oldsmobile will sell like hotcakes in the fall, such a step forward, so streamlined, such great new colors. How he hears everything from a designer up there, a pal of his from General Motors Training Institute, what a draftsman this man is, and what a slick guy. How this is only the beginning of the new things to come.

"Jane, am I boring you?" Daddy says all of a sudden, putting his face up close to her face. She moves away.

"No, Dick. I'm listening. I'm always listening."

Annie jumps up and down, saying, "Tell ME, Daddy, tell ME!" She flings herself onto Daddy's legs in a way I can't do, as I'm too big, and you never know when you might accidentally knock him off balance, or hurt his bad feet—and she's looking up in the way I'd like to be able to throw my head back and look up into a Daddy face that looks down and smiles into my face in a way that I've only glimpsed, in the small salute.

Annie knows how to be cute for them and make them like her. I'll get her later.

Daddy spins around and starts clump-CLUMPing across the parking lot to the car. We put down our root beers and run after him the way we always do, in a long line strung out, with Daddy way ahead, clump-CLUMP hurrying, then me skipping and trotting, trying to keep up while looking back at Annie running to catch up, then Mama and the baby, her yelling, "Dick! Dick! Slow down! Wait for us!"

As we pull onto the parkway grass at Love Field, he's saying how Ford could never come up with innovations like these, how the whole world's going to see how General Motors is the best with the new models this fall. How Oldsmobile and Chevrolet make the Great American Cars, and how Cadillac is the Very Pinnacle of American Style and Class.

We often drive around just to feel the breeze, to put off going back to the still air of the house. We often park out at high and windy Love Field on a sultry evening to watch planes fly in and out, propellers whirring, against the setting sun. A few other cars are out there doing the same. There's a crowd of retired small fighter planes from the war lined up on the edge of the field, painted with bared-teeth faces and pinup girls. Uncle Ted owns one of those and took Daddy and me in it once to fly up all over the city, high and low, looking down over our house, buzzing Mama and May-May, who were out in the yard hanging clothes on the line, waving at us. People came out and looked up, the way people always did at this time whenever a plane would fly over. Dogs ran in circles and barked.

A high-flying skywriter over the airport spells out a puffy-dissolving *Drink Dr Pepper,* white, then pink against the darkening blue-and-orange-striped sky. The stripes fade to pale and gray; the blue darkens. Stars come out, crickets, lightning bugs, a crescent moon.

I keep thinking of the word *streamlined. Stream-lined.* A line that's streaming, that's moving through air like a stream of water, like a streamer over Fair Park, not zipping, not lunging forward, not wavering, confused, not jerking out of balance, or hurrying, or falling, but a line dancing through air easy as a breeze, *knowing where it's going,* and going there with style and with grace.

I keep thinking of the Girl flying like Wonder Woman in her own personal *streamlined* plane, knowing where she's going, high up, away from people, looking down at their tiny dollhouse lives, doing whatever they do, and then just flying away to somewhere else with ease. Small, and visible only to me.

Now Daddy's saying it's part of a world of new inventions on the way! He speaks names of inventors, the smart guys making these new things, how we're getting air conditioning in the whole house soon, and after that, television!

"You just don't care, do you, Jane? You don't care a helluva lot about anything I say to you!" he says.

"Oh, please, Dick . . ."

"Why do you sit there looking like that?"

"I don't see why you have to act so extreme about everything," she says. "Can't we just have a quiet conversation?"

"You don't get it," he says, "You don't get it! You're living right in the middle of it, and you don't get it!"

It's completely dark now, other cars pulling out. Daddy starts the car, talking again, how those GM guys say air conditioning *can't be done* but that it absolutely has to be done for down here, how he knows he could figure good working car air conditioning, no matter what they say! "They'll see! It'll be a new world now! This whole country will be completely changed!"

Mama keeps nodding her head. But all the way home, her face seems to say that all of whatever it is he's talking about isn't going to change a thing.

FOR YEARS, I TRIED TO GET BACK into bed with Mama, but she would not let me in, no matter how I would beg and cry and tell about nightmares and shadows and being scared.

She'd roll over and make sounds. I'd wonder if she knew I was there, I'd beg to stay, and then we'd have one of those whispered arguments, with me crying and pleading, and her finally walking me back to my own room. We would not want to wake Daddy.

Daddy's breathing would stay the same. He wouldn't move, hunched under the covers, at the top end, his freckled red face mashed to the mattress in the venetian blind–striped moonlight, slight voiced snores threading in and out like scratchy violins.

At the other end of Daddy, the white scarred feet would stick out off the bed, having kicked off the covers and the metal blanket brace placed to keep the covers from weighing on his pained, fused-ankle-stiff feet, which would seem to glow like frighteningly knife-sharp greenish white fish in the submarine gloom.

I wondered if the feet were hurting while he was asleep. I wondered if he dreamed of hurting feet.

The feet-fish seemed to look over and nod to me in some sly understanding, in spite of that scrunched-asleep face on the other end, helpless and different from when the black bird-eyes were awake and looking at me. I never got into or even touched Daddy's bed. I sat down between the two twin beds. The floor cold, the carpet itchy, I crawled around like a dog, making myself a spot.

Daddy's blanket fell off on the other side, not touching the feet, so I crawled over, eased the blanket down, wrapped it around myself, and stretched out on the floor there between their beds, then looked up at the venetian blind–striped night sky. I could see one star, one star to wish on, a lone star.

We lived in the Lone Star State, which sounds like *The Lone Ranger* I heard on the radio every week. Lone Star Oldsmobile and Cadillac was GranDad's business where Daddy went to work at *the office* with the cars. There was something special about Lone Star, something special about us, it seemed to me.

But Daddy was unhappy about something at Lone Star. Even though he loved hanging around with the guys in the service department, the guys on the sales floor, sometimes joining in on jokes and pranks they would do, even things that would go seriously wrong and cause trouble, still there were things at Lone Star that made him come home upset—things that people would not talk about.

He liked to bring cars home and do custom work— change things on them. He would sometimes go up to Detroit and talk to people, then come home saying, "General Motors is worse than the goddamned army."

And Mama would say, "I wish you wouldn't talk that way."

"Don't you realize what this means?" Daddy had shouted as we stood in the showroom, waiting for our car to be brought around, one day, his hand on Mama's elbow, pushing her closer, as if to force her to look in and appreciate the new and revolutionary importance of the gleaming arrangement of pistons, valves, belts, wires, and tubes that was before us, our fun-house mirrored faces looking back from every curving chrome surface, a big placard saying PROTOTYPE—COMING NEXT YEAR—ROCKET V-8 ENGINE—CAR OF THE FUTURE!

"Don't you see how important this is?" Daddy's pointing nose and finger, his red freckled face, so eager, black eyes leaping as if at something to eat, his hand pushing her.

"Don't you see everything is changing now?"

Mama pulled away.

"Don't you realize, Jane?" He seemed to want to clutch her arm and dive right into the shiny insides of that engine, but she did not want to go in there with him.

Mama liked to go to Lone Star for the courtesy car, when we went shopping downtown for school clothes or for Christmas. She parked her station wagon in front, and all the salesmen would come to greet us as we walked around the bright, modern showroom, so friendly to my elegant mama and to scabby-kneed me, in our dressed-up downtown clothes, and they would point out the newest of the big gleaming cars on display, cars everywhere, the parking lot, the used-car lot, cars and more cars everywhere you looked, and photographs and drawings of cars on the walls, and even a little toy red car for me that I never actually got to play with, that had pedals inside.

Daddy would be there, clump-CLUMPing around, looking at papers in his office, talking on the phone, kidding around with the mechanics in back in the service department, the men in uniforms with names on the pockets, working on engines with hoods up, or with cars up high on those big cranking things, and calendars and pictures of ladies in bathing suits on the walls above the big boxes of tools.

I would slip away from Mama and follow Daddy around the service department, listening to the men banter and talk about Kettering and Burrell and Skinner, about Pete Estes, names I didn't know. They'd stand looking into engines, talking cylinders, crankshafts, and what "they're working on up there!"

Daddy loved working on cars, showing off cars, polishing and looking at and selling cars, and driving cars as fast as he wanted to, just as GranDad loved the cars, bicycles, motorcycles, boats, planes, tanks. His study was full of models.

When he'd bring cars home to work on in our garage for an entire weekend, he'd act so happy, pacing with shirtsleeves rolled up, clump-CLUMPing around the garage where the car lay belly-up as he peered into the clean, shiny engine as if at something alive, thrilling, and good to eat, saying, "Is that slick or what?" and holding grease-stained hands away from the white shirts and business clothes he'd always wear, because he hated to have dirty hands, as he hated to be hot. Sometimes he'd shower and change clothes, then go back to the garage to work again, then do it all again, never wearing shorts or jeans or going shirtless.

Aunt Lee always said you couldn't love things that couldn't love you back. But in our family we did.

Down at Lone Star, Uncle Ted would be there, but rarely would he talk to us. He'd say hello and hurry away.

GranDad, always a snappy dresser, would be sitting in his big front office with its modern leather chairs and framed pictures of old-time Oldsmobiles and Cadillacs, with his dark wavy hair, wide silky tie, gold tie clip and cuff links. We'd sit around while he seemed not to know what to say to us, and then he'd tell the courtesy car man to drive us downtown.

Mama liked for the two of us to be dressed up in hats and gloves and be driven to Neiman's, Sanger's, Titche's,

Harris's, Dreyfus's, James K. Wilson, all the big down-town Dallas stores, by the dignified uniformed colored chauffeur in the big black courtesy car limousine Cadillac. The driver opened doors, bowed, said, "Yes ma'am, yes ma'am" about a million times, but I could see he didn't really want to talk to us. I examined the little Cadillac symbol shield. *Why* are *there tiny ducks on it?* I wondered.

Mama would talk on and on about what Nana would think of this or that store, or this or that dress, how we should go by and show Nana what we'd bought, how if Nana were there, she'd make us walk to every single store to be sure we couldn't get the same dress for less, how Nana is this amazing, energetic, thrifty, clean Scottish woman who might be found on her maid's day off scrubbing her pots and pans on her kitchen floor because the maid didn't get them anywhere near clean enough.

Mama would say that Nana is the one with "real class," is the "brains of the operation." She would say that we are not the old land and cotton people or the old ranching and cattle people in Texas, how we are not the oil people or the banking or real estate people, but we are the people who sell everybody their Cadillacs. And how it's all because of Nana that Cadillacs are so big in Texas, how our family is synonymous with Cadillac in Texas, how everybody knows that we are among the nicest rich people in Dallas, how we are so lucky and special to have a family business like this, because we still think about the Depression, and you never know what might happen next in this world. So we are so lucky and special, even though we're really only car dealers and newspaper people, and how all of this is because of Nana's being so smart and so stylish and having so many friends.

And this all must be true, because everywhere we would go, the salesladies would know Nana and would ask about her, their voices all high and singsongy, the way Mama's gets with bridge-club friends, saying what good taste Nana had, what a nice person Nana was, and not a snob like some others, how Nana was their favorite, best customer, and remembered all their names and birthdays.

"Oh, are you her grandaughter?" they would say. "Your grandmother is famous around here!"

Then driving home, Mama said how she knows she's Nana's favorite daughter-in-law, even though Daddy's not Nana's favorite son, because Nana said poor Daddy has "always been just awful," and because Nana'd always liked Ted best. And Mama said that I am Nana's favorite grandchild because I'm the eldest, and the little ones give Nana a headache, because even though Nana's a wonderful person, she is just so nervous, and on and on about who are the favorites, until I didn't want to listen anymore.

Then the courtesy car took us to the downtown Dallas Athletic Club for lunch with Daddy, and they let me order the twelve giant shrimp with red sauce for a dollar fifty.

An ancient colored man seemed to be in charge, small, wiry, and very black, with white hair and a face like a tree. He greeted us, while Daddy called his name several times and seemed to want to joke around with this old man. And the old man would just smile sternly and nod. At the table, he took our order, and when he left, Daddy leaned over to Mama and me and said, "That old *spook* knows everybody in this town."

"I wish you wouldn't talk that way," Mama said.

Daddy blinked and snorted and ordered a vodka tonic.

I pretended not to see, not to hear. I looked around at the polished dance floor, the white columns. I chewed on a shrimp with red sauce, and another and another, as I watched them both.

After lunch, the courtesy car took us all back to Lone Star, where Daddy clump-CLUMPed toward the service department again. As he was going through the door, I saw Uncle Ted coming the other way, walking fast, and the two of them bumped into each other hard as they both tried at the same time to get through the door first. Uncle Ted went through, and somehow Daddy lost his balance, spun around once, twice, and then fell down hard, one of those long, struggling falls. Mama and I both jumped toward him.

"Oh, excuse me, Dick," Uncle Ted said, and then he just went on walking out to the parking lot.

One of the salesmen pushed a chair over to Daddy and then looked away while he struggled with pulling himself up, cursing and violently pushing Mama away when she tried to help him.

"I don't see why you have to act like that," Mama said.

"There's a lot you don't see, Jane," he said. And then Daddy clump-CLUMPed away to his office and slammed his door shut. So now we'd have to pretend that this hadn't happened.

THE BLANKET GOT TO BE ITCHY, my arm had fallen asleep, and it was getting light outside, but I could still see the one star out there through the blinds.

Daddy started trying to call out, but he seemed to be asleep, or partly asleep, or starting to wake up. I stayed horned toad–flat there on the floor.

Daddy sat up on the other side of the bed. I scooted closer to the bed on his side, then up underneath the creaking springs. *Please God, don't let Daddy see I'm here!*

Mama turned over, making a sound.

Daddy stood up, breathing heavily, moaning to himself. He pulled the sheets and blankets off the bed, then, clutching the huge wad of them, limped heavily out of the room, as though his feet were especially bad.

I lay listening to him clump-CLUMP into the bathroom down the hall, then close the bathroom door and lock it the way he always did, even when alone. He came out finally, clumping into the kitchen. Noises in the kitchen. I waited, sleepy again, not scared of shadows anymore, since something as real as Daddy was stomping around the house.

Mama turned over again. Then it sounded like the back door closed. I crawled out from under the bed, tip-toed into the hall, my eyes used to the dark. I looked into the living room at the wood bin. Daddy didn't seem to be in the house at all.

Looking out the back porch windows, I saw the dark figure of Daddy standing in the moonlit yard, looking up at the sky, still holding sheets and blankets, and turning slowly around and around. He was holding something else in one hand; a bottle glinted in the moonlight as he turned around again with a moan. He was saying something in a regular voice. Then he was saying something in a loud voice that sounded like crying, at the sky. The dogs barked and whined. Then Daddy was clump-CLUMPing out to the toolshed where he often would work on model boats or planes, on which he would often paint with a tiny brush the name Astro Solo.

I waited a long time, nodding with sleep. The light didn't come on out there, and Daddy didn't come back.

Back in my room, I saw that hunched black thing was just clothes on top of a chair. I got into bed, put my arms around myself, the way I wanted to hold on to them, the way I wished all of us could hold on to all of us.

The Age of Reason

*D*addy sits at one end of the dinner table, Mama at the other. I sit between them on one side. On the other side, opposite me, sits a baby, the elder of two babies, in a high chair pulled up to the table. The other baby is still in a crib in the back room. The maid is in the kitchen, waiting to be called.

There are place mats and stainless steel. Our napkins are in our laps, and we sit up straight at the dinner table. We do not sing or whistle or read at the dinner table. We do not interrupt. We do not tap or kick the chair legs or swing our feet back and forth at the dinner table. White bread is stacked on a plate. Salad plates are set before us. Iceberg lettuce, section-cut red tomatoes, a pink dressing—I poke my fork at it.

"Don't play with your food," says Daddy.

"Eat your salad," says Mama.

Normally, I would argue, saying "I hate salad!" and trying to bargain for something.

But just then, Mama says, "You should eat that salad instead of so much bread and so many cookies."

"That's right, you know," says Daddy. "You are getting fat."

So that's that.

Everyone is tense, because for the older baby across from me, tonight's dinner is a test: Will she or will she not be able to eat properly enough to stay and have a place at the table throughout the meal? This would be a first.

It doesn't look good for the baby, as she has just caused a bit of cut-up tomato to fly across the table and land on the bread plate. And Daddy saw it land.

Daddy groans. Daddy doesn't like having a baby at the table. Mama reaches and takes the tomato bit onto her own plate, saying, "That's all right. It's just one little thing, Dick."

A few drops of tomato wetness are sitting on the plate, threatening to spoil the perfection of the white slices. But maybe he doesn't see it.

I look across at the baby. She hasn't noticed what's happening yet. She's a happy baby, almost two now, with bright black eyes. Everyone says every single day how she is so cute, which makes me want to do something to her.

I eat a few tomato bites and push my lettuce around. Daddy devours his salad in seconds, ready for the meat of the meal. Mama eats slowly, cuts up her lettuce with care. The baby drops her baby fork on the floor with a clang. Daddy flinches, looks at Mama. Mama picks up the fork, then stands and picks up her plate and mine.

"Jane," says Daddy.

"Yes, Dick?" says Mama.

"Let the maid do it."

"That's okay; I need to get something from the kitchen." And she walks out with the salad plates, then returns quickly, carrying dinner plates, followed by gigantic May-May, the white-uniformed black maid, carrying a platter with meat loaf. May-May is as tall as Daddy, so dark that sometimes I can barely see her Indian-sharp features, and hugely big. Her uniform doesn't fit right, apron crooked, slip hanging out. I see Daddy noticing this. He has a look on his face. Daddy doesn't like May-May, says she's a slob. But Mama says May-May loves the babies and is a good soul. Mama sits. May-May goes back to the kitchen, cut-open loafers flapping, then brings out mashed potatoes and peas.

Daddy begins slicing the steaming meat loaf, his bird-like eyes appraising its blanket of tomato sauce and slices of bacon on top. We pass our plates.

"Jane, how many times do I have to say I want it pink in the middle?" says Daddy.

"It *is* pink in the middle," says Mama.

"You call that pink?" says Daddy.

"It looks pink to me," says Mama.

"Well, next time." He takes a long breath, exhales it, then speaks very slowly. "Could you please make it pinker than this?" he says. He isn't that mad yet.

Mama takes a plate for the baby and starts cutting up small bites. I am seven now and I cut up my own food. The baby bangs excitedly on her tray. Daddy leans and suddenly grabs her little arm. Her eyes widen. We all freeze.

"Now, do you think you can settle down and eat right?" he says, holding her arm, glaring into her face. Her little face crumples. She starts to cry. Mama shoves a bite of mashed potatoes into her mouth. She stops crying and works to swallow.

We receive our filled plates and start to eat. I watch each of them, and I watch the baby staring wide-eyed at Daddy. She's starting to catch on.

I am waiting for my moment. Thanksgiving is past, and Christmas is coming. I'm in second grade now, not a baby anymore, and I hear the things other kids say. I am ready to hear the truth. Even though I pretty much know the answer, I need to hear it from the two of them. I've taken my questions mostly to Mama up to now, but this time I've waited until they're both here at the table, because Daddy will often tell you things, and I am always looking for somebody to tell me things.

For example, one time Daddy showed me how to use the index in *The Book of Knowledge,* and he told me to always find things out for myself and to always think about things for myself, and not just take what other people say.

And one day last summer at the dinner table, Daddy told me about the solar system. I had asked about the man in the moon. Was there such a thing as a man in the moon? Was this a man living inside the moon, or what? And if so, what about the moon being made of green cheese? How did that fit in? And what about the cow jumping over the moon? Could that happen?

I couldn't imagine the cows I'd seen at Aunt Lee's farm jumping over much of anything. So which of these things was true and which not true?

When I said this, Daddy had looked over at me with sudden interest.

"You see this?" Daddy had said, holding a fat red radish right in my face.

I glanced at Mama, who seemed to think something was funny. But Daddy pushed back his chair, went clump-CLUMPing into the kitchen without his cane, grabbed a grapefruit, an apple, an orange, a lemon, and came back to the table, May-May behind him, looking out the swinging door with a face of alarm: *What could he be doing now?*

Then this rare thing happened. Daddy leaned forward to me excitedly and started showing and telling me about how all things in the huge universe revolve around each other, how all things are affected by each other, how the sun is this gigantic ball of fire, the moon a small cold planet that mirrors it.

Mama said, "Oh, she can't understand all that, Dick!"

"Yes I can! Yes I can!" I shouted, jumping up and down in my chair, hoping he would never stop.

And he did go on and on, looking right into my eyes as if I were a serious person, not just a little kid to be brushed aside, telling me how the Earth we live on is actually a wet green ball constantly whirling around and around, and yet we don't feel the whirling and whizzing through space because we are stuck to the Earth like magnets by this thing called gravity, which even the wisest men in the world don't really understand. But the wise men are studying it right now!

Daddy picked up rolls and olives to show how all the

planet worlds are zooming and rolling around the super-hot sun, while the sun is boiling up a billion explosions all the time, even though we humans are walking around on Earth every day and not noticing a thing.

He drew pictures on napkins, talking low, leaning forward to me, confiding the secrets of the universe into my eager ear, including little-kid me inside his mysterious smart-daddy circle. It was thrilling. I would ask questions, he would get pencils and rulers and answer, and Mama would keep on protesting from the other side, trying to put a stop to this.

After dinner, I ran out to the backyard to look up at the moon and wonder at the millions and trillions of stars. The dark yard didn't seem so scary with all those stars out there, shining and twinkling above in a sky full of promise! In spite of everything, I'd have to love Daddy forever for this!

I decided then to at least go ahead and like Daddy, on a trial basis.

But Mama didn't like this, for some reason. Why didn't she like for Daddy to talk to me like that? What was she so worried about? Why didn't Mama want me to know things?

The baby is putting her fingers into the mashed potatoes, then into her mouth. Peas fall to the floor and bounce. Daddy groans. Mama jumps up. The baby looks from one to the other and starts to cry.

For some reason, I want to save her.

"Kids at school say there's no Santa Claus," I blurt out loudly, even though this is not my perfect moment yet.

"Who says that?" says Mama, "Is it Nathan?"

"No, it's not Nathan—just kids at school."

Mama looks mad. The baby is fussing and twisting in her high chair. She knocks a glass of milk, which spills across the table, then rolls off and shatters on the floor. *Crash!*

"Good God, Jane!" Daddy jumps up as if a bomb has gone off, and gasps as if hit by it, then knocking back his chair, which falls on the floor with a clatter. He grabs his cane with one fist, tottering, almost falling, grabbing the table.

I duck down. The baby freezes for a second, holding her breath, then makes a long, high-pitched wail. Mama stands, calling for May-May, who rushes in with a towel, as if she'd been waiting just behind the door.

"Out! Take her out of here!" shouts Daddy, clump-CLUMPing away from the table, turning his back, as if he can't stand to watch while the dining room explodes into a million pieces!

The poor baby has failed again. She shrieks in protest as Mama picks her up and carries her to the kitchen, then to the bedroom, banished.

May-May cleans, down on the floor, shaking her head.

I eat what's on my plate as fast as I can. We hear the baby screaming from the back rooms, but everyone settles down again. Then the littler baby wakes up fussing. May-May goes back there and closes the door.

We three eat in silence, Daddy wolfing his food the way he does, as if starving, Mama frowning and picking at hers.

Finally, she speaks. "It's Nathan, isn't it? I'm going to speak to his mother."

"No, it's not Nathan!" I yell. "It's not!"

Mama doesn't answer. Maybe this is an opening.

"But it's true, isn't it? There is no real Santa Claus, Mama, not really. Is there? Why won't you tell me? Because how could he fly around to all the houses in the world in one night? And how could he know what everybody wants for Christmas? How?"

"He just does, that's all. Maybe you don't know everything there is to know! Did you ever think of that? What about all those presents you got from Santa last year? You liked getting all those presents, didn't you?"

"Yes, but what about . . ."

"Well, maybe if there's no Santa Claus, we should just forget about Christmas this year!"

Mama's angry now, her forehead wrinkled. Why does she look like something's hurting her feelings?

"What makes you think you know so much?"

"I just don't see . . ."

"You have to believe," she says. "It's important just to believe. You have to."

I look at Daddy. He's watching the two of us with a little smile. I figure Daddy might understand. Because there is just something about Daddy.

But Daddy looks me right in the eye and says, "I think you should consider the fact that your mother might be right."

Mama laughs, but I don't get it.

Well, I think, *Daddy wouldn't lie to me.*

Once Upon a Time There Was the War

The first time I remember stealing something was at Fort Riley, Kansas, where we lived when Daddy came home from the war, and after that everything changed. That was when Mama first seemed to not like me. Instead, she liked that new baby best.

Once upon a time before that, when it was just Mama and me alone together in all the world, and the real voice of my mother was the voice I heard then, when during the War all she had was me, me just a baby to her, a part of the life of her body space and time, and a possession of hers as well, almost like a pet or an accessory to her. Back when it was just the two of us, Mama and me alone, Mama told me the world.

She told me how before the War, she and her friends cruised Dallas in convertibles, the red leather staining their linen summer whites, how they danced the Lindy and the Big Apple at the Adolphus and the Baker hotels downtown, their pictures in the *Dallas Morning News'* society pages for every little thing, how they chain-smoked their Camels and their Lucky Strikes, needing only one match, getting lit off each other, how they went to schools up east, went to New York, saw the Cotton Club and the

Battle of the Bands at the Savoy, then came back to Texas for small home weddings, which were more tasteful in the Depression, when so many were so poor.

She told me how they played bridge in their slips in Granny's big Beverly Drive house, fans going, windows open, ice melting in minted tea as they listened to Hitler invading Poland on the radio. How that world went with Daddy, away in the war, *Pearl Harbor Day* written into my baby book in her school-penmanship hand when Daddy, already an officer from New Mexico Military Institute, where he'd been sent away for being a wild prankster problem child, put on his uniform and went with all the men far away to the war.

Back then, it was just Mama and me for years, all points of our two-tangency making up the primary-core *us* of the then-known universe, that certain voice of hers evoking the emergent becomings of me. Mama and me, Mama and me alone.

Mama and me at the dresser, her braiding her own waist-length dark hair, and then my lighter child hair, every morning without fail, putting hers into the coiled braid, mine into the two tight pigtails waving stiffly rubber-banded in the breeze.

Mama and me in mother-daughter dresses and coats, going to church, to Granny's house, to Nana's house, Aunt Meg's house, Aunt Annie's house, all around Dallas in the old black cars with the creaking clutches and the running boards.

Mama and me driving to the different army bases to see Daddy, saying "Now I Lay Me Down to Sleep" wherever we were bedding down, sometimes in the car, camp followers—Fort Bliss, El Paso, Presidio, Fort Riley, Valley Forge—empty two-lane blacktop forever, cows and cotton and fences and desert and oil rigs whizzing by, windows open, the vent blowing sparks from her cigarettes into the backseat, her skirt hitched above her knees in summer, before air conditioning, the radio-scratchy cowboy songs, the big-band music, then pulling up at another strange place, her grabbing her sewing machine out of the car trunk, making cheap slipcovers to maybe stay awhile.

She chewed gum and wore saddle shoes and skirts and sweaters back then, and she popped her gum and laughed easily, and strange men were always looking at her, but she was with me, and talking a constant stream into the human tape-recorder ears and eyes of infant-child me completely tuned to what her voice and her whole body might be saying about what was happening to the two of us now, and what was going to happen next, as if to pin down through telling every detail of our busy existence, letting me in on the order and meaning of events in our small two-together life, me rarely seeing or playing with any other kids. All this to the point that I'd pay little attention to where we were going or to what else might be happening in the outside world, but only to every gesture and pulse beat of the source of the universe that was her, that was *us*, singing along with the radio, just happily and mostly obediently following along, getting into her big warm bed, soothed nightly by the heartbeat of her heavy-breathing, grown-up, sweet-sour-smelling body then, back then, when we didn't have Daddy and these babies taking her attention away from just Mama and me.

Mama and me in the army-base store at Fort Riley, counting out our ration stamps every week for the checkout lady. Mama and me at the movies in Dallas, the big fancy Majestic downtown, where a man in a bow tie played the organ between shows, and then we'd gaze up at the black-and-white stories and newsreels of people in the War, cheering for our boys, booing the bad guys, the *Jerrys* and *Nazis* and *Japs*. Because they started it.

So all our men had to go away to kill all the Jerrys and Nazis and Japs. And that was a lot of people to kill, so no one could make it stop, this evil machine grinding away out there, blowing up towns, chewing up babies and grandmothers, all our men gone away to dark, sad, wild-hair-kerchiefed other countries where people speaking in strange other tongues were unlucky enough to have been born.

Mama and me at the kitchen table at Granny's big Beverly Drive house, where Papaw was serious, almost about to cry, and was giving Mama some papers to keep, saying those papers proved she was adopted by him, and not *a Jew*. He said "just in case."

Afraid it might be coming to suck us in and make us suffer like people in newsreels were suffering, we fought against being afraid. *We believed,* hands and arms linked, lockstep, all together, the same music, direction, purpose, and goal; we sang along to the bouncing ball, to the surge of energy when everyone realized together that everyone else was singing, too, letting all the singing inside you come ringing out as loud as you wanted, safe in the crowd, in the dark—"The Man on the Flying Trapeze" and "The Sunny Side of the Street"— singing and believing in our boys, our flag, silver linings, that jaunty little ball showing us what and how to sing next. We clapped and cheered; we belonged; we sat back into the very meaning of *us,* holding on to that beat to which we could go ahead and live our good soldiers' positive-thinking, team-playing, true-blue lives, in step, hand in hand to the marching music, the upbeat, swing-beat music, the clear and simple music of that time.

Mama and me wearing hats and gloves together in a downtown department store where I had to be careful to hold on to Mama because I could so easily find myself mistakenly grabbing onto the skirt of a strange woman with mean green eyes high above me, frizzy red hair sticking out from a pointed hat like Mama never wore, making that strange woman look electrocuted right in the midst of the bright, noisy confusion of rows and racks and blank-face mannequins, lettered placards, dizzying piles and stacks of shirts and dresses and coats and pots and pans and toys, shiny products high and low, people rushing, clerks with glasses on ribbons and hairnets and ruffles at the neck, saying "May I help you? May I help you?" and then sending the little tube canisters zinging around the store on wires I could see from the *mezzanine,* where I finally would find Mama ordering cloth unfurled and cut from a bolt like ribbon for giants, and where Mama would take way too long picking out patterns and buttons and bindings and threads and zippers and snaps and hooks.

I'd lean over the banister, saying *mezzanine, mmez-zzanniine* until it turned nonsensical, watching the zinging tubes of money and paper crisscrossing the whole space of the amazing, buzzing, clanging, cash register–ringing department store.

All I wanted was to get my turn upstairs on Santa's lap, telling how I wanted a real rubber baby doll like I saw in the girl upstairs's apartment at Fort Riley. But sitting there, I looked up and saw a real man looking down, winking at me, black hairs in his nose, and I froze and didn't tell anything.

"She's shy," I heard Mama say, and "She's big for her age."

Mama walked so fast on the street past the plate-glass windows showing Christmas scenes, I was running to catch up.

"So does that mean Santa gets toys from the same place the men get jeeps and tanks for the war?"

"No, that just means the North Pole elves can't get rubber for toys, because all the rubber's being used up for Daddy and the other men in the war."

"But if Santa can fly, and knows who's bad and who's good all over the world, then why can't Santa just, *POOF,* make some rubber of his own?"

"Because that's the way it is. We have to pray for the war to be over, and then we can have those toys again."

"Does Santa have something to do with the war?"

But she stopped answering. And I wanted to ask how did Santa bring toys to the kids in the unhappy war countries. Is it just for us, the lucky ones, lucky because we believe—and over there they don't believe? Are they being punished for something over there? If we couldn't have rubber dolls, then they must not have a lot of things. Santa could bring food and blankets like the Red Cross. Would he bring toys? Would they still be expected to be good all the time, with the war?

Mama and me at Granny's house under her Christmas tree in look-alike quilted satin robes, smiling for the camera, taking pictures to send to poor Daddy in North Africa, acting happy, waiting for Santa, living in that small King's-X interval, knowing that that day of world peace was on its way, and we just had to trust and wait with the true-believing women friends, the aunts, the grandparents, the maids, the card games and dominoes, the making do with homemade toys, homemade Christmas lights with painted globes and black electric tape, with Sunday bacon fat–fried chicken dinners with biscuits and gravy and fruit salad, the victory gardens, the army blankets, the having the measles with a big red QUARANTINE! sign on the door, the radio, the Victrola, the war news, the letters and telegrams, grown-ups reading the letters and telegrams and newspapers to each other in hushed and excited voices, me not understanding a thing about Germany, Japan, North Africa, Italy, Hitler, the Jews, Roosevelt, MacArthur, Eisenhower, Patton, but being mad, sad, or worried right along with the grown-ups because of the war that was their war, the war that their youth poured into, the bottomless-pit, endless war that stole their youth, but to which they gladly gave their youth, and valued that giving gladly to the war of their America and that of all their friends.

To not go and give gladly was to be no friend of theirs. They were all agreed on being all together about everything about it, in spite of men captured, men coming home in wheelchairs, or with no hands, or burned red all over except for goggle marks, or just not coming home at all.

We got good at this waiting that was our life. We dreamed of World Peace, when Our Boys would have killed all the bad Jerrys and Nazis and Japs, and the war would be over, and all the daddies who had not been killed already would come home.

I dreamed my tall heroic, First Cavalry Division daddy would come riding up our sidewalk on a silver horse, teeth and medals flashing, all of us laughing, jumping, waving arms! Daddy would reach down and scoop me up onto his horse to ride with him. And all the toys and cartoons and photos and bouncing balls would come magically alive like in the movies, singing, bouncing along the sidewalk beside happy, smiling, me and Daddy! Daddy and me.

After that there would be World Peace, and no one would fight ever again, or kill one another, or drop bombs, or probably even raise their voices, or disagree or *act ugly* or be rude or throw things or even have to get sent away from the dinner table, but then everyone all together would just work and believe and be good and be happy, happy, happy all the time, all the time, no exceptions allowed at all.

That was when Daddy was just a photograph and a story about the War. He was Faraway Soldier daddy in North Africa with General Patton.

But then later, he was poor broken, war-wounded daddy at Valley Forge Hospital, where finally I did get to see him, after a long car trip and much talk about going to "see Daddy."

But the real Daddy we saw then was small and strange and quiet in a stiff white plaster cast that covered him all over, an itchy white torture-jacket, his thin neck and arms sticking out like a turtle stuck on its back to die. And he spoke in a thin, sad voice, not to me at all, but only to Mama, not the Daddy I expected looking over from far away over Mama's shoulder at me on a chair in the corner with a big square carton of melting vanilla-bean ice cream on my lap while they talked in low grown-up tones I couldn't hear, two together, and me left out.

Mama and I were at the Walgreens counter eating club sandwiches after that, and a nice man in uniform came and talked just to me. Mama was looking at his ribbons. He asked Mama, "Are you married?" And she said, "Yes, I am," looking proud of herself. I wanted to stay and talk with that man who seemed to want to talk to me, but Mama made us leave.

That was before the real Daddy came home and I got kicked out of Mama's big bed.

Then, when the real Daddy finally did come home, he ruined everything. I had to sleep alone, far away in my own room. Then she had that first new baby, so everything changed between Mama and me, and she wouldn't tell me things anymore.

Daddy came home again and again—home to our first Dallas apartment from the war, then away again for operations, then home again to Fort Riley, to teach tank warfare, where Daddy was sort of okay for a while, with us having that first new baby there, a tiny red thing of no use, as far as I could see.

At Fort Riley, I was always being left with a maid named Frankie, who was mean. I knew Frankie hated us because I saw her face one time when Daddy was talking at the table about someone who was not supposed to be in the Officers' Club. And then Mama said "Hush," and then Daddy said he didn't care. And then something mean was in Frankie's face.

After that, I saw Frankie pinch our new baby and make it cry. I was going to tell Mama about this, but Mama never believed me.

Frankie told me if I touched down there, I would get worms. I said she was *not my mother*, and then Frankie slapped me while I was wet in the bathtub, which hurt.

Frankie said if I pushed my chair back like that, I was going to fall backward and knock my teeth out. I said I would NOT! And then I did fall backward and I did knock out one tooth right in front. *And I saw Frankie smile. How did she know that?*

I had Cookie, the first dog, to play with in the yard, but then Cookie had to be "put to sleep," because Daddy's commanding officer's mean little boy teased her until she finally bit him. All the grown-ups thought that little boy was the nice one and Cookie was the bad one, but they were completely wrong! I wanted to tell them that, but Mama was too busy to listen, and it was too late. So it was clear that grown-ups do not know everything.

But I carried my Raggedy Ann everywhere then because of her smile face on one side, her asleep face on the other, and because of the secret heart printed on her chest, which I could look at anytime I wanted to see it whispering *I love you.*

What I really wanted was a rubber baby doll like the one the girl upstairs in our apartment building had from before the war, with all-over soft rubber skin instead of a chipped hard plaster painted face and hands and feet and a limp, dirty cloth body like my baby doll. The girl upstairs's doll made my doll seem used up and sad. Her doll felt almost like that real baby Mama brought home and spent all her time with now, even though all it did was sleep and eat and fuss and cry.

But we couldn't have a rubber doll like that because of the war, and that girl wouldn't let me hold her doll for long. I had to wait for World Peace.

That girl was older, and had a lot of toys from before the war. She had a dollhouse full of tiny furniture, tiny dolls, with little bedrooms, a living room, a kitchen with tiny wooden cabinets, doors that opened and closed, even dishes and lamps. I wanted to be left alone with this dollhouse, to turn each thing over in my hands, work the moving parts, but all that girl wanted was to make me go into her mother's closet and play dress-up.

Before we went in there, I saw the thing I had to have.

It was a tiny white toilet with two tiny moving lids with tiny moving hinges. If only I could get enough of holding it, working the moving parts, then maybe I could put it back later.

But did I really think anything? My hand just reached out and took it, the taking getting behind me, like swallowing too big a bite and just getting on to the next thing. It was small and so easy to slip into a dress pocket. Maybe no one would notice such a small thing.

But they did notice. The next day, the girl and her mother and my mother stood over me in a big quiet room for what seemed like forever and kept asking, "Why did you do it?" with their sad, mad faces too close to mine.

"Why, why, why did you do it? Why? Tell us the truth! Tell us the truth!"

All I could do was say, "I don't know, I don't know why."

Mama said that I had "broken her heart," because she was "so disappointed in me," and after that her face was different every time she looked at me. She just didn't like me anymore after that.

She started watching for me to do something bad, yelling, "Do not steal!" But I was only looking into her purse to see what was kept in there that she always had to have.

Now it's Mama and Daddy, and it's Mama and babies, and it's Daddy alone, and it's me alone, out on my own, out looking for somebody to be my friend.

And even now, everywhere I look, I see things I could steal.

I CAN SEE THE LONG-AGO DUSTY ROAD and the hill I walked up from the Fort Riley apartments one time to get away from Mama, who was with the new baby, and who was mad at me, always mad at me—and away from that other woman sitting in the yard, who said I was a *bad girl* and that they were going to cook and eat my pet frog for dinner.

I can see myself walking up to the high grassy fields to wait for Daddy. I can see the torn-up dirt road up there, deeply rutted and layered in dust that rose into the wind, swirling up and scattering the cloud of gnats that followed me up there, getting into my eyes and nose. A fat brown grasshopper blew onto my skirt and clung there as if to a friendly giant.

I looked back and saw the flat land, the late-summer dry grass, the faraway dome of light sky, the toy blocks of apartments where Mama was busy fixing dinner, and I did not see another person anywhere. It was a long way out there for me.

I was four at this time and not a baby anymore. I had my frog in a jar with me, and my frog was my friend. I opened the jar and let my frog hop away toward a tree, so no one could eat him. I said, "Good-bye, Frog."

No one knew I was out there alone, and no one saw me run, run, run up the hill to meet my daddy ("Pick me up, Daddy, pick me up!"), the wind whipping my dress like in a flying dream. I was waiting for my daddy to bring in the tanks at the end of the day. I didn't know where the tanks came from, but I knew they just appeared up there every day—first the distant roaring sound of them, then the first one appearing seesaw-tilt wobbling at the top of the hill like a dollhouse tank, like the green lead miniature tanks with moving parts that Daddy had on his desk at home.

It toddled down and crawled, and then another and another olive green robot toad roaring and rolling over the top of the highest hill, then a lower hill, and then rolling toward me, the top parts swiveling, towering more and more hugely on the dirt road before me, and then they stopped. And then the toads' tops popped open and some men came out.

"What have we here?" and "Who might this be so far from home?" they were all saying.

Then my daddy was getting out of a jeep that drove up beside the first tank, with another tall man helping him, and then another, and one of the men picked me up and lifted me up to the top of this huge tank, like onto the back of an elephant, then into the trapdoor and down into the small dark space full of glowing dials and lights. Then they drove the tanks again, riding with me down toward home.

The men knew how to do things. They handed me up and down, in and out. I was so little to them, they could just lift me, put me on their shoulders, toss me around in their big warm men's hands. I would have done anything for more of this.

"Daddy, Daddy, pick me up, Daddy, pick me up!"

But Daddy could not pick me up when his feet were bad like right then. We walked home, back to the apartments, where Mama was with that fussy new baby they said would be somebody for me to play with, but she was much too small.

I ran along beside Daddy's tall, stiff legs, his two canes at that time, his uniform, his medals and ribbons, the patches like hearts on his sleeve, all saying that he and all the men were part of something big, an us-protected circle within which they knew how to believe, join up, join in, and be part of things. They could do what was required to belong. I wished I knew what to do to belong.

On tiptoe later, I looked at the medals and ribbons laid out on Daddy's dresser. My hand just reached out.

When He Saw Me

While awake, Daddy cannot be still. His knees are moving, his fingers are tapping and drumming to the rhythm of something inside him. I spy on his left hand one day, with its short fingers, clean nails, pink skin with brown freckles across the back. Mama says he has small hands for a man of his size, and that when he was young and would get into fights a lot, his small hands were a problem for him.

His hands seem to belong to someone young and innocent, not the person we are all so afraid of when he comes home from work on a bad day, comes charging in from the garage, and we would have known from the way his car hit the driveway and by the speed with which he would have made it to the back door in that walk he has that is not exactly limping, but making lurching forward look purposeful—we would know, we would just know, the way you know when you swing a bat that this one's going to be a foul, and even though the bat hasn't hit the ball yet, you know it's too late to change it, there's nothing to be done, because it's already in motion and this one is just going to be a foul.

And everything has to be just right. If something at

dinner was wrong, he would throw the corncobs on the floor, for example, there being no plate set out for them the way he wanted, or he would hurl a whole tomato aspic across the room, because didn't she know he had to have something to chew on?

But mostly, Daddy likes to eat better than he likes most things. He lunges into each bite as he eats, surrounding and attacking each forkful as though in an act of capture, going faster and faster, as though accelerating toward some climactic moment, and when he does this, his eyes seem to glaze over, as though not only consuming but also being consumed, merging with something in which to be lost, the way he told me one time he was lost in the morphine they gave him when his feet were crushed in the first place, and he spent years in hospitals and body casts like the one at Valley Forge, where I saw him that first time. I heard he later cut that itchy cast off himself and went running around yelling, like he wasn't supposed to do, hurting himself again, so they didn't know what to do with him. Nobody ever knows what to do with him. They just had to put him in a new cast.

At home, all you can do is to get out of the way in time. Anything might happen. Usually, he just breaks things. Sometimes he falls down. He even breaks his own bones a lot.

But he doesn't seem to care about hurting himself, because he wants to have things a certain way. Like when they operated on his feet the first time and he would not have a general anesthetic, because they wouldn't promise not to cut off the worse one of the feet, because they said he would never walk on them because of the pain, but he wouldn't let them do it. After that, he did make himself walk, even though the feet were always hurting, especially that one worse foot, and he is constantly moving and twitching and jigging them. At a movie, he cannot just sit there, but is up and down the whole time, getting popcorn and drinks, going to the bathroom, or just walking around, and while in his seat, his feet are moving up and down in the aisle, or his knees are going back and forth, and then sometimes something in the movie is not just right, so we all have to get up and leave right in the middle.

Even sitting at home, it is the same way, feet moving up and down the whole time, in those brown lace-up, oxford-type shoes.

The shoes have to be of the softest leather, the best, sometimes handmade, and they must be hard to find, since the two feet are different sizes and shapes since the war, so he either has to buy two pair or he has to have them specially made to measure. But then his feet hurt all the time anyway.

His feet are so stiff and so square, they look almost like wooden feet, and he walks on them in a way that seems just as if they are wooden feet, because the ankles can't move, so they have this stiff look. If you could see them without shoes and without those thin dress socks he always wears, then you would see how wasted and white and woodish they appear, and why he walks on them as if he is walking on stilts. In a way, they actually are stilts that have been fashioned in the early days of plastic surgery, but made of bone and flesh and also nerves, with pink raised scars all around the tendons and the square heels and the ankles, bony and lumpy in an oddly defined sort of way, man-made approximations of feet.

And of course these feet are always getting injured and reinjured, like the time when Mama and Daddy went to Nassau with their friends, and Daddy didn't believe them when they said there were stinging sea urchins on the beach, and so he wound up with a swollen foot full of stinging sea-urchin quills, as well as with a bad sunburn, because he also didn't believe that he couldn't stay out in the sun as long as anyone with his redhead's skin, and so the next day he was stuck in his hotel room while everyone else was out on the beach again, and he didn't know what to do with himself in the room all day.

He got curious about a little metal trapdoor that was in the ceiling of the bathroom of his hotel room, so he found a screwdriver and undid all four screws, and the metal trapdoor fell corner-down right on the instep of his now triply injured foot, so he wound up in another hospital.

He came back from that trip angry, breaking things every day, and he paced up and down the kitchen on one cane, eating three whole packages of Nestlé's cooking chocolate, and when he did that, he got the same look on his face that I had seen before when I watched him pull a bottle out of the wood bin that was in the brick fireplace. I saw him turn that bottle up, and as he drank, I saw him lunge toward that bottle with his face, as though he were Alice plunging in that instant through some looking-glass boundary in his own mind, and his face had the look of standing in a strong wind.

When he first came back from the hospital at Valley Forge, he was in leg casts and couldn't get around except on heavy wooden crutches, so there wasn't much he could do except make models of boats and planes and tanks and things, over and over again.

There was one model boat he was working on for a long time. It was a good one, made of balsa wood, and he would sit for hours absorbed in working on it and not moving much at all. But then one day there was a piece he couldn't find when the boat was almost finished. We looked and looked, but he couldn't get that piece and he couldn't get anyone else to get it right that instant. He got so mad that he took his crutch and smashed that model boat into bits and pieces, and then it was ruined.

He had really liked that boat, and had been working on it for a long time and had bought the stuff to paint it. It was going to be blue and gray wih a red stripe, and I had helped him to pick out the colors, but now he had crunched it into a hundred pieces that could not be put back together. He'd ruined everything.

I didn't want to talk to him much for a long time after that, which made him even madder. After those casts came off, he went from crutches to using two canes, and his feet hurt a lot then, and he had a hard time learning to balance on those two canes and would fall down a lot, such as the time when he had the two canes and it was dark and rainy and the car lights and the streetlights were shiny on the pavement like streaky-colored mirrors, and we were all hurrying, and my mother said to him, "Don't cross now; you'll fall." And the look he gave her, I thought he was going to hit her, but instead he leaned on those two thin canes with all his weight and he lunged out into the street. It was raining hard and there were cars, and he went lurching across as well as he could, but his weight was on those two thin cane tips, and one slid out from under him and he fell down hard, slipping and sliding in the street, with cars screeching and skidding on the mirrored wet pavement, but he glared right into their grilles, baring his teeth and yelling and cursing, and then he looked back at my mother and me as if we were the same as the car grilles, and then he struggled up, saying not to help him, goddammit, and to get away from him, and then he hit at the car nearest with one of the canes, and then he took off his nice new overcoat, which was now all wet and grease-stained, and he threw it in the street, and then he was mad and wouldn't talk to anyone for the rest of the night.

I was getting to where I didn't want to talk to him all that much, either. Not too long after that, when it was my fifth or sixth birthday, he gave me a pair of tall wooden stilts, and he made a point of saying that I had to learn to use them all by myself, but I never did learn to use them, and those red-and-green-painted stilts are still leaning reproachfully against the back wall of the garage. Once in a while he will get this look in his eye, and ask me why I never learned to use those stilts.

After that, he went back to the surgeons and said that he had changed his mind and that he wanted them to go ahead and amputate that foot that was always hurting him the most, but now he could already walk, so they refused to do it, so he has to live with himself like that.

He always wants to get any things that might be bothering him away from himself. He will fling those things, just hurl them away, and out into the abyss of intolerable imperfections out there orbiting aimlessly, forever banished from his awareness and from his sight.

And if he can't hurl the things away from himself, then he will thrust himself away from the things, and out of the scene at hand right that instant. For example, it might be that a friend he had known for thirty years, having gone to high school together, or having spent the war in hospitals together, or something like that, and it might be that Daddy and this friend would be sitting in a country club dining room with white tablecloths or even in a café on the border, with Mexican waiters in aprons standing around, and this friend might just say something that might strike Daddy as indicating a fundamental breach of some kind, or maybe he would think it indicated some sort of betrayal or personal insult, as he was constantly on the alert for such things, and then my father would suddenly shoot from his chair, knocking it backward, would throw the wooden table with all its cutlery and crystal to the floor, and then would go charging out of the room as fast as he could in that stiff-legged walk he had, and then he might never speak to that old friend of his again, just to show that that was how strongly he felt about it.

And suffering the consequences of showing how he felt about it was something that he didn't mind doing, and the fact that people didn't know what to do with him or how to handle the situations he would cause didn't seem to bother him, as if that was something that was just in his body, as if the way he had to live in his body was such that he had to show and act out everything. As if that was just a fact of reality and what other people chose to do about it was their own affair.

Sometimes that worst foot bothers him so much that he has to go back to using one crutch around the house, just for a week or so. One day while he was doing this, I was five or six, and I didn't want to go to school. I was hiding out in the backyard hoping they would just forget about me for long enough that I could miss the bus and skip school for just that one day, but my mother was yelling around the house for me and was getting mad, until finally she started yelling out the back door for me. Then Daddy came clumping out, still in his bathrobe and on one crutch, and furious that I would dare to defy them like that. I realized that I had made a big mistake. I hunched down behind the newly cut woodpile, hoping that he wouldn't see me, but after calling out a couple of times, he headed straight for me. I could see him through the spaces between the stacked logs near the top of the pile, and I was looking around for an escape, and then his crutch sank into the ground and he fell.

He fell heavily, right into some uncut branches, and scraped his hand and arm. Lifting up just a little, I saw him through the woodpile furiously struggling with his legs and feet and with his bathrobe and the crutch, his face turning redder and redder, and then he picked up a hatchet that had been left by the uncut wood and he started hitting his crutch with it. He got up on one knee and hacked and hacked at that crutch, until he was chopping it in two.

I hunched down low behind the woodpile, and he just kept on hacking and hacking and hacking. It seemed as if he had forgotten about me and about the yard and even about the crutch and everything, and that all he was thinking about was the hacking that went on and on, and there was no other place for me to hide. And then everything stopped.

I got up slowly to where I could peer between the logs and see him, and I could see that he had stopped hacking and was looking at the foot that was right there in front of him. It was the worse one of the two, and he was just staring at that foot with that hatchet in his hand. And that was when I knew I had to get out of there right that minute, and so I jumped up and ran from behind the woodpile and across the yard, and that was when my father looked up and saw me.

Lennox Lane

Now we live outside the city limits in a Dilbeck ranch-style house spread as far as a small two-bedroom could spread across our suburban-pioneer acre-and-a-half lot. White-painted brick, wood shingles, gravel drive, three-board white-painted fence all around, roses and more roses climbing and blooming along the fence, up on the house, onto the roof on one side, blood red roses every one, small, tight blooms, branches lined with thorns, and hardy climbers all.

A sprawling prickly pear cactus that my mother backed into and accidentally sat on one day while dragging a sprinkler across the newly seeded lawn in her apron and high heels is dead center in front, next to the fence. She was mad all summer about Daddy's laughing so hard while picking out the spines.

I know that cactus does bloom, pink petals opening to relentless sun glaring across the narrow ribbon of sticky tar and gravel country road, bluebonnets and buttercups nodding on the parkway in spring, flowering briefly before they get mowed.

At this time, there are blankets of bluebonnets and cactus in front yards north of town. Late summer and fall, tumbleweeds roll along the road out front, stick in the glossy black tar, and are mashed into the tar by the occasional car or pickup truck. They pile in drifts against the fences along our country roads, our country mailboxes, different sizes of tumbleweeds, different types.

There are still septic tanks and telephone party lines.

There are woods and creeks and culverts to play in, and neighborhood kids and dogs and cats and even chickens wander the yards at will. There are rattlesnakes and tarantulas, scorpions, horned toads, bees, wasps, hornets, and ants of several kinds.

Daddy goes back to work at the job he had before the war, at Lone Star Oldsmobile and Cadillac, his father's business. And when all the men come home from the war and buy a car or two, they make good money.

Some days, Daddy comes home from work in a good mood, and some days not. And what he might do then, you never can tell.

Here I am, sitting on the steps in the garage one day, when his car barrels up and suddenly stops a few feet from where I am sitting. I want to hide, but it's too late, so instead I try to act casual. To my surprise, he clump-CLUMPS up to me, hands me a lollipop from his pocket, grins, says, "Here, kid," and then clumps on in the door.

Now Mama is putting us to bed after dinner and looking like she's been crying, and we don't know where Daddy went, roaring away in his car.

Now it's bright white morning again, with everyday let's-get-busy schoolbooks and socks, with hurry-up, everything-is-just-fine voices, May-May humming and singing with the kitchen clanging and kitchen sizzling, and time to start hurrying again.

Every day I run-run-run as if along a string—*do this, do that*—to get myself out there to dangle in windy space on the corner, waiting for the school bus—have to get there on time, on time! And I'm never ready to do everything on time, the way she wants it, the way all grown-ups seem to want you to do things, and the way even Santa Claus and God must want you to do things, but I'm always running as if tied behind a moving car.

I was eager to go to school in kindergarten, and even in first grade. A boy across our worktable told me that his brother told him that in second grade everything would change and not be fun anymore. And then the teacher separated us for talking too much, and after that we weren't friends anymore. And he was right, because now I'm in second grade, and even though I can already read most things, whatever it is that's happening in second grade, I'm never ready. They make it go too fast.

"Hurry up!" Mama says.

In the bedroom I pick up a sock and look it over, wondering if all this time I've been ignoring some secret indication of right and left. A worn place on the heel is there, and the defuzzed threads crisscross in a way I never noticed before.

I put the sock on one foot. I look down at the other sock, the shoe, the shoelaces, and here I am again in the time-stopping bog that seems like my own more natural state, a somehow shameful and stolen state of blank staring at the limp foot-pattern flatness of a sock suspended over my one bare foot, and at an untied shoelace falling like a napping grass snake across the other already sock-accomplished foot.

I look at the tops of my feet, my knees, my legs, the palms of my hands, the blue veins. In and out, in and out, my breath is going, on and on, as if I have nothing to do with it. My heart is thumping through my whole body, and I must be thumping and breathing all the time like this, even when I'm not noticing it. Even asleep, my body must be throbbing, buzzing, keeping itself alive every second to the tips of my toes, my fingernails, my hair. But I'm not telling it to do this. It's alive on its own, with me inside. How does my body know what to do?

I wonder if it all might stop during the night when I'm not watching. *If I should die before I wake.* It seems we pray so God won't make us die in the night while we're not looking. *I pray the Lord my soul to take.* But no! I don't want somebody taking my soul, leaving my body for bugs to eat! And then what? Would I be in heaven? Would Mama cry? Would Daddy be mad?

I don't want to go to heaven! I want to stay on earth!

Outside the bedroom window, a dragonfly left over from summer sits on the screen as though exhausted, but his mission incomplete. I tap the window and he jumps off. Then there is a short time, a long time—I don't know how much time, but it seems all time dissolves into watching a silvery green dragonfly helicopter from branch to branch of the no-longer-flowering bushes. Will he die soon?

"Are you in there daydreaming?" Mama says from far away down the hall.

The dragonfly darts away, then darts back, as if having forgotten something over here, then darts over there, then darts to a different spot, as if now a decision is going to have to be made. It seems that dragonflies are as busy as everyone else.

"Are you ready yet?" she's calling me from another room.

I look down at the second sock, start putting it on.

"If you miss that bus again today, I am not going to take you," she calls.

And what would happen then? I wonder. Would she really let me miss school every day if I didn't make it to the bus on time? I don't think so. But that would be fine with me. I'd rather be left alone to play barefoot in the woods and the fields behind our house. (Visions of rabbits and horned toads and quail skittering away from my invading feet, visions of the abandoned chicken coops.) Then what about the next day? And the next day? Would she let me go on that way, missing school, having said it?

Everything would be different then. How far would it go? Would that one change make everything else change completely, like in *The Wizard of Oz*? Dorothy was missing school all that time, but the story doesn't mention her having to make up work when she went back. Did they ask a lot of questions? Was everybody mad?

And what about Pinocchio? He did set out to go to school but then got sidetracked into having too much fun, and that turned out to be bad. And he kept forgetting about telling the truth. Then everything changed for him, like in a dream.

"I'm coming in there," says Mama from far away.

And what about Alice? When she followed that white rabbit, did she drop out of school and get behind? She didn't seem to be having fun. Just like Dorothy, she was trying to get back home to her own real world. How come none of these kids has to go to school? Maybe all those stories are about dreams, and this is something that you're supposed to know already. Is that real? Can you go into another world like that? I think some stories are real and some are not, but grown-ups do not seem to want to tell you which are which.

"I don't want to ruin it for you," they say.

Ruin what?

Or they cock their heads and smile and say things like "If you believe it, then it is true."

But that is not what I want to know!

It seems like the main thing grown-ups want is for you not to find out anything about what's real. They close the doors. When you come into the room, they stop talking.

I asked a boy at school about this, but he just laughed and said that I was a big baby, so of course I'm supposed to know something about this already. And *you can't ask!*

So here I am, in a kind of box, walled in on one side by school and my mother's voice shouting, "If you miss that school bus . . ." (Visions of the trundling sunflower-bright country school bus bristling with noisy children passing me by. Visions of walking through the high grass fields behind our house, trudging alone up to the school, slinking into my seat late, curious eyes turned onto my red-hot face, my mother-chosen dress.)

On another side, there's the window, which in summer would be an open window to all outside, trees budding and blowing, fresh-cut grass smells wafting through the screen, grasshoppers, frogs, crawdads, horned toads. But now there's only this one leftover fading green dragonfly, and the silver shine of sunlight across the chilly screen.

On a third side, there's the room, my bed, the baby beds, the blond varnished dressers with dime-store decals of busily rushing Dutch girls in wooden shoes and aprons and sideways bonnets hiding their faces, carrying tulips and water buckets and brooms. (Visions of picking out the decals with my mother from the overflowing wooden filing cabinets on the dusty plank floor at the back of Mott's Five and Dime. Visions of my mother with apron and bucket and sponge, sticking the slippery wet decals onto the dressers and the beds, sliding them into place, blotting them, smiling at them, smiling at me as if these busy Dutch girl decals were going to be so good for all of us.)

And there are all the many people around me all the time—Mama and Daddy and May-May and grandparents and neighbors and teachers and aunts and uncles and cousins and sisters and maids, and even lots more people than that, things always going on that I don't understand. They all seem to know things and have secrets they are not going to tell. And you're not supposed to ask. And they all seem to want things, to care so much about everything about me being a certain way.

Now I'm in this box; later I'll be in another box. Why am I here now and not someplace else?

If I could spend enough time alone and barefoot in the woods, away from people, would magical things start happening to me like in those stories they read to me, the Girl slipping through a looking glass, a whirlwind, a rabbit hole? Could a dream world take over like that? Could the Girl take over? Is there another place to go?

Surely such things couldn't really happen. They wouldn't allow it. I'd get too far behind. I'd have to go to summer school to catch up. They would not allow it.

Clubhouse

Winter starts coming in with the first December days. I hear hammering outside. Nathan!

I climb the low three-board fence to find him at the edge of their woods next door, working on his clubhouse.

"Look," says Nathan, pointing, and we watch as a cottontail disappears into the woods.

"He came out to see why I stopped hammering! He's practically my pet now," says Nathan.

"Maybe he's the Easter Rabbit," I say.

Nathan laughs. We both laugh.

"I came before."

"I saw your apple core." He starts hammering again.

"What're you doing?"

"Fixin' leaks. It's fixin' to rain."

"Where'd you get the wood?"

"You know that new house? They let me have these nifty shingles." He doesn't look at me, talks like a grown-up around the nails pinched in the corner of his mouth.

I walk around his little pounded-dirt clearing, kicking fallen pecans into where he's made a pile. In Texas, winter's only a hint of cold yet in early December.

"Have you got your tree?"

"Yep, a big one, but we haven't fixed it up yet."

"We're getting ours tomorrow," I say. "Maybe when we go to the movie."

"What movie?" Nathan and I talk about movies a lot.

"Something about a miracle."

"What is a miracle anyway?"

"I don't know—something in the Bible, I think."

"Oh yeah."

A drop of water hits my nose. I look up—dark clouds, wind picking up, getting cold.

"Here comes the rain!" says Nathan. Every rain is an event.

It comes down fast, a sudden storm, cold needles of drops.

"Get inside!" and he scurries off the roof and into the low door of the clubhouse—a door too small for grown-ups. I scramble in after him. It's dark, the only light through gaps between boards and patches as it darkens outside, and water drizzles down on the corners, making puddles on the uneven dirt floor. We sit on small fruit crates.

Nathan strikes a wooden match, and the musty air fills with a burning wood and sulfur smell, the yellow light, the thrill of this forbidden act. He lights a candle stub he's stuck in a tuna can, rests it on a shelf on the wall next to his stack of cigar boxes filled with treasures and trading cards.

"They let you do that?"

"Do what?"

We hover together, shiver and laugh as the candle lights our faces, rain dancing loudly on the roof, puddles spreading out. He opens a box with matches, stolen cigarettes, a corncob pipe, a dime-store penknife, other secret stuff.

"Want to smoke grapevine?"

"I don't know. What is it?"

"Oh. Never mind," he says, putting it back on the shelf. "I don't want to get in trouble with your mom."

"What's grapevine?"

"Oh, it's really nothing. You wouldn't like it."

"Because I'm a girl?"

"Well . . . yeah."

"But that's just what my mother says!"

He doesn't answer.

"Nathan," I say, "do you think the Easter Rabbit is small like that or big like a person?"

"I don't know," he says, not looking at me.

"Once I thought I saw the Easter Rabbit, and he was as big as a man. But now I don't know."

"Maybe you saw a man in an Easter Rabbit suit," he says. *(I never even thought of that!)* "Because it seems to me if the Easter Rabbit's real, he's got to be a real rabbit, maybe like a extra-big jackrabbit."

"But how would he carry all the eggs?"

"Maybe he lays the eggs like a chicken."

"But then why don't baby rabbits come out of the eggs?"

We laugh.

"So do you think the Easter Rabbit is real?"

He peers at me, considering. "No, not really." He lowers his voice. "I think grown-ups made it up."

"But what about Santa Claus? Do you think he's real?"

"Uh ... I don't know about that." He looks at the ground.

"Daddy told me when he was a kid he saw Santa Claus."

"Yeah, at the department store, right?"

"No, no, in his living room on Christmas morning—saw him come down the chimney and everything!"

"Your Dad?" He looks at me now. "He told you that?"

He picks up a knife and a piece of wood and starts carving on it. "I don't think so," he says to himself.

"Cross my heart and hope to die," I say, making the cross-my-heart sign on my chest with my finger.

"Stick a thousand needles in your eye?"

"Yes!"

"You have to say it!"

"Okay, cross my heart and hope to die, stick a thousand needles in my eye, he told me that!"

"Your dad did that, huh?" He's bent over his carving now. "Why?"

"Oh, nothing, I thought it was just your mom."

"What?"

"Oh, nothing," he says, holding up his carving. It's two U-shapes with dots in them.

"Tits, man, tits! Pretty good, huh?" He laughs in a mean way.

"What do you mean 'just your mom'?"

He starts carving again, not answering me.

"Tell me!"

The way I see it, Nathan and I are partners in an ongoing investigation of the unknown and mysterious grown-up world, so reporting back our findings and observations is a matter of great seriousness. And I want to know that this unspoken pact is still on. So why is he acting this way?

"You're lucky you have parents who love you," he says quietly.

K*NOCK KNOCK KNOCK KNOCK KNOCK!*

We both jump. The little door opens, and Mrs. Calder is there, leaning down with a big umbrella, shouting over the rain.

"What're you-all doing out here? Honey, your mom is looking for you! It's dinnertime! Go home! Go! A little rain won't hurt you! Nathan, you come in with me right now! Is that a candle? You know you're not supposed to have matches out here. . . ."

I run out, climb the slippery wooden fence, run, slip on wet grass, fall down, get up, run, run, run, and by the time I get home, I'm drenched.

I stand shivering inside the back door, smelling dinner, and disaster, hearing Daddy yelling about GranDad and Uncle Ted as I come in the back door.

Oh no! Daddy is mad—I better hide!

They don't see me at first; then they do. Mama hushes him.

"Where have you been?" she says to me in a voice that is trying to be mad.

"I . . . I was just . . ." Uh-oh! *What will Daddy do?*

But when Daddy turns and looks at me through the doorway, sees me standing there dripping wet and shivering, he smiles, as if he enjoys seeing some adventures.

"What are you up to, kid?" he says, grinning.

You never can tell.

A Moth, a Toad, a Bat

Mama bends to kiss me, and the long dark braid falls across the light from the rooms beyond. Daddy and I have been to a movie and are taking off our coats. It's late for me to be up.

We three are in the small entry hall—Mama, bending down now to me; Daddy, whipping off his coat, impatient at being really much too warm in such a coat, then Daddy standing aside, watching Mama and me. I'm holding my coat across my chest, looking down and away, but still seeing the two of them the way a plant sees the sun, even turning my eyes away from their two lines of vision, hot searchlights sweeping around, to each other briefly, then converging, focusing their hot attention, both at once, on me. I pretend I do not notice being scrutinized by their grown-up eyes.

I see the dim nightlight at the far end of the hall, where the babies are asleep. I've usually already been put to bed back there, if never asleep, by this time of night, but listening, praying, rocking, singing, running and rerunning the entire everything of what has so far been revealed.

Mama's ready for bed in the see-through red nightgown. I can see her nipples and her belly button, and her hair down there and everything. Daddy and I are both seeing them at the same time.

"Go and put something on," Daddy says to Mama. Mama laughs in a funny way, turning with a sideways mouth. Daddy puts his coat into the closet, looks over his shoulder as though taken by surprise, then closes the closet door with a jerk, as if something's secret in there.

Mama's hand, as shiny as the yearbook-beauty face I watch her smooth at her mirror with the nightly cold-cream, is on my shoulder. Mama turns, casting a passing glance at me, and whispers to Daddy.

"How did it go?"

I pretend not to hear what they say to each other. I stand looking down at an anchor-stamped coat button. The navy blue thread is frayed, starting to break away.

I pick at it.

Why didn't Mama go to the movie with us? Why did just Daddy and I go to this particular movie? Because I heard her talking on the phone about this movie and about some kind of a problem about me.

I saw the front curtains move as Daddy and I were turning in, the two of us side by side on the car seat in the dashboard light, me up front where Mama sits, instead of me in the back with the babies, trying to figure out what the grown-ups are talking about up there. I looked over at Daddy's sharp profile against the windows half-open for the balmy-cool mix of Texas December air streaming through, blowing across both of our thoughts and feelings, which were hovering together, it seemed to me, Daddy and I gliding through a city suburb, a rural highway, unlit country roads—a rabbit in headlights on the road, a moth, a toad, a bat, a neighbor on a bicycle, a dark-skinned maid at a bus stop whose eyes met mine.

As the driveway gravel crunched at my realization that this time and chance of my being alone with Daddy was ending now, there were so many things I wanted to say, things I wanted to ask. As the headlights swept the front of the house, shadows running across the lot, I could have sworn a curtain shivered in the wake of some quick-motion back into the house, Mama in there watching for our return, as if there were some reason for this unusual thing of Daddy and I going out at night.

Now they're standing here, as if waiting for me to do something. I tease thread from the back of the button. *Why do some threads come loose?* I wonder. *Perhaps this button will come off, fall and roll away under chairs, be lost.*

"Fine, I think," Daddy murmurs. Daddy's standing next to Mama now, his hand lifted to touch her arm.

His eyes quickly glance over, not to my eyes, never really to my eyes when Mama or anyone else is around, it seems to me, but more to the placement of the object of me next to and on the other side of Mama from where he stands.

Mama stands between Daddy and me, her hands poised as if a holding position, at the center of our three-some. I look away from the headlight-beam grown-up eyes and the hot, humming center of *us* that seems to me to be located somewhere between them.

I want in. I want to be good.

Daddy's shifting from one foot to the other foot for the third time now, his bad foot bothering him, I can tell. Then they speed up time, as if we have to keep up with something that's supposed to happen.

If only I could have asked Daddy why that man who you could see wanted to be the daddy in the movie kept acting as if there were something so wrong with that little girl in the movie who didn't believe in Santa Claus.

Something sad and embarrassing and wrong.

And that they couldn't really talk about.

At first, I was surprised to be taken to a movie with this kind of little girl in it, because she was not at all the kind of little girl they want. I wanted to know more about that girl.

Daddy will sometimes tell me things. But at the movies, there are too many things Daddy will not sit still for. He can't sit still for long anyway, because of the feet.

He'll leap from his seat like he did tonight when that Santa Claus man first came on and said, "You are making a mistake! You are making a mistake!" as if this were something important.

I was about to ask Daddy, but Daddy was up and gone by the time the mother in the movie was hiring the man to be the department store Santa Claus in the big New York City parade, and the man decided he would do it because, he said, "the children mustn't be disappointed." But Daddy didn't wait around for that part.

By the time Daddy came back, it seemed that something was wrong with the little girl's mother that put her in a bad mood all the time. And of course the little girl could not feel good until her mother felt good first.

I'm aware that I have not yet been excused. Released. Dismissed. I look away from the two of them standing here waiting for me to do something they already have in mind. I try to ease away from that one hand of hers that is returning now to hold casually but firmly on to my shoulder, holding me in place.

Mama leans down to me, changing her manner and her voice. The braid swings loosely down, and so does the nightgown. I see the small breasts tight against her body, the nipples pink erasers vibrating as she talks.

"Well, how was the movie?" she's saying brightly. "Was it a good movie?" And she's smiling and nudging me as if to play a little game, but I don't get it.

"Did you like that movie? Did you and your daddy have fun? Did you thank your daddy for taking you out for such a nice time?

Mama's eyes catch mine, little lights, little hooks in them, as she leans the full moon of her irresistible face down to right in front of my face, and as she is speaking so closely to me in that voice that grown-ups use for talking to babies and small children, and to dogs and cats and birds in cages when other grown-ups are around. When Daddy is around.

Daddy's shifting from one foot to the other. He looks down at me with his black bird-eyes.

I'm tempted to go ahead and like Daddy, not only on a trial basis. Sometimes I want to like him. Sometimes it seems Daddy wants me to like him. But then sometimes it seems that Daddy wants me to know that he doesn't care if I like him or not, because it's all about something else.

On this particular night, he did spend the whole evening taking me to the movie, and then out for ice cream, and not even once saying anything about my being too fat to be allowed to eat ice cream. Even when the woman with the hairnet at Preston Road Pharmacy brought the ice-cream sundae just for me and only the coffee for him, Daddy didn't say anything, even when both our eyes rested on those soft vanilla-bean scoops, the satiny fudge sauce, the whipped cream, the cherry on top. When I took the first toothache-cold bite, I waited in my head to hear Daddy call me "Fatty," but he didn't say it, didn't even give me that look. He didn't take bites with his coffee spoon without asking, either. He just let the ice cream be mine.

Instead, Daddy started telling about when he was a kid like me, how the kids then would go to the drugstore after school, how things were in those days in drugstores and in candy stores, when one penny would buy a paper bag of licorice sticks you could chew on for a week, when the boys wore knickers and caps and played Red Rover and marbles and kick the can. He told me how he worked after school in his father's cycle shop, where men of the small town in Utah—where he was born, the eldest son and namesake to his misfit Italian father and his red-haired Scottish Mormon mother from a prominent Salt Lake City pioneer family—would come by the shop and talk to his father about the new bicycles and motorcycles. He told me how they held the motorcycle races—the first West of the Mississippi, he said, his voice becoming quieter and quieter—and how men who later became famous as race-car drivers or as big shots at General Motors, or for this or for that, came to those races from all across the country, and how he knew them all by name, and how they all knew him.

"Is that really true?"

"Yes, that is all really true," he said, and his eyes looked a certain way that made me know it was true.

The excitement for him lay with the new machines, the Iver Johnsons, the Harleys, with the famous men of the time, Edison, the Wright brothers, when the new machines were changing the world, and knowing his place there in his father's forward-looking small business. He seemed to have a vision of something about his father saying, "You didn't see him when he was young."

His eyes looked off, seeing something standing there next to us, believing in it. He even stopped moving his feet and knees, and I could sit there watching him in the mirror behind the counter until I could almost see my big, gruff, half-crippled daddy as an eager freckled boy in knickers among tall men, and I was letting down my guard with him.

He was forgetting about paying attention to something about me, was being friendly, as if I were a regular person, not someone he had to pretend something with, so that I was forgetting about ice cream, and forgetting to wonder why we'd done this unusual thing of going out together, Daddy and me. And when my ice cream softened, I stirred the chocolate and vanilla together cake batter–smooth, and I gave my daddy a bite.

I saw the surprised look in Daddy's eyes, his forehead smoothing, his mouth working the cold spoon. And then Daddy and I both smiled right at each other, right into each other's eyes, and right at the same time. And then he said we had to go.

But now here he is, standing by the door behind Mama, foot tapping–ready to end our good-night scene, while Mama's leaning over to peck me on the forehead. He has a crooked grin.

I should have asked him some things while I had him to myself. I know that soon they're going to turn out the light and leave me in that dark room where something sits in the corner watching and waiting for its chance.

In the movie, the little girl had no daddy. She had only a mother who talked in a serious voice, telling her there was no such thing as Santa Claus.

That was surprising. I looked over at Daddy, but he did not look back.

And in the movie, the two of them were not looking for a daddy, and yet the mother seemed to be so worried about things like fairy tales and Prince Charming, about believing in things that were not true. "No fairy tales!" she said.

Then along came this man from across the hall who wanted to be the daddy. You could tell. And the man was nice. But then the man seemed to think something was wrong with the mother and with the little girl, and he wanted them to change.

Then along came this other man with a white beard, who told everybody he was Santa Claus. And he got the job. The little girl pulled his whiskers in the store to be sure that not believing was really the correct policy. But I knew that was silly, because he could have had a real beard and still not been Santa Claus.

So then after that, people started saying this man was more than "a little bit crazy, like painters and musicians," and they all started arguing about whether the man was crazy or whether he was Santa Claus. Then they sent him away to a hospital to sit around in his bathrobe looking sad.

I kept looking over and wondering why Daddy brought me to this movie where the little girl and the mother did not believe in Santa Claus. Was he now going to be the one to tell me the truth about this? Did Mama know about this?

But Daddy hunched down eating popcorn, his eyes bright as he looked at the screen, watching the man trying to cheer up the mother and the little girl. But the mother did not want to be cheered up, so the little girl couldn't be cheered up, either, because, of course, she had to wait for her mother. So then Daddy jumped up again.

Then there was a part at the end with a trial, a judge, and a lot of grown-ups talking, where I did not understand why, if that bearded man in the movie really was Santa Claus, were all the grown-ups in the movie and in the audience laughing so hard when those big sacks of letters to Santa Claus were emptied in the courtroom. Was it all a big joke?

Was that man really Santa Claus or not? What is the

answer? I really want to know the answer! *Why is it so hard to get the answer to this question?*

And I want to know more about that little girl.

I look up into Mama's face. The clear dark eyes that seem so secure in some secret knowing. The high, serene forehead that has no doubt. The cool smiling lips that are not telling. Her beautiful yet invincible face. Her invincible yet sweet face. Her blandly sweet and yet knowing face. Her hand is on me, as her hand is always on me. I am hers.

Daddy's watching me from far away again now. Something not unfriendly is in Daddy's eye as he watches Mama and he watches me from high and far away.

I feel my eyebrows might be slightly lifted, and I try to lower them in a natural-appearing way.

"It was a good movie," I say, working to brighten up my voice, but it comes out sounding all wrong. I try to join in, but we all three know now that she had to tell me to do it.

If only I could have a big brother or even a big sister, someone older, or just someone—*I need someone*—who will tell me at least what it is that we are pretending.

That movie was telling me something. It was clear from that movie that if that little girl was going to have a happy mother and a happy daddy and a nice happy house with a swing in front—and you cannot just go around being happy until you have all these things in place—then that little girl was going to have to go ahead and believe in Santa Claus and in all the things in which we're supposed to go ahead and believe.

"I had a nice time. Thank you," I say to the floor. I grin,

showing a good-child face. They stand and look as if they do not know what to do with the problem of me.

I slip away from Mama's grasp. I slide away from their disappointment. I slither away from their poised huddle and down the hall to our children's bedroom. I pull the door almost closed with one lizard hand.

I put my coat on a hanger into the dark closet, careful to be quiet, to go with little light, and to jump quickly back from the yawning closet cave before anything in there can thrust out a claw and grab me. I hold my breath against the shadows, taking care to tiptoe so as not to wake the two little sister babies Mama's so crazy about now, in the way of the good and well-trained responsible eldest reptile child that I am.

In the bathroom, I brush my teeth and wash my face. I scrub until my cheeks sting. I wring out the washcloth, fold it, and place it in exactly the way I have been taught to do, all the time perfectly aware of the fact that something scaly with one eye in the middle of its forehead has been watching me all this time from the shadows in the hall—something that is waiting for its chance.

On tiptoe, I can see the eyes of me in the mirror. I don't like my eyes, and yet I look.

Is that the face that is me? I don't look like my dark-eyed mother. My face is red, freckled, the eyes light, the eyebrows lifted. I prepare to look, as if afraid of seeing something watching from behind. I can't look at myself without myself looking back.

I hear their voices. I hear my name. I hear them say "she," as if something's wrong.

In the hall, I stay on the path of light from the bathroom until I see the lamp next to the bed. I walk slowly and casually, because I know that if that thing in the hall sees me hurrying or being afraid, it will jump me. And when it jumps me, it will have a big grin on its face.

The Sheik of Araby

After we say "Now I Lay Me Down to Sleep" and God bless everybody, and Mama goes out, I lie in the dark, hearing the babies' moist breathing, and I listen to the sounds of the two of them walking around the house—her light, clicking heels—even her slippers have high heels—and his heavier-on-one-foot clump-CLUMPing, a great injured bird looking for a place to land.

I hear the jingle-crash of keys and coins hitting the dresser. I hear their talking rising and falling, the words unclear, but the tones and rhythms, their back-and-forth, are the night music of our lives, weaving in and out with one radio song after another—"Sentimental Journey," "Night and Day," "Tumbleweed," "Stardust." I sing along, often rocking and singing myself to sleep.

On this night, I don't hear fighting or yelling or crying. There's no slapping, no falling down, no slamming doors, no phone calls, no Daddy's tires squealing, skidding gravel all the way to my midnight bedroom windowpane on this night, either, after they think I'm long asleep, like the babies.

They are quiet in there for once, and seem to be getting

along. I think they've closed their door. I wonder what they're doing in there.

I want to be part of the *us* that includes the two of them. I hold myself in readiness to be what they want, and I watch them, am never not watching them, holding onto myself.

They don't know I'm not asleep in here the way they think I am, but am keeping watch, fighting the giving up, the stepping off that too-deep step that sometimes starts a floating down to hit the ground, to waken with that sudden *What's happening?* jerk. They think when they put me to bed and turn out the light, that's the end of it. But that is not the end of it.

I can still hear their muffled talking in there all the long way down the hall, but it's getting quieter. Then they turn off the radio.

Silence. Darkness. Silence.

I lie in my bed like a small worm curled upon itself. I am this small worm. And I am lying alone on a chilly beach near the edge of the black ocean of night washing across the whole world outside of our house. The ocean laps darkly at the edges of *us*.

I hurry up and pray for Jesus to keep me from dissolving away into the dark, saying "Now I Lay Me Down to Sleep" a few times, but this makes me afraid I might "die before I wake." I say my own prayers, over and over, like a chant.

I sing "Jesus loves me—this I know, For the Bible tells me so," and then I'm rolling around clutching the covers, trying to focus tightly all my longing into a single prayer arrow arcing shakily upward by the force of *I do believe. I do! I do!*

A speeding silvery glimmer, sparks flying in its wake, my arrow gathers speed, pushes right through the ceiling, the trees, the clouds, the syrupy moonless night, all the way out to some farther-beyond-outer, lighter and glowing-brighter place where transparent-paper cutout figures of God on His Throne, and Jesus and Mary and Santa Claus and the Three Wise Men and Ozma of Oz and the Blue Fairy are standing together, underwater-ishly undulating up there among purple-and-gold-tinged clouds, sparkly stars and comets, little heat-wavy things, small puffs of blue smoke, all surrounded by angels, cherubs, fairy godmothers, all looking down at me from a sky so far away with sad smiles, as if they have things to say to me, as if they would like to explain all kinds of things to me, but something is holding them back.

I tighten my whole body to make them know how hard I am believing in them, and how sincerely I am trying and begging and wishing for even just one of them to come down from that hidden world you have to be afraid of all the time, to please come and shed some light around me, some Truth into me.

I pretend my arms are tied behind my back, and then that my arms and feet are tied to the corners of the bed. I rock back and forth, straining against imaginary bindings, toward I don't know what. Surely they'll see up there how much I do care, how I am not just one of the regular people who don't care. Surely they'll look down and see I'm doing all I can do to be as worthy as anyone has ever been worthy of the sort of special appearance that all the Bible stories they read to us in Sunday school testify to their having made in the past to certain other people—usually in the desert, but not always.

I want this special appearance. I need this special appearance. *Please, God, let me be the one to receive this special appearance.*

They will, of course, understand that I am still too young to go to the desert.

I imagine being the Virgin Mary and having God appear. The Holy Ghost. What is that? Then later, she has the baby Jesus. I don't get it. And what's the difference between an angel and a ghost? They say angels are real, but then that ghosts are not real. But what about that Holy Ghost business?

Surely some minor angel will favor me. I know if I keep doing this for a long-enough time, I will be worthy and surely one of them will appear. I would be happy with just the briefest appearance of an angelish something. Anything. *Give me anything!*

Because then I can make up my mind about some things.

It's the Three Wise Men that I'd most like to talk to. Who are these Three Wise Men? How did they know about the star? How did they get to be so wise? What are the things the Three Wise Men know that make up all this wisdom, and is this knowledge still around for someone like me to find out? And are the Three Wise Men still alive, or are they up in Heaven the way I imagine, along with Jesus and all those others? *Come down, Three Wise*

Men, and help me to understand! Tell it all to me! Please! I am waiting and waiting for you!

I keep on doing all of this for quite a long time.

I wonder if any other children do this, or think these things. Maybe children all over the world are doing exactly the same thing at the same time, but it's just that no one talks about it—too shameful.

I'm not sure exactly where that arrow goes. Does it dissolve upon arrival in such a place? Does it disappear when I stop seeing it? Or are all my arrows saved up somewhere? In Heaven? At the North Pole? Saved up until they amount to something up there? Do they know about me up there? Are they watching me from up there? Making lists?

They say Santa Claus knows if you've been bad or good, and keeps a list, so that means he must somehow be watching you all the time. "You'd better not pout, you'd better not cry! . . . He sees you when you're sleeping . . ." But how? Does he watch you in the same way that God and Jesus watch you, from up in the sky, playing with moons and stars, sitting on clouds? From behind rocks and trees? From inside your own head?

In Sunday school, they say that God and Jesus hear your prayers. But how do you know if they're hearing you or not? How do you know you're not just making the whole thing up? *How do you know you're not talking to yourself, in bed, alone in the dark?*

I banish this bad thought.

There's no sound, no sign. I lie still, absorbing this. Then I go ahead and feel around on the interesting parts of my body for a while. Sometimes this part or that part is more tingly and interesting than the others. I think my mother would not like this if she knew. I figure God and Jesus and whoever else must not be paying that much attention right now anyway.

My navel is interesting lately. When I tickle it, especially deep inside, it makes other things tingle as well, each in a different way. Then I start in on tickling some of those other parts. This is not a completely new discovery, but lately it's gotten a lot more interesting. I think about Nathan, who lives next door. I must ask Nathan if he's noticed things like this. But Nathan'll be the one to bring up this subject. He always does.

I think about something Daddy said. I turn over and stare at the window. The moon is up and beaming mistily through the blinds, as if the Blue Fairy were coming through to tell Pinocchio how to change from being a wooden puppet into being a real boy.

I always used to be trying to kiss my elbow to turn into a boy. Boys seem to have more fun, and they seem to know things.

The boys at school talk about Santa Claus in a sarcastic way. Most of the older boys already seem to have their own world, separate from and scornful of much of the grown-up world. And scornful of *girls.*

I go back and forth about all this. This is the second time I have put my doubts on hold.

The first time, we were in another house, a small, modern, carpeted, flat-roofed Stanhope Avenue house in town, as sleek inside as a new car. I wasn't in kindergarten yet, the second baby wasn't born yet, and I could never remember whether that first baby, tiny then, was a girl or a boy.

There was a vacant lot behind our house where older boys played ball, and I would hang around this boy named Billy, who had once stopped them from knocking down my snowman. I had dreams in which Billy was mixed up with Mighty Mouse. At the vacant lot, near Easter, I heard Billy say it was really your parents who hid the eggs.

Also, I'd heard Mama on the telephone saying, "Well, if it rains, we'll just have to hide the eggs in the house." But then when I asked about it, she looked surprised, and she said, "Yes, of course there's a real Easter Rabbit."

Daddy came in to say good night to me the night before Easter, and I asked him. He said the same things Mama said, but with his little teasing smile, and he started tickling me, saying he was going to count my ribs. *Tickle tickle tickle tickle tickle!*

"How many ribs do you think you've got?" he asked.

"A hundred and sixty-thirteen!" I screamed.

He started counting, "One, two, three, four," and the more he counted ribs, the more ticklish I became, until I was giggling and squealing insanely, hoping this would go on forever, and afraid it might, and also closing my eyes to a feeling of something new.

Then Daddy stopped, all of a sudden jumped to his feet, grabbed his cane, and clump-CLUMPed out of the room as if something bad had happened. *What?*

The next morning was Easter. I always wake before

they do, and I wasn't supposed to leave my room yet, but I did.

I'd recently realized grown-ups don't know what you're doing if they're not looking at you. Although you have to watch out for the sides of their eyes.

I sneaked out from where the baby was asleep, then tiptoed across to their room, where they were both breathing deeply and covered with bedclothes, Mama's face just peeking out, sideways on the bed. *Is she looking at me? Am I real yet?* I tiptoed closer. Her eyes were closed, her mouth open. A moving and gleaming beneath the lids made me think it might be a trick. *How can she not know I'm standing right here? Would she be mad?*

I touched her hair, ready to jump back. I reached out one finger and touched her eyelid. She did not move, but lay there on the bed at my chin level, breathing the same, even when I gently lifted her eyelid to see if the eye was awake inside there. I was ready for Mama to get up now, to come out, to make the world start up.

But the eye of my mother was not seeing me. The eye was rolled over and looking like something that could scare you, looking whitely inward at dreams. Her breathing changed; she rolled over. I jumped back.

I tiptoed into the living room.

Looking out the plate-glass sliding back doors, I saw it had rained, so I figured if the eggs were hidden in the house, that would mean it had been the two of them who had done the egg hiding, and not the Easter Rabbit.

That would mean it had been the two of them coloring

eggs in the night and then cleaning up the mess and hiding it all away.

That would mean that the two of them, up late, sneaking around behind chairs and under tables, had placed the eggs in the obvious places around the house, a blue egg here, a gold egg there, the two of them together, maybe laughing and joking, having a little fun just for the two of them. Would they have crawled around together? Fallen down giggling about the game? Would they have hugged and kissed each other there on the floor like people I could imagine, like people in the movies? This seemed so much more exciting than any Easter Rabbit.

I'd hardly ever seen such a thing. They don't want me to see them having fun together, as if something bad might slip out if too much fun is allowed. You have to watch, because if one of them starts having fun, the other will put a stop to it.

Sometimes in the car on the way out to dinner on Thursday night, the maid's day off, with me in back with the babies, a low sun glowing orange across the walking-running striped rows of black-dirt cotton fields out Preston Road, throwing orange-and-blue shapes into the chrome on the car window, rosy gold onto Daddy's freckled elbow in front, Mama might start to sing, as though we were all going to join in with "Row, Row, Row Your Boat," or "Three Blind Mice." She acts jokey, her singing coming out like talking, as if just this once showing us how to have some fun.

Then Daddy would laugh in this way where his teeth stayed covered but his mouth went up at the corners, as though a silly mistake had occurred, his head pulling back with chin down, an unfunny laugh, not joining in. Then he'd step on the gas. Especially if she started in on "The Sheik of Araby," laughing and teasing, Daddy becoming angry red about this song for some reason. But then she might think she could jolly him into something from when they were younger, and would keep on singing: "The Sheeeeeeeeeiiik of Aa-raa-beeeeeeeee, betweenthesheetswithdirtysockswithoutashirt, Oh heeeeeee made loooove to meeeeeeee, betweenthesheetswithdirtysockswithoutashirt"—you say that part really fast—and so on like that.

I would not see what was so funny about this, or what was so bad about it, either, but would just watch the two of them.

I'd think of running between the sheets hung out on the line, hiding from Daddy, who'd come home from work in a rare good mood one day in spring when his feet weren't too bad, clump-CLUMP, clump-CLUMP, clump-CLUMP, chasing me across the backyard, me running, a sharp thrill in a breathless chest, between the clothesline sheets, Daddy clump-CLUMP, bursting through the great white flapping, grabbing me!

Me! Caught! Swept up! Perched, lurching and bobbing, on the giant lame-gaited shoulders! *Clump-CLUMP, clump-CLUMP, the fear of his feet, of him falling—always the fear of him falling*—carried helpless, gasping, squirming, yet grasping onto him, bouncing across the yard toward the house—*throw you in the oven and cook you for dinner tonight!*—shrieking in terror and joy that he might be going to do a thing so extreme with me.

Who knows what these moody giants might do? They killed and ate the black lamb Aunt Lee had sent home with me one summer for a pet, and Daddy thought that was really funny. Easy to imagine them stuffing me kicking and screaming into the flaming oven like the witch in "Hansel and Gretel."

"For your own good," they would say, laughing hysterically at their own private joke! The oven is on, the kitchen, the heat! Easy to imagine the two of them with forks and carving knives, devouring the flesh off my bones the way wolves and witches and giants in stories are always eating children up.

But then Mama would not join in with any Daddy-chasing-me games. She would watch with a nervous face, would talk in a down-turning voice with little tucks in it, making us stop that playing, as if something might be wrong with it, as if she couldn't trust what might happen if Daddy or anyone else started having too much fun. Then Daddy would turn and stomp away, hurrying into the back of the house with his stiff-legged, one-foot-heavy limp, not coming back until dinner-time, and then acting as if nothing had happened.

But it's also true that Daddy couldn't get up and down from the floor easily because of his feet, so I might have to imagine just her hiding the eggs by herself while he read the paper in bed. Or would they have argued about the proper colors, how to do this and that, yelling until somebody slammed a door?

Looking out the plate-glass windows at the wet grass in the backyard, the vacant lot behind, all of a sudden, incredibly, I saw him! The Easter Rabbit!

Yes, it's true! The actual, real-life Easter Rabbit!

Mama and Daddy had not started up the day yet, no grown-ups anywhere in sight, and yet there he was, walking along the wet sidewalk on the street behind the vacant lot behind our house. I was seeing him with my very own eyes, the Easter Rabbit, no doubt at all about it. It was definitely him.

As tall as a man, with white fur, as solidly there as rocks and trees, he was *ho-de-o-do* striding down the street in long loping steps, top-hatted head bobbing, as if the big world that I wonder so much about were nothing but a lot of hilariously happy silliness where people black and white are whistling while they work, saying *okeydokey*, winking at you, pulling nickels out of one another's ears, and where a person can go around skipping and singing *Zippity-doo-dah* all the day, and nobody thinking a thing about it.

Then he disappeared behind another house.

I didn't even look for the eggs. *Maybe he hasn't been here yet,* I thought. I turned around, heart pounding, and ran right back to bed, the way I was supposed to do, easing my door closed, jumping under the covers, squeezing my eyes tight.

So the boys on the block were wrong, and Mama and Daddy were right, I thought. *So it is the kind of world in which you can have Easter Rabbits and Santa Claus, and Jesus, and angels, and maybe witches, devils, ghosts,* monsters, werewolves, and vampires, as well—and not another kind of world, in which you cannot have any of those things.

So that means you have to be good.

At Granny's House

Granny's house stands in giant-Elm-tree shade on a corner of Beverly Drive, ivy all over, with a slate roof and wood trim painted gray-blue. Daddy calls it "Tudorish" as the rainy morning clears and we drive up next to Gran-Dad's Cadillac with its LONE STAR dealer plates parked out front, and Mama says, "Dick, please."

We already had a quiet little Christmas morning with sticky ribbon candy at our house, and now we're having it again. It's a Christmas Day party at Granny's house.

Granny, for whom the wild old days of party-town, new-oil-money Dallas, Texas, was just yesterday—for in the 1940s, the '30s and the '20s could still be seen in the people, their clothes, their habits and stories, their music still in the air—from that time when bootleggers in Model B Ford sedans cruised the wide Highland Park alleyways on Saturday nights, high school boys jumping out with deliveries here and there, while oil men, developers, and their lawyers played high-stakes poker, with only silver dollars allowed all night long, and Dallas was small enough that you could still feel you knew everybody in town.

Granny loves nothing more than a party in her big house, loves dressing up in all her jewels, loves making everybody laugh and have fun. Sometimes she brings out costumes, or makes her dinner guests put on red wigs before they can get a plate.

Granny often seems like she's just waiting for the next party to start. I've walked in the side door when Mama would drop me off on a slow afternoon, only to find her alone, furiously smoking, drinking, and playing solitaire at a card table on the side porch, *one-two-three-four-five-six-SEVEN, one-two-three-four-five-SIX*. She'd look up as if wishing for someone to please drop by, then she'd go to the bar, and then she'd insist on teaching me how to play solitaire, showing me how to win, and if I didn't win, showing me how to cheat once, twice, three times, counting how many times I'd have to cheat in order to "win" the game.

I'd walk into the living room on any afternoon and find the maroon velvet sofa bolster pillows propped up, costumed, bewigged, rubber-masked, with jewelry and cigarette holders tied onto their stuffed gloves and sleeves, ready and waiting for the next party.

Granny says Oliver was mixing drinks at the bar at my age, and everybody thought that was so cute, but now he's not her sweet little boy anymore and won't do it. I asked if I could mix drinks too, but Mama says, "No!" I asked Oliver if it was true, but he got up and left the room without a word.

Oliver's Mama's brother, which makes him my uncle, but he's only seven years older. I always think that he's like the older brother I've been looking for, and that we'll be friends.

Now that it's Christmas Day and everybody has to be nice, I look for him as Granny greets us excitedly at the front door, Papaw behind her with his *Ho-ho-ho-ho* Santa-Claus laugh, lots of cheek kissing, offering drinks, as we walk into the big dark house full of old maroon Sarouks and Kashans, carved chairs, Chinese lamps, and, upstairs, satin comforts and floating secrets with bedroom doors closed. Granny's house is full of people and fun, and full of strange things that don't match, not like Nana's house, which is silent, light, and full of perfection.

Daddy leaves his cane at the door and clumps around. Mama talks to Aunt Meg. I wipe off Papaw's kisses, which are too wet. There's a light on in the black-tiled bathroom under the stairs, where we used to hide. Maybe Oliver's hiding in there. He's done it before.

"I have a surprise for you!" Granny's saying, walking away toward the kitchen, teasing over her shoulder, winking, flashing black eyes at me as I run after her into the bar, where she talks to Cleveland, who's dressed up for serving drinks. His yellowish oak brown face with its sad dark-ringed eyes splits wide in the gold-toothed grin he always gives me when he's out trimming bushes in overalls and a straw hat. His wife is no-nonsense Nona, Granny's lifelong maid, small, round, plum-dark, and always in a bad mood.

In the kitchen, another party's going on. Granny jokes with Nona. Nona's sister Johnnie gulps her drink and tries to hide the glass as we walk in. Johnnie looks completely different from Nona, straight hair, small nervous eyes, skin as light as Granny's. They say "Merry Christmas" and ask what Santa Claus brought me. Granny always says she has more black friends than white.

"What's the surprise? What's the surprise?" I follow Granny around, and she keeps winking and teasing. "You'll find out!" She says.

I see Daddy heading for the bar as if there's something he just can't stand. Clump-CLUMP, clump-CLUMP, he hurries in his pounding lurch. I look around for what might be wrong now.

In the living room are people with cigarettes and drinks, Granny's friends I know from snapshots taken in New York, in New Orleans, horse races at Ruidoso, and they're talking about the new Cipango Club, where there's a phone jack in every red leather booth, and you might see John Wayne and Ward Bond and other movie stars dance with the girls on tables crazy drunk.

Nana calls me over to give her a big kiss, saying maybe Santa Claus came here, too, while GranDad holds his new camera ready and pops his black eyes like a man in the movies. Mama and Aunt Meg and Uncle R.E. and Aunt Annie and Uncle Eddie sit and stand together on the back porch with cousins who are all babies. All they ever want to do is watch babies, play with babies, and talk about babies, babies, lots of babies fussing and drooling all over the place. Oliver still has not appeared.

"Well, we bought all this ribbon candy and it wound up being a huge mess from the wet weather," I hear Mama say, clearly admitting that that ribbon candy was not brought by Santa.

Granny takes me around and shows me off to her

friends for the men to wink and whistle the way men did back then, and pinch my cheeks and pull nickels out of my ears, and say, "Jeffee, you are too young to be a grandmother," and the women to say, "What a pretty child," and "What pink cheeks!" and "What grade are you in?" All her friends laugh at Granny's jokes. "She's such a cute woman," her friends all say.

Granny says she's the only person in the world with the name Jeffee. She says she was her daddy's favorite. She tells stories and sings old school yard songs in her deep, trembly voice, even with just me spending the night with her, which is a lot, because when Papaw goes out of town, Granny can't stand being alone, so I often spend the night, because the babies are too little to talk to. So I am Granny's favorite because I'm the eldest. She told me that. But Granny teases.

Granny says she had a Scots-Irish uncle named Peter Berry Campbell, who was hanged as a horse thief in Itasca, Texas. Her sister Aunt Annie says that's not really true.

Granny says they were so poor as children in Fort Worth, after their dad was killed on the railroad tracks, that they had no shoes and stole from the apple wagon for food. Another sister, Aunt Lee, says Granny just likes to make it a good story.

Granny says her cousin was a vaudeville star in New York City, another sister, Kate, a world-champion boxer's girlfriend, and that she herself was the It Girl at the speakeasies there.

Granny says Seabiscuit whispered a secret in her ear,

and maybe one day she'll tell it to me. Granny likes the horses.

Granny says it was terrible what they did to Al Smith. I see Mama and Aunt Meg rolling their eyes.

Granny says she is secretly a witch with magic powers and can make people do whatever she wants. She winks at me.

"Mostly Papaw," she says, and Papaw laughs redly, his big *Ho-ho-ho-ho* Santa Claus laugh, and wetly, coughing, snorting, dabbing his eyes and nose and the corners of his mouth with his damp handkerchief, and soon all the friends and guests are laughing and teasing, too. With Granny, you're always having a good time. At least you're always having some sort of *a time*.

In a little while, Nona and Cleveland are cleaning up coffee cups, glasses, ashtrays, and the friends are leaving, saying, "Merry Christmas," saying "Now you can have your little Christmas," and "Good-bye, honey," "Good-bye, darling," "Good-bye, sweetie pie."

I'm still walking around looking for Oliver. Baby Annie follows me out to the side porch where Granny plays game after game of solitaire on quiet days. Her bright little face looks up at me, wanting to play, but I tell her to go away.

Then I'm sorry I did that, because she runs to Daddy, and he picks her up and cheers her up. I wish Daddy would cheer me up. Daddy likes Annie better than me, as well. It seems that everybody likes Annie best. It seems that there's nobody for me. I think Oliver must be upstairs.

There's a fireplace with a tall black mouth where coals

smolder, though windows are open now. I examine it, wondering how Santa could have squeezed down that chimney. I want to ask Daddy what he thinks of that, but I don't see him now.

The mantel is draped with cedar branches, silver fairy-reindeer stuck in here and there, and it's hung with thick white cotton nurses' stockings, lumpy with oranges, pinecones, walnuts, and drooping to the hearthstone floor. Next to it, Granny's tree has white soapsuds along the branches, like snow, and is decorated silver and blue, different from our tree. Above the mantel is a painting of people around a table in old-fashioned clothes, all looking sideways at one another. A woman holds a fan. I always look at this painting. Something seems to be missing from it.

The people all seem to want something, but they can't say what.

Now we have Christmas all over again, and beautifully, with Neiman-Marcus boxes and wrappings, new clothes and dolls and eggnog, brunch in the dining room with pancakes, strawberries, spicy sausages, and scrambled eggs.

Daddy comes and sits across from me, and I'm hoping nothing will make him get upset, turn red, jump up, go clump-CLUMPing right out of the house. But now he sits sloppily in his chair, laughing like everything's so ridiculous. He puts a Santa's elf clown hat on his head. His elbow slips off the table spilling his drink, but Cleveland's right there to nod, bow, smile, and quickly clean it up. I see Johnnie passing rolls with a mean smirk on her face.

I see Mama talking to Aunt Meg and Nana, all look-ing at Daddy. Nana looks disgusted. Mama looks hurt, about to cry.

GranDad rushes over and snaps a picture of Daddy, and then another of the women looking like that, and Nana gets mad at him. He's always doing that—taking pictures at the wrong time.

Aunt Meg comes and sits next to Daddy, gives him a cup of coffee Nona brought, jokes with him in her know-ing, chipper way. She winks at me.

Granny and Nana go back to talking about Granny's blue glass swooping birds sitting around the dining room with beady eyes. Granny told me once they came from a faraway city where people drive boats through streets made of water. I asked Daddy once if this is true, and he said, "Yes, actually it is."

Granny's telling Nana about the low-hung chandelier Granny says comes from "poor old Dresden," which is another faraway city that Granny might have made up. It has cherubs and flowers all over, and little glass fruit and flower baskets that dangle and vibrate as if about to fall.

When plates are being served, Oliver suddenly appears in the dining room and says it looks to him as if one of those baskets will fall right onto his plate, and when he says it, he looks right at me. Our eyes meet with the joke. And then everybody except Granny laughs, and I cannot stop laughing. I laugh so hard, I start choking, and Aunt Annie starts hitting me on the back.

He must have been upstairs all this time. I see how he's growing up beautiful, with soft brown eyes, always thinking of something funny, smiling to himself, staying on the edges of things, so I think that we are alike and should be friends, but he won't show that. When I try to catch his eye, he will not look at me. But he and I have a secret from last summer, a thing we never talk about, a thing no one else knows.

Papaw's still laughing, so I pipe up and say, "Papaw laughs just like Santa Claus," and then everybody laughs again, except for Daddy, who is now devouring a plate of food, and except for Oliver, who won't look at me.

After lunch, I try to get him to play. I dance around and hum a little song, thinking he'll be forced to glance over, but he looks away quickly when I turn around, then acts as if he thinks I don't see that, or as if this is telling me something I'm supposed to already know. I call him "Uncle Oliver," and I see a corner of a smile. So this must be a little game of his.

I dance closer and bump up against him. He glares down as if he really does not like me at all, not even the littlest bit. But Oliver has no reason not to like me. He's supposed to be like a brother to me. Everybody says that.

I know he does like me and is trying to hide it, because of last summer, when I was spending the night here.

Sometimes I can tease a little light into those distant eyes. It's the same light that comes into Daddy's eye when he teases. I tease and tease toward that little light, trying to get him to laugh, or look, or play, or to do something, to do anything, to break the spell.

I keep on dancing around the living room, the way the Girl can dance, like a tap dancer in the movies. Then baby

Annie and cousin Dottie, who is her size, both come over and start dancing around, too, tripping, giggling, and everybody is clapping for them. They always have to do what I do. So I stop doing it.

And then Papaw, *Ho-ho-ho-ho-ho*, wants me to come sit on his lap, and I can't get out of it. I see Daddy clump-CLUMPing out of the room. Papaw gives me a piece of candy. GranDad snaps a picture of this. Why is he always doing that?

Papaw holds me too close, pushes himself on me, bounces me around, keeps kissing me too wetly, so I pull loose, jump down, wipe off his slobbery kisses, and tap-dance away from him.

Then Oliver goes up the stairs without saying a word to me or to anyone. I stand at the foot of the stairs and make a face at him as he goes up, sticking out my tongue.

Granny comes out of the bar with a drink in her hand, sees me doing this, and says, "Stop that!"

I stop, surprised to see her standing over me wild-eyed and pointing up at the sun-and-moon grandfather clock that stands looking down from high above us on the stair landing. Oliver, just passing it, looks back at us, then disappears up the stairs.

"Don't you see that clock is about to strike?" she yells, loudly enough for the whole house to hear, as if we're onstage. But they all keep talking. I just look at her.

"Don't you know if that clock strikes while you're making a face like that, you could get stuck, and your face could stay that way, mean and ugly for the rest of your life?"

"That clock?" I say.

"Any clock!" she proclaims even more loudly.

"But . . . is that really true?" I say, checking around, but Mama's not looking over here.

"Yes, of course that's true," says Granny, "Would I ever tell you something that wasn't true?"

She leads me back to the living room, where GranDad and Daddy are now taking everybody's pictures next to the tree. Both of them have new cameras, which they examine and compare.

Usually, GranDad takes pictures when something awkward is happening—he sneaks up and slyly snaps an argument or an accident, to everyone's irritation, but now they are posing.

Everybody puts on big smiles, their many voices chanting "Cheeeese" as we hear the clock striking. *Bong . . . bong . . . bong . . . bong . . . bong . . . bong . . .* Six o'clock.

"WAS THAT A TRUE STORY?" I study Granny's face as she tosses *Grimm's Fairy Tales* onto a chaise and leans to kiss me good night, eager to get back downstairs. I am spending the night at Granny's while Mama and Daddy go out to another party.

"Well, nobody knows if it's true or not. What do you think?"

"Somebody must know."

"You think so?" Her black eyes crinkle.

"Granny, are witches real?"

"Sometimes I think so." She smiles into the mirror.

"Have you seen one?"

"Maybe you've seen one and you don't know it." She winks, then leans in toward the mirror and freshens her makeup by holding the flattened red lipstick in one place and moving her wide, mobile lips back and forth and around over it.

She brushes her wiry dark hair, dabs on more perfume, then winks at the mirror as if someone's in there, and I see the two Grannies lean in and flirt with each other.

She's ready to get back for the few friends dropping by later for drinks, after the party you can hear getting louder downstairs, where they chatter and laugh about things that are not for children to know.

The doorbell rings down there. After Mama and Daddy left for another party, at first I ran upstairs and knocked on Oliver's closed door.

"Get out of here, you brat!" he said, kicking it shut.

Then we both went down to say good night to the company. They all smiled down, saying I looked "good enough to eat."

"What about 'Jack and the Beanstalk'?"

"Now I think that one might be true. I saw a giant about as big as a house one time at the fair." She brushes off her shoulder, checks her dress. "Looked like he might come get me! I saw the Siamese twins, Cheng and Eng— two men stuck together for life!"

"And what else?" I've heard this before, but the Siamese twins might be just one of Granny's stories. My cousin Dan said that.

"A man with only half a body and the sweetest face

I ever saw! I saw the fat lady, too! Huge rolls of fat! I dropped my purse so I could look up under her dress! I love freaks!" she says, bugging her eyes, and blots her lipstick with a kiss on my forehead.

"There! That'll give you sweet dreams."

"But what about the witch? Is the witch part true?"

"Time for you to be in bed, young lady."

"But is it true?" I want her to stay, but she closes the door.

A Chinaman dresser lamp spotlights her makeup, powder puffs, perfume bottles, Jungle Gardenia and Chanel No. 5, the carved ivory elephants, each one smaller than the next. Then I try on Granny's bracelets and beads.

I crawl under her bed to find the *True Crime* magazines full of grainy pictures of famous criminals, famous detectives, Texas Rangers, people in handcuffs, guns and knives with tags, bullet holes, and half-naked bloody women and men lying in odd positions in small rooms, scary, sad, and dead.

I think of Nona's sister Johnnie, the way we found her asleep in a broom closet one time, after we'd walked around calling her name for an hour. Granny made it into a funny game. Whiskey smell poured out when Granny opened the closet door. Cleveland laughed, Johnnie moaned, cursed, woke up, pulled down her dress, gagging, but Nona's face was plum purple, lips working, her angry eyes wet. Granny said to Nona, "That's okay, honey," and they all dragged drunken Johnnie out to Cleveland's big black car.

I tiptoe through the dark hall to look over the banister

into the smoky pool of percolating piano music, laughing, singing and Ho-ho-hoing below. *I'm the Girl who watches without being seen, observes the whole world from her lonely tower.*

I don't see why I have to go to bed in the chilly upstairs like a baby and Oliver gets to stay up at the party, just because he's older. I'm older than those babies! Just once, just once, why can't I stay up and be at the party?

On the landing just below and across from me, the grandfather clock strikes—*Bong . . . bong . . . bong . . .*—ten times, and the whole party stops, hearing it. The clock has a smiling sun face and a sideways moon face chasing each other around all day and night. Now the moon is at the top.

I lean over farther and see Oliver sitting on the bottom steps down there, watching the party. I can see the top of his head, his knees, his Sunday shoes. He's sitting alone watching, like I do. He has no one to talk to, no one to play with, like me.

I wad a piece of paper from the desk and throw it down. It's a direct hit! He looks up, his face open in surprise for an instant. I grin, wave, make a face. But he acts all huffy, goes off to tell on me. Maybe he'll come up later.

I smell the liquor and cigarettes and feel the bumbling gestures, and instantly I know it's Granny's hands on me, her deep whiskey voice waking me. The house is quiet now.

Papaw comes in, too, clearing his throat a few times,

taking off suspenders, shoes, his pants. It's late now. Papaw leans down to kiss me. I roll and jump off the bed, dodging him.

"Oh, let her stay in here," he says.

"No," I hear her say. "Not this one."

I heard Mama say, "Don't you put her into bed with you!" before they left. She always says this, because Granny always does let me get into the big bed with her and Papaw, where there is lots of giggling and tickling.

"Do not let her get into bed with you!"

And Granny said, "Okay, Dear, okay."

Usually, when we hear them coming in, I jump down and run, run, run back to my guest-room bed. And Papaw gives his *Ho-ho-ho* Santa Claus laugh. And Mama says, "I hear that!" And Granny thinks this is terrifically funny. She likes to go against the rules, and be like a child. And I love this. But Mama does not like this one bit.

Tonight, Papaw puts a little black hat on his head and goes into their big bathroom–dressing room, where he can be heard snorting, hawking, coughing, spitting, and then talking and chanting in a low voice behind the closed door in a strange other language, and he stays for a long time.

Granny brings her drink and her cigarette and takes me back to the guest room, where she lies down on the bed next to me. I want to ask her more questions about Oliver, but what she wants to tell me is about how many friends Papaw has, how Papaw would be a much richer man today if he had not helped out so many people, how Papaw is the sweetest man in the world, and how most men are not sweet and not good—especially Daddy and GranDad and Uncle Ted, who are not good at all, but are terrible people, selfish, jealous, and mean—and even most especially Granny's first husband, Homer, who was the meanest, coldest man you ever saw.

She turns over and shakes me when I start to fall asleep to be sure I am hearing all of this, and I wake up.

"Is Oliver going to bed now, too?"

"He's already asleep," she says.

Then she starts talking about Oliver, how he was such a sweet baby when they adopted him, poor little thing, but now he's changing, and she'd like to put "a brick on his head." How Oliver talks to her so ugly now, how she hopes I'll never talk ugly like that, how she's getting old and will soon die.

Will I be sorry when she dies? Will I promise to name one of my children after her? She's starting to cry.

I promise that I will, letting my eyelids fall.

Then she says how Oliver was a tiny baby no one wanted, half Jewish and half not, and when the young parents died in a car wreck, neither family would take him. "Terrible people," she says. But he was exactly what Granny and Pawpaw wanted. His real name was David. She says all this is a secret and not to tell.

She tells me this whole thing every time I spend the night with her, and always late at night while I am falling asleep, waiting for a chance to ask about Oliver, and she gets drunker and drunker and more and more upset, maybe even after that on and on and on into the night.

"What does *Jewish* mean?" I ask, opening my eyes.

"Pawpaw's a Jew," she says.

"But what is it?"

"Don't go to sleep yet; open your eyes."

"I'm just resting them," I say, closing them again.

I want to ask more about Oliver, but I start drifting off while she goes on with what a good man Papaw is, how he puts on his Jewish costume and reads his Torah every day and night, how he prays in secret away from all of us, in their big bathroom–dressing room, even though nobody makes him do it.

As the night goes on, she tells how Papaw's father escaped from the Tsar in a hay wagon, came to Texas, sold pots and pans out on the frontier, when there were still Comanche wars, then bought wild horses, bridle-broke them, sold them back in the city, then did this all again and again until he could send for his sweetheart back in Poland. They settled in Dallas, cofounded their Orthodox synagogue, had children, including Papaw, then almost had heart attacks when Granny and Papaw married, but she was not going to cook like that!

She tells how Papaw started out as a poor kid selling papers on the Dallas courthouse steps, but now he has friends in the newspaper business in New Orleans, Beaumont, Houston, every town in the South, how he can walk down the street in New York City and meet a friend on every block.

And then she laughs and says that Jewish men make the best husbands, and she shakes my arm.

I remember how once in the car Daddy said that

Granny got so mad at her Dallas Country Club friends that she almost turned into *a Jew.*

I open one eye and peek at her. I want to ask her again, What is a Jew? But she's opening a door in the bedside table, taking out a small bottle, slurring her words now, but going strong, louder and louder.

And I am interested in Granny's stories, in all of their stories. And they all tell me their stories. But right now, I just need to rest my eyes.

Papaw comes to the bedroom door in his striped pajamas and makes his little whistle signal, which seems to mean *Watch out!*

"Come on to bed, Jeffee; it's late."

"You go on to bed. We're having a lovely time in here, aren't we?" She looks at me. "Just don't you worry about us!"

"All right, but don't be long now." And he goes to bed, clearing his throat about fifty times.

Granny drains her glass again, shakes my arm again. Then she starts in with what she always gets to—about how she couldn't help it that she had to leave her first husband, my mother's real father, even though divorce was such a disgrace that she had to lie to her own mother. She says Homer worked for the *Star-Telegram,* was from a nice Fort Worth family, had gone to college, and was always going to church, but he was such a mean man and told her every day she was nothing but trash, gave her the silent treatment for weeks, and was even in the Ku Klux Klan.

"What's the Ku Klux Klan?" I manage to ask, my eyes closed.

"It's a club for mean, ugly men, and you don't need to know about it," she says. I want to ask more about Oliver, but she's talking too fast, saying how Homer did not know how to have fun.

She says how for years she'd told this Homer man she was going to find somebody else and leave him, and when she did find Papaw, at a big party for newspaper people, and Papaw sent her a dozen roses, then she said to Homer, "Ha! See there! I found somebody!"

Then Homer said, "Yeah, a Jew!"

The Braid

Mama's hair grows long and longer, down to her waist, where she trims it off even, brushes it out, and then she braids it in a long, thick braid. And then she twists it and coils it and pins it up against the back of her neck. And Mama's hair is dark like mine is, but it is fine and silky and smooth against her head, not dense and wiry and full of cowlicks like mine is.

She wears it like that always, right through times when such hair is not in style, and Mama is a very stylish woman. She wears it in the braid right through the pompadours and pageboys, and everything else. She just keeps on braiding that long braid and then wrapping it around and around in back and pinning it with the black wire hairpins, and then anchoring it with the giant tortoiseshell hairpins, almost as if that coil is holding herself and all of us in place as well as the hair. No matter what is being done, Mama just goes right on doing what she has always done and knowing that it is the best.

And it is the perfect thing on her, because Mama's face has a greater evenness on the two sides than any you have ever seen. And she has a high, wide, smoothly rounded forehead, which comes square to the hairline, where the hair flares gently away before being pulled back into the coiled braid. Such a high, smooth forehead demands hair with seriousness, with innocence, with all the authority that hair can ever have.

And she always wears it up, and always neat. If any ends are pulled loose, or are blown loose by a wind of greater force and roughness than any to which Mama has ever intended to be exposed, then those ends will be quickly tucked in again.

When she takes it down, she pulls the hairpins out with one hand, moving rapidly, searching, and gathering, and removing pins, and placing them hurriedly on the dresser, and with the other hand she holds together and manipulates the coiled braid until it is ready to come down. When the braid comes down, she removes the rubber band and starts running her fingers through, separating and undoing it. Then she brushes it out upside down.

I like to watch Mama's hands braiding that long, thick braid, her body leaning to one side, head tilted over, she and I both watching it lengthening in the mirror, her fingers moving in and out in that particular dance that produces the braid, bit by bit, holding and adding on, holding on and adding, and then tying it off, winding up the end with a tight rubber band—making the end into a hairy little nub to be tucked underneath and never seen, so that the circle of the braid at the back of her head appears to be continuous, with no beginning and no end.

I often sit on the edge of Mama's bathtub and watch as she brushes out her hair until it crackles with electricity, and then as she divides it and smoothes it and starts making the braid. The bathroom smells of lotion and face powder and of the particular smell her hair had when she brushed it out like that. Sometimes I help with a strap or hairpin, and I study the way she goes through all the motions exactly the same way every time, looking for clues on how to be a woman. But looking in the mirror, I can not help but see how small and graceful and smooth Mama appears, and how tall and clumsy and red-faced I am, looking back at myself with dismay, hair flying in all directions.

When the braid goes up, Mama's face goes through a subtle change that I cannot describe, except to say that her neck seems to elongate—in that moment, it seems that she is as self-sufficient as a cat. She seems to have a secret that no one else can share, a secret that lives in the house with us but that only once in a while can be glimpsed, and then only out of the corner of your eye. You would almost swear a shape was there, but when you try to look at it, there's only an empty space.

Mama can braid so fast and with such deftness and control that it seems to me she could do it in her sleep— could do it without noticing what she is doing. In fact, she braids not only her own hair but also mine and that of my younger sisters—she'd do this every single morning, and again at night if our hair needs to be recombed for some social event.

We sisters wear French braids, which are braids that start small, with a small amount of hair on the sides of your forehead, and then, as they are woven closely down on your head, more and more strands are added in a gradual accumulation, until every hair on your head is caught up into these two tight ridges running from front and back on both sides, all the way down your head, and then the two pigtail extensions stick out behind your ears. Ours are braided so tightly that they curl back toward the front, and our scalps get to be tough. Mama goes to a lot of trouble to keep all the hair in the family under control. She does not tolerate any flyaway hair or messy hair or hair in the face. Often she asks me if her own hair has any strands escaping or hairpins slipping out of place, and it is part of my position as the eldest of three daughters to help keep an eye on this for her, as well as on the same situation with my younger sisters.

Once in a while, I come across a long single hair that has somehow escaped with its full length and is lying curled around and around itself, unnoticed, black and spidery, on the white bathroom tile. I pick it up and hold it and marvel at its length and its singleness, and once, knowing how much effort keeps them disposed of, I kept one of these escaped hairs. It was a particularly long and heavy one. I wound it up on my finger and put it into my little box of found objects, which I felt had to be kept. And then I hid the box, because she keeps the house so neat and clean, and sometimes she throws my things away.

Except for when she is combing or washing it, I don't see Mama's hair down. Living with her, you don't have the sense of being around someone with all that hair, because it is always done up, except for rare occasions.

One day she picks me up from school with her hair still wet from washing it. When I get in the car with my books and see that long, tangled, wet black hair streaming over the back of the seat like some strange animal, I am horrified. I can't stop looking at that hair and at her, and am afraid some of my friends might see it—somehow it seems to be something indecent. She laughs at me and gives me a funny look, and she tells me that when I was still in a crib, she had once leaned over to pick me up with her hair wet and loose, and it fell, sudden and dark, across the crib and I would not stop screaming for an hour after that.

When we have a grade-school fair, Mama dresses as a fortune-telling Gypsy wearing her hair down and around her shoulders like smoke, and has lots of veils and bangles and things on, and with her dark eyes and pierced ears, she really does look the part. I keep walking past her booth and looking and looking at her, and she calls out to me to come in and have my fortune told, but I just keep walking past. She has it dark in the booth, with candles, and it looks as if her hair is moving behind her as the candles flicker, and every time I walk past, she calls out again, and I don't know why, but I don't want her telling my fortune. I just want to look at her again and again without her seeing me doing it. But she is always seeing me. It seems to me that there is never a time when she doesn't see me before I can see her.

As it is getting to be spring, Mama and Daddy are going to a big party where everyone is supposed to dress like Hawaiians, and she tells me that after dinner she needs my help getting dressed. Like always when they go out, there is an atmosphere of bustling and subdued excitement, with whiffs of perfume all around the house.

In her bathroom–dressing room, the air is humid from the bath she has just taken, and heavily scented from the oils and lotions and makeup that have been opened and used during the course of the preparations. She and I can see and talk to each other's reflections in the long foggy mirror over the dressing table, in which her face is lit as if onstage, and mine is dimmer and behind hers, a watcher and an assistant.

She has gotten a grass skirt somewhere and has strung masses of flowers together and has also bought a dozen bottles of Touch & Glow suntan-color makeup because she does not have time to get a deep tan. I am to help with putting this makeup on her back and where she can't reach.

Her skin is so white against the black hair. It is an opaque kind of gardenia white, not transparent and blotchy like mine. The whiteness of her skin as she stands there in the bathroom in her underpants makes her seem all the more naked, and as I smooth the orangey tan makeup on her back and shoulders, being careful not to get any in her hair, and then on her legs, I feel funny, because ordinarily there isn't that much touching between us, and because it seems to me that Mama's nakedness is being covered by the makeup and yet uncovered at the same time. She makes up her face and neck and arms, and the color change seems to transform her curving, compact, almost Oriental face and body into something tawny and muscular. She puts on the grass skirt, and then Mama lets her hair down.

She bends over, brushing and brushing her hair until

it seems to be moving of its own will and the bathroom is filled with its animal smell. Then she suddenly straightens up and shakes out the now-flying mane, letting it fall around her shoulders and down her back, moving now with a kind of power, a music to which the air sways and bounces as she moves. The hair seems to be breathing. She looks at herself in the mirror with an expression I have never seen before, and I stand back in the shadows to watch Mama.

Word Study

We hear the school bus's honking horn.
Oops, you forgot to hurry up!
"What on earth is wrong with you?"
Obviously, something is.
"Why aren't you ready for school?"
I do not know the answer to this question.

The kids from our stop are already on the bus when I get out there, and they jeer and laugh with lots of noise as I climb on, like always. I laugh like I don't care. I see Nathan, but we don't sit together on the bus. He sits with the boys in the back, where they alternate between urgent whisperings and explosions of sarcastic glee.

I sit alone nearby, the only girl on the block. I look out at fields, fences, trees, creeks, houses, the clattery wooden bridge on Walnut Hill Lane I'm afraid will break down and crash into the rushing creek below.

I hope it'll happen, because I haven't done my word-study homework. I imagine how we all might save one another, escaping from the wreck, getting to know one another and becoming friends. I look at the other kids at each stop, each one climbing on to the cheers, jeers, jokes, or silent looks of the boys in the back. It's the same every day.

Our little country public Walnut Hill Grade School has just been taken into the Dallas city limits. It's small, and our class includes all kinds, from a couple of rich kids whose big houses are hidden behind tall trees and gates to a family of dirty-faced, towheaded boys who it's said sleep three in a bed and get beaten up every Saturday night. Their pale, thin-lipped faces look out the windows or at the floor.

A boy named Timmy with glasses and flat hair gets on every day to complete silence. Everyone looks at him. Someone whispers, "His dad was killed in the war." He glares redly back.

We live with the war still, not really knowing anything about it. The boys draw fighter planes and tanks with their crayons and call each other "Nazis" and "Jews" and "Japs," and the one being called this becomes deeply hurt. And then the teacher gets unusually mad.

Our teacher's young and pretty and has red hair. She writes numbers on the blackboard while I look around for whom to ask what to do. Not the teacher—too busy.

Not Nathan—too far across the room, and we don't talk much at school. Not any of the boys, who will laugh.

Not Gloria—the only one I talk to, because she talks to me. She sits across from me at our worktable, has naturally curly hair and patent-leather shoes, and is not really my friend, because when I draw pictures in my workbook, she says in a certain kind of voice that I am not supposed to do that.

But I have to do it. The pictures need me to draw them.

All of a sudden, the teacher's handing out sheets of paper with numbers on them and saying we're supposed to do them, and we have ten minutes. I stare at a long page of arithmetic problems. I missed something. I don't know what to do.

"You'd better hurry up," Gloria whispers.

I don't know what they want. I don't know what to do. I was not listening. I am afraid to ask. I sit with pencil over my paper, not moving, head pounding, the clock ticking. *Why do I have to do this?* I want to sneak out, run home, hide in the woods and watch hovering, darting dragonflies, but I am trapped.

"What is wrong with you?" says Gloria, "You'd better hurry up!" She's finished hers. How does Gloria always know what to do?

The teacher says "Time's up!" and starts gathering papers.

Gloria hisses, "You'd better hurry up."

Then the teacher's standing there, looking at my blank paper with drawings in the margins. The teacher gives me a worried look. Gloria looks like she feels sorry for me and is glad.

"Is something wrong?" says the teacher, leaning down to see my face, which I am trying to hide. She puts her hand on my forehead.

"Do you have a headache?"

I nod. *Yes, that's it—a headache.*

She tells me to put my head down on the table.

I put my head down again and wish I could escape

like those kids in books. I try to remember the words for word study, but the pictures I need to draw to keep from crying are flying around on the ceiling. *I hate school!* Gloria keeps looking. I can feel her seeing whatever it is that's so shameful about me.

It seems there is something wrong with me. I missed something. I keep waiting for something. There seems to be a part of me that refuses to allow the whole of me to move forward one single inch if certain other parts are not saying *Okay! Okay, we got it that time! Okay, it is time now to move onward with all of us, every bit of us, all accounted for, ready and here in step at last, and all together now!*

Other people do not appear to be having this problem. Grown-ups of course, but even many other kids seem to know what to do and just join in. I keep waiting to be told. I keep thinking someone will explain things to me, but it does not happen that way. That someone who will be my friend never comes.

So what can I do but pretend and hope no one will notice.

After that, on the playground at recess, we're all just let loose, the teachers leave us alone, and everybody runs wild, chasing, capturing, fighting, and the boys always pulling the sash off my dress.

It's a big bare field of a playground, sloping down from the small stucco, tile-roofed building. There's a long bank of swings on one side, a long bank of black walnut trees on another, a chain-link fence all around. There are old seesaws, heavy and splintery. There's a dingy sandbox, a jungle gym. All is gray steel and weathered wood, on pounded, cracked black dirt with patches of johnson-grass, clover, chickweed, stickers that cling to my socks, dandelions, and here and there an anthill I can scuff into and watch the ants go nuts.

Once in a while, some kid rides a horse to school.

The girls play hopscotch on cement sidewalks next to the building, using found white rocks, which last longer than the store-bought chalk we steal from classroom blackboards. Sometimes I play hopscotch, but mostly I watch the boys.

I see Nathan out there with other boys, playing ball, and he holds his own. The boys seem to have a lot more fun.

SCRUB IS A SOFTBALL GAME everyone plays in the neighborhood yards and vacant lots every chance we get. When you play scrub, you might start out in the field and rotate in through all the positions to get up to bat, and if nobody gets you out, you could stay at bat for the whole game. There's no rule about how long the game lasts, so on the other hand, if you keep getting put out, you could spend most of the game standing out in the field.

There are no teams and no score. Any number can play, and it's every man for himself.

Everyone plays scrub at school, too, bigger games, harder, with kids from all different grades, the big boys. In spring, everybody suddenly starts playing scrub every day. I like the game when it's not with the bigger boys. The other day I got hit square on the nose by a fly ball, so now

I flinch. I can't throw far enough, but I can pitch a bit, and do okay at bat, so I get by.

Tiff Minton's better than most of the boys. Tiff has older brothers, and all the boys treat her with respect. She has a face both tough and kind, large dark eyes, streaked-blond Prince Valiant–cut hair, which swings as she hurls a powerful ball all the way in to a boy named Larry, who grabs it perfectly at home base, the two of them absolutely heroic in my eyes. I think about Tiff as much as I think about the boys. Her eyes are quiet and observant. Her hands are cut up and rough like a boy's. We are friendly to each other, but I don't know what to say to her, any more than I know what to say to anyone.

When the bigger boys come out, that kid named Larry's the main hero out there in a fast game, pitching, catching, scanning bases, yelling, signaling, snatching his flying gum wad from the air with his teeth mid-wind-up, the dusty wind whipping his hair and shirt around his scrawny body. Even some of the teachers come out to watch him. Grown-ups talk about him. My dad filmed him. One day, the teachers call Larry to come in off the field. Larry gets in trouble a lot.

Once he tried to show me how to pitch. He held my hand in his and stood close, sweaty-smelling and tall as a grown-up. He was nice to me. And his friends teased him about this, but he didn't care. He just kept on being nice. I kept standing near him. But then he walked away with the other boys onto the field.

I watch for Larry at school. I think about Larry's lanky grace in bed in the dark. Larry wouldn't be scared of the dark like I am. I imagine him telling me the things he knows, being my friend, being on my side, but I only see him at school, often sitting outside the principal's office, where he nods to me.

One day leaving school, I was walking behind Larry and a boy named Sam, who has blond hair that always looks dirty and bruises on his face, and I heard Larry say, "I told her! I told her! But she wouldn't listen to me!"

I walked faster to catch up behind them. I heard Sam say, "Ah, they don't care. All's they care about is the rich kids," his lip curling down. And then they both looked back at me, and I stopped, and the two of them walked away.

THERE'S A GIRL NAMED GEORGEANNA who plays well with the boys, and I watch her, wishing I could be as fearless, but I don't know how to join in. She leads a pretend adventure game, and I follow along, asking, "Can I play? Can I play?" until she turns around and looks at me, her face blank, distant. One of her eyes is green and the other blue.

"What is wrong with you?" she says.

I go over to the sandbox, where two boys are digging holes and piling up sand. When I sit down, one of the boys looks at me and says in this sneery voice, "Are you rich?"

"Uh, no, I don't know . . ." I don't know what to say.

"Then how come your mom drives a Cadillac?" he says, looking like he knows something bad about me.

I go play on the swings. I can swing by myself. I can

swing so high and so hard, I can feel the swing-chains pop at the top and the back legs come out of the ground.

Out in the center, there's a heavy steel Maypole-shaped merry-go-round that spins and wobbles, that swings not just around and around but also loosely in and out toward the center post, the seat often banging hard into the center post while careening around, constantly in motion, a whirlpool of excitement, kids constantly dangling off. Mostly, the bigger kids play on it.

A couple of the older boys will position themselves around inside the rim, taking the job of keeping the wooden seat away from the center post with their feet. There are Maypole-type steel supports holding this circular seat to the top of the pole, that you can hold on to, but you have to be ready at all times either to jump away if your section of the seat happens to swing into this center post or quickly take over the keep-away position.

There's a wide rut in the black dirt all the way around, so it's hard to roll away if you jump or fall off, and you get kicked by all the feet going around. For most of the boys and a few of the girls, riding this thing is a test. It's always in motion, and every rider affects its shifting orbit. You have to run and jump and hope that someone you have already signaled to will help you scramble onto the splintery wooden seat. You have to spy a space, a moment, an ally, and you have to be fast, or another kid will grab it. There are accidents and fights. Some kid is hurt on this thing almost every day.

If his tears fly fast from a stony face and he brushes it off, then everything's okay. If that kid cries or whines in a babyish way, or blames somebody, or goes in to tell the teacher, he is branded weak and unworthy from that time on. The same with everything on the playground— if you want to be out there with any respect, you follow the code, unless it's a matter of life or death. If there's blood, or a broken bone, evidence of something serious and real, that has to be dealt with by the grown-ups, then that injured kid gets respect, and everyone's his friend and writes on his cast.

Today, there was a compound fracture, complete with blood, screaming, and white bone sticking out—one of the towheaded kids. I was standing right there, watching Nathan grab onto a steel support in motion and then stand up on the seat, giving it a push, and I was trying to get up the nerve to do the same, but the thing was too full, swinging too fast in its unpredictable-monster orbit, bristling with arms and legs.

I saw the small blond kid about to get caught between the swinging seat and the steel post. I saw the blond kid stick out one skinny leg to try to stop it.

I saw the world crack open, *POP!*—the red blood and the white bone, like a snapped pencil, so fast—and the screaming, the screaming! Not like your normal screaming. I wanted to go back and see and hear it all again and again, because I could not believe what I thought I'd heard, thought I'd seen.

All the kids jumped off, stopping the thing's motion. Older girls playing jump rope came to look, ran to get the teachers, many grown-ups came running out, and I was able to stand with Nathan in a group of the big boys.

I saw the whole thing, and with the boys I talked about it, relived it, reviewed it, acted it out, and with the boys I laughed about it.

One of the teachers named it.

And then everyone, kids and grown-ups, went around speaking the words—*compound fracture, compound fracture, compound fracture.* The teachers explained in class how *compound fracture* means that the bone is not only just cracked in two but also first bent and then split and then sticking out through the skin for everyone to see. Scars that will be there for life.

Everyone in school had to say *compound fracture* as many times as they could. I said it to myself over and over. I sang it into a little song on the way home. And I thought about the boys and I laughed all over again.

I ran into the house to tell those words to my mother: *compound fracture.*

The Sewing Room

If I come home from school and I can't find her in the yard or anywhere around the house, she's probably in the sewing room.

I grab an apple off the table. I tiptoe down the hall. I call out. Is she back there, not answering? I hear radio sounds, then sewing machine sounds, then smell cigarette smoke. I can be alone with Mama in the sewing room.

But now Daddy's voice is coming from back there; he's mad about something. Then I hear her voice, low, as if to make him calm down.

"It's as if everything is for him," I hear him say.

I wait in the hall and listen. You have to watch out for when there's something wrong with Daddy. He rarely goes into the sewing room, usually with a huff and a quick exit if I'm in there, as if he's caught someone in the bathroom and just turns and leaves, as if he can't stand for one second being in there where she's so intent on something besides him, or as if he just has to get out right then from such a small, cramped space where there's not enough room for two people, let alone three.

"Oh don't be that way, Dick."

"They don't give a goddamn about me!"

Then Mama says he should not say *goddamn*, and that she doubts that ... something ... And then *BANG!*—a loud noise.

I know that sound. Daddy has thrown or broken something.

Stay away. Listen. Duck into the hall closet.

I swallow a mouthful of apple whole, and blocky bits hurt going down. But I like an apple in the hand, which makes me feel like the Girl.

I hear him clump-CLUMPing out through their bedroom, out of the house. I hear a whining sound he makes in his throat, then the slamming door. I hear him starting up his car, roaring away.

I come out. I open the door. I see her back stiffen. "Go outside and play!" she says.

Mama likes to work in here, removed from the rest of us, bending her head to something she's making. There's always something like curtains or a dress she's making. Sometimes she knits. In the years just after the War, she was still knitting Argyll socks, washing them, pinning them to patterns, taking great care. In every house, there's always a sewing room.

I come in sweaty and plop down in the low chair next to her quilted satin-covered chest and the shelves full of patterns and buttons and hooks and thread and tape measures and seam bindings and pincushions and zippers and boxes of bobbin.

I take another bite of apple and chew it this time. She does not look over.

"Mama?" I say. *Has she been crying?*

"Yes, here I am," she says. "You found me."

Here she is, her high forehead smooth and shining onto the fabric, her small face and intent dark eyes lit from below by the tiny bulb shining onto the tiny needle zipping dangerously in and out with the other tiny needle from below, and the little "foot" that she expertly raises and lowers with one hand reaching around to a back side lever on the machine. The stitching and the machine humming continue and then pause, continue and then pause to her own coded rhythms, as if she's playing on some musical instrument. Her one hand on the fabric stitching place, expertly holding while inching forward, her other hand on the wheel, her one foot on the pedal, her other foot cocked beneath her, she's riding that machine into a place of her own, where none of us knows how to go. And I can be alone with her in the small room. She seems almost happy, thinking her own thoughts in here.

It's different from talking to her anywhere else. Her focus is on a piece of cloth already cut and pinned to her perfect plan. She might give other sorts of answers than the ones I get at the dinner table, for example. And once in a while, there's a bull's-eye kind of moment in which she tells me something, and looks at me as if she really wants to tell me what is real, but this is quickly covered by one or the other of us. So I keep on trying to find things out.

And I get a different voice, a lower, plainer voice—more like the *just us* voice from earliest times that seemed to be the real voice of my mother.

If Daddy might be around the house, might be bursting

in at any moment, then it will be somehow in her voice that we both are being aware of that.

"Mama, is something wrong with Daddy?" I say, and then I'm sorry I asked, from the way her eyes look.

"Do you think that's any of your business?" she says.

I don't know what to say. I wait.

"What are you doing?"

"What does it look like I'm doing?"

Sometimes I have to sit there for a while. Sometimes when we are alone together, and Daddy or the babies are not there to ruin everything, and I'm being just Mama's good child, and she is exactly busy enough with making something the way she always likes to be making something, then I can ask one small thing at a time, and Mama might let me in a bit, might talk in the voice I remember, the voice I look for.

I have to sit quietly, letting a long time pass, as if I had nothing to do and wasn't thinking about a thing in the world, because if she thinks I am already thinking about a question, she won't answer it. Mama keeps her answers close.

A lipsticked cigarette smokes itself away in there, smoke rising loosely tubular, swaying cobralike above the ashtray between us, smoke shifting with every gesture of air, every move of hers or mine, floating this way, that way—smoke trapped at the top of the small windowless space in sultry cirrus drifts.

Her mouth pursed with pins, she talks out of one side, her voice low, curling in, ear cocked to the radio—an ad, "Call for Philip Mor-ris!" and then an ad for *Sam Spade,* on later tonight. Mama likes *Sam Spade.* Something pleasant crosses her face.

After I've waited the right amount of time, as if I have no reason and do not really care, I can ask a question.

She stops, knocks off the long ash, takes a long drag.

"Mama?"

"Yes," she says, and then: "Hand me that tape measure."

I do it. She measures one side of the piece she is working on. She looks pleased, puts her head down to her task.

"Mama?"

"Yes, what is it?"

"Will I go visit Aunt Lee again next summer?" I say it as though I have nothing at all in mind. Actually, I don't, but just want to get her talking.

"Oh, I don't know," she says. "We'll have to decide that when the time comes."

I hear May-May in another part of the house, going out the back door with the babies. Almost time to start making dinner.

"Mama?" I say again.

She looks at me sharply. Her eyes scare me.

"Don't you see me sitting right here? Why do you keep on calling me?"

"I don't know."

"Well, please stop calling me! I'm right here!"

"Mama, even if there is a Santa Claus, those Santas in the department stores aren't the real Santa, are they? Because Granny says Santa can be in different places at once like that, but I don't think so." I say all that as fast as I can. I still just want to see if she will tell me the truth.

She looks at me. "And why don't you think so?" she says.

"Because how could he be in all those places at once? And besides, the Santa we saw at Sanger's had brown eyes, and he was not fat enough to be Santa. And then the Santa we saw at Dreyfus's was fat and had freckles and blue eyes. Yes he did! I saw them! And besides, Nathan says so."

"Says what?"

"Says the department store Santas are not the real Santa!"

"Oh, he does, does he."

"Yes. And I think that must be right."

Silence. She flattens a seam with the side of her thumb. Her face is the face of someone who knows things. But her mouth looks sour.

"I thought we settled this."

"But, Mama, tell me! It's not really real, is it?"

"Of course there's a real Santa Claus, and if Santa could hear you talking like that, you wouldn't be very happy with what you'd get for Christmas this year, young lady." She's looking at me the whole time now. Her eyes seem to exert a force upon me.

"But that man at Sanger's wasn't really Santa Claus, was he? And there was a different Santa at Titche's when we went there!"

She looks back at the seam. "Well, no. Okay, the department store Santas are not the real Santa. The real Santa's just too busy at the North Pole this time of year, so those people are some of Santa's helpers, dressed up to talk to all the children about what they want."

"But I thought Santa's helpers were elves."

"Well, Santa has all kinds of helpers." She seems pleased with this answer.

"But Mama, have you really ever seen the real Santa?"

She looks at me again. I seem to see something scary standing behind her. Why does she want to keep pretending like this?

"Well, no, because he comes in the middle of the night, when no one sees him. But we know what he looks like."

"But how do we know?"

"We know, that's all. Because some people who have seen him told us about it. Why can't you just believe it?"

I don't know why. But why won't she tell?

Sometimes it'll be in her voice that it's not just her and me, but that someone else is listening in, even when Daddy's not around and no one's nearby that I can see. Someone is going to be hurt by me. Is it Santa watching? Is it God? Because I don't want Mama to start talking about God.

She bends her head closer to the piece of cloth and her mouth holds more tightly to the pins she has there. I sit quietly and watch how she has a way of putting her forehead to the task that looks like something's pushing her head down, but from the inside. Decisions have already been made.

There is always a kind of knowing about her, and in the sewing room the complex bisque of Mama and her knowing is thick, perfumed and ancient. She is a good woman, my mother, dutiful, strong, always busy. She makes me want to be good.

She does what she is supposed to do. She says what she is supposed to say. She never tells what she is not supposed to tell. Without doubt or discussion, she lives the part she has agreed to live. There's determination in it, and loyalty.

Her face is clear, with a blandness to it, a smoothness of forehead, of mildly smiling lips, an absence of expression grounded in some act of will. But the eyes are intelligent. Decisions have been made. I am not to question. I am not to interfere with the space of goodness and light around her. She seems to own goodness.

In the sewing room, there is no room for anything but the kind of goodness that Mama owns.

I get up and go outside. I climb the fence and go to Nathan's clubhouse, a rough box the dimensions of the old garage doors and scrap wood that make it up, but he's not there. I stick my apple core on a nail at the door.

Mrs. Calder's in their yard, hanging things on the line. She says Nathan's at Cub Scouts. Fritzi, their old, crazy, always penned-up fox terrier, charges at me. *Bark! Bark! Bark! Bark! Bark! Bark! Bark! Bark! Bark! Bark! Bark! Bark!*

I go back over the fence and play fetch with Hap and Hazzy, two brother and sister honey-colored cocker spaniels that are our dogs at this time. They play together all day, rolling in the grass. I tease and tease, trying to make them fight with each other, but they will not fight. I run back and forth across the yard. I am the Girl.

The Girl leaps over the fence, the chasm, the roaring

river! The Girl escapes the hungry wolves! No one can stop the Girl!

The older baby comes running to play with me and the dogs. Her name is Annie, which is also the name of other people in Granny's family. She always wants to do what I do, have what I have. *But she has already taken everything of mine.*

I tease her. It's easy to get her to the point where I can just look at her a certain way and she'll cry, and nobody can tell it was me who did it.

"No!" I yell in my meanest voice. "You're just a baby!" She stiffens in the grass and screams. I lure the dogs away. She toddles back to May-May, crying.

Then the smaller baby starts fussing, as well. Her name's Trudy, because it was I who wanted to name her after that girl everybody was always talking about who was in *The Wizard of Oz,* and May-May spoils Trudy the most. May-May hugs them both and pets and kisses them and lets them lie all across her huge pillowy body. I think they are someday going to find out that no other grown-ups will ever let them do this when they get older. *It's disgusting*, I think.

"Why you have to be like that?" says May-May, looking at me with her mad face. May-May likes the babies better than she likes me, just like Mama. I am out here on my own. I am the Girl. I stick out my tongue at all of them, and May-May yells again, and the babies cry, but I don't care!

Like a Drawing

Bright sparks dance and twirl; bits of ash curl and lift on billows of rising heat. Flames snap in and out of the blackened incinerator, itself planted in a piling heap of powdery ashes, paper, raked leaves—spring cleanup, a chilly day—all this out near the dog pen, near the woods. Each spark shoots, then blooms, a live thing dying.

Scraps and twigs glow orange, then crack, pop, fade all the way to bits of nothing as I watch, peer in, hot-faced wild child circling the flames, close, closer, closer, close as a dare.

"Stand away from that fire!" Mama calls from the other side of the hedges, where I'd thought she wouldn't be able to see me.

And here she comes, carrying her small hoe, head down, walking the square flower bed, arms going, her whole body working up to what is on her face as she stands mother-high over me, and with that look.

She takes her hoe and drags a careful V-shaped trench around the edges of the ashes, walking it around, leaving her back-and-forth good-mother footprints like dance instructions in the ashes and dust around the incinerator, closing the circle.

She doesn't have to speak. We both already know the meaning of this line of hers already drawn here and everywhere—the line between me and everything else.

She doesn't have to point to the line. She doesn't have to say the thing she says or look at me the way she looks at me with that face of hers.

I look back. I do not know how to come right out and say the words to certain things in the face of her.

I just stand, and I watch her walk back across the yard, busy, always busy, head down to her important present task.

She doesn't have to look back at me. She can go right back to her flower bed, where bulbs and seed packets are laid out on the ground, according to plans of my mother's that were in place long ago.

I scuff some ash into her little V-shaped trench with my scabby bare toe. The incinerator fire seems to go flat now. The power fades, the force. It seems to recede now, and to turn into something like a drawing on paper of some long-ago incinerator fire.

I turn and walk into the woods.

I Call Him Nathan

The first time I saw Nathan, I thought he was tall. His eyes slanted over at me. His head tilted as if with a question. He stepped onto higher ground next to the mailbox, where he looked down at me.

It was blinding-hot summer then, and I was nearly six. I'd been playing the Girl under the weeping willow in the yard next door to ours, and had been dancing around the Calders' faded blue Ford, wondering how come we were so friendly with the Calders when Daddy said people who bought Fords were idiots with no taste.

And there was this strange boy fooling with the Calders' mailbox. Had he been watching me? I walked over.

"What are you doing?"

"Getting the mail." He pulled out a small stack.

"That's the Calders' mail."

"I know, I'm getting their mail for them."

"Who are you?"

"Nathan. My name is Nathan." He said it the way a grown-up would say it. He said it like someone from somewhere else.

"How old are you?" I asked.

"Six and a half," he said, his hand on the lid—a rough hand, scuffed knuckles, bitten nails.

"I'm visiting the Calders." He closed the mailbox, starting for the house.

"Are your parents visiting the Calders?"

"Nope. It's just me."

As he walked away up the driveway, I saw how his ears stuck straight out, and the sun shone bright red right through them.

He's a bony, pale, thin-skinned, undersized but scrappy little kid, much scarred, ugly, red at the joints, with sticking-out ears and a swollen lip and eyes that look as if he's been beaten on, or like he's been crying, or both. He has stiff dun-colorless hair full of cowlicks that stick up like Dagwood's in spite of being combed flat every day with greasy hair stuff, and it seems he's always acting the way he thinks happy and nice people would act.

But he actually is happy and nice most of the time, in a way, at least to me.

I've never known Nathan to lie, though there is a lot he won't tell about the different worlds he came from. He just tells about how he kept getting sent back.

And I never see Nathan cry, except in a fight, of which there are many. But Nathan always wins in a fight because he goes crazy, becomes a purple dervish of hitting, kicking, pinching, biting, cursing, giving out a high-pitched tortured-animal whine. Even much bigger boys back off.

Just before Easter, Nathan and I overheard a bigger kid's dad whipping him with a belt in their garage as we were just leaving their fancy house and yard. This was a kid we never saw around the neighborhood. He was always in the house and was a little bit fat. The father was weirdly angry and was whipping that kid because he'd gone down in defeat to a runt like Nathan.

The kid had been showing us around their property, bragging about things, picking on and teasing and trying to get a rise out of Nathan, eyeing him as if having finally found somebody he thought he could beat. It did work; he got the fight, but then, of course, Nathan went crazy, and the kid backed off. This was always happening. They didn't know Nathan like I did.

When we heard his dad whipping him, we decided to feel sorry for that kid, even though he was a jerk. We walked the steep white-rock creek bed on the way home, looking for crawdad holes to come back to later, collecting crystals from the long veins of quartz in that part of Bachman's Creek in our ongoing search for gold. Because Nathan always said he knew he was going to find gold.

Nathan was the first kid on our block to ride a bike, the first to build a tree house. He can shimmy up a tree with no low branches, jump straight down and land like a cat. He's not like anyone else around here. He collects things. He has a BB gun, cap pistols, holsters, firecrackers, a Scout knife, a Texas flag, a rebel flag, a *Don't Tread on Me* flag, and a chipped plaster Palomino like Trigger from the State Fair on his dresser. He won it at the baseball toss. I was there and saw him talking to the grown-up carny people with their missing teeth and tattoos, showing them his arrowheads, like he was one of them. I follow Nathan everywhere to be part of his adventures.

He lines up his treasures on shelves around his room—arrowheads and fossil shark's teeth found at Scout camp near Cedar Hill, rattlesnake rattles he got in a trade, rocks and stamps and coins and comic books and baseball cards and other trading cards and pinup-girls in stacks of cigar boxes in his clubhouse—and is not really your friend in a trade. He'll look at you like a creature from outer space and make things go his way.

Lots of things he'll never trade—like the bird and snake and cat bones he's gathered in the fields, cleaned, wired, and glued together. He has old marbles and buttons, rusty penknives, broken pipes and lighters, busted wire-rimmed glasses, tools, bullet casings, and shotgun shells he found while walking the creek beds, the windbreaks, the barbed-wire fences way beyond where Mama will let me go, bringing his found objects home, showing them all to me. When he goes out, he selects a few items to carry for the day. He combs the countryside for storied treasure, going far beyond our area to play with the colored kids and the Mexican kids who live farther out there, saying how he really likes them best.

He comes home talking Spanish and slang he gets from the colored kids, calling everybody "*man,*" and his mother gets mad about that in a way you hardly ever see.

Nathan came from an orphanage to live with the Calders for good after that. They'd wanted a child, and finally Nathan was what they got. They said he wasn't what they had wanted, but when they saw him at that orphanage, they just couldn't leave him there. And then they couldn't send him back, because he'd been sent back so many times.

Nathan calls his mother "Momsidoodle." Her real name is Epsie. Epsie—Mrs. Calder is what I call her—is an angular woman with horn-rimmed glasses, sensible brown shoes, and cardigan sweaters, and she actually enjoys the company of children.

Last summer, she was out there in the heat running back and forth in the road with one after another of the kids on our block until she'd taught every one of us to ride his or her bike. She laughs and laughs about little things. She is what they used to call a "good soul."

Mama likes Mrs. Calder, but she doesn't like Nathan. I can tell. Daddy thinks Nathan is okay but says the Calders are ruining him because they feel sorry for him. But I've never felt sorry for Nathan.

Some kids in our neighborhood won't play with Nathan because he just doesn't fit in. And maybe because you can never tell when he might all of a sudden go crazy, or all of a sudden start saying in this weird voice how one day he is going to go looking for his real mother, and when he finds that "nasty bitch" who sent him away, he's going to stretch her out on a cranking torture rack, and turn and one-more-turn that crank while she begs and cries. He will laugh while she begs and cries. He will have it all planned. He'll burn her with matches and slice off her "tits." He'll cook those tits on a huge bonfire, then feed them to some vicious black dogs he'll have around the place he plans to have, and lots more things like that. And when Nathan says things like that, he gets redder and bigger, his eyes turning black. And this can go on and on unless his mom is in the next room saying, "*Stop that!*"

I just wait for it to pass.

The Fish Pond

*H*igh on a slope of thick grass above wide, curving Armstrong Parkway, two-story fat white columns, double doors, two car–width driveway up the side to a three-car garage full of Cadillacs—more Cadillacs and Chevys parked all down the block. It's Easter Sunday at Nana and GranDad's house.

Brick walkways, boxwood, English ivy, a bed of purple pansies, the smell of frying chicken coming from the back door and wafting out over the covered porch, and there's the sizzling, the laughing, the talking, ice clinking in glasses, children chasing one another in grass-stained organdy pinafores, screen doors slamming, and there's Elise sweating over and forking sizzling chicken from two popping iron skillets onto greasy paper bags.

Elise whispers she's saving a wishbone just for me. Daddy grabs a drumstick, stands over the sink bolting it, burning his mouth, Elise saying, "Just get out of my chicken, Mr. Dick!"

You walk through the kitchen, a butler's pantry, and a breakfast room before you get to the garden room at the back, where a crowd of grown-ups stand around with drinks. At first, we all mill around in church dresses and white cotton gloves and patent-leather shoes, aunts, uncles in suits, cousins, Granny and Papaw, friends of Nana's, everybody with big smiles, eyeing one another.

I see Oliver across the garden room, and I see him see me. He turns and walks away into the living room. I go around the other way.

While the grown-ups are talking and the little ones are picking out Easter baskets, I go into the foyer to look at Nana's snuff box and pillbox collection, which is in a glass case under the stairs. I pick out in my mind the ones I would like to take. From there, I drift around into the living room, but Oliver's already gone.

Nana's house is more perfect than Granny's house or our house or any house I've ever seen. It's filled with antiques, paintings, books, toys, music, flowers, cut-crystal dishes of candy. There's a wide curving staircase in the front hall with a polished brass banister you're not supposed to touch. Everything is beautiful. We used to come to Nana's house after Sunday school every week, but after all the babies born at the end of the war grew big enough to constantly chase each other and fight, Nana would always be standing on the staircase, saying she had a headache. Then GranDad started taking us to feed the ducks on Lakeside Drive instead, and then to Beck's Fried Chicken after that. Now we come here for Thursday-night dinners, or for Christmas, or for the big Easter egg hunt every year, like today.

I wander through the house, looking at every single thing. I don't dare steal anything at Nana's house; I'm just checking out the many things to look at, everything so interesting and so grand. There are cherubs and porcelain ladies in fancy dresses—the Dresden and Meissen that Nana talks about collecting. All the women talk about the things to have in your beautiful house. You have to be careful not to break or to stain or to scratch or to leave your greasy child prints on anything at Nana's house. I have become an expert at erasing my tracks, even worrying later about having left a clue. But I never steal anything but candy.

In the living room, I go first to the amber cut-crystal candy dish with the little swirl-top chocolates on one side, on the other side the cellophane-wrapped jelly nougats. It's like a secret pact between me and Nana that my favorites are there for me to get into before anyone's thought to watch me. I put a few in my dress pockets.

I sit down at the big black grand piano where Nana once said she used to play and sing, but now she doesn't play and sing anymore. And I wonder why not. I touch the keys, hearing Nana talking in the next room. Everyone listens when Nana talks. Everything Nana says seems to be serious and important, even when she's making a joke, instead of just funny like the things Granny says. And when you're listening to Nana, if you start to feel worried something's wrong, or might soon go wrong, even though she's only talking like anybody talks, telling her story, you have to just ignore it. Everyone ignores it because we all know this is Nana talking, and nothing on earth could ever be wrong with Nana.

I pretend not to be listening while Nana talks about her sister Zella, how Zella was "the pretty one," and how she,

Nana, was not the pretty one—too skinny, a face too long and "horsey," teeth too big, hair too wiry and red—and how GranDad came to their house to date Zella first, but how she, Nana, snapped him up. And I don't even look over at her when she says how, when they had the firstborn son, by which she means my daddy, Zella would spoil him and make him hers, and how all her family loved spoiling him, but how she, Nana, hated that. Then Nana talks about old family fights between sisters and brothers who never spoke to one another again.

Mama says, "A shame they couldn't just forgive and forget."

Then Nana looks stern and says, "Well, if they could do that, it wouldn't have meant much to them, would it!"

When she says this, GranDad, who is standing in the middle of the room with his camera ready, turns around and snaps a picture of her. Then he walks out of the room.

Mama looks surprised, and then both of them look right at me, and I pretend I wasn't listening.

Nana always talks about who is pretty and who is not. She looks at me and says, "Such a pretty child." And then she says, "Don't be like Zella." But I've never seen Zella and don't know what this means, so I just pretend not to listen while Nana keeps on talking about her family in Salt Lake City, so many people I've never seen, just like Granny talks about her own old family, but different, too. Nana tells about the Mormons back in Utah, whose people went there in covered wagons, like in the movies, how they will just give you anything they have, and then she says, "I'm not a good Mormon," and lifts her chin and looks sad.

Now Nana is telling Mama that her cousin in Utah researched their family back to Scottish kings and queens. Then they stop talking again and both look at me. I leave the room.

I step carefully up and down the wide, curving staircase, being good, not touching the brass banister, holding out my dress. *The Girl is a princess in a grand palace, beautiful and beloved by her people. She commands all that she sees.* Pale carpeting on the staircase goes up to the beautiful rooms.

When I sleep over with Nana, I stay in a guest room up there that's far away from their rooms, but for some reason I am never scared of the dark at Nana's house. The beautifulness of everything comforts me. Also Nana reads to me from *Pinocchio,* and *The Wizard of Oz,* and talks to me about the meanings of the stories without hurrying to do something else, like about how Pinocchio had to go back home and know that he did love his father Geppetto, who'd made him, before finally the Blue Fairy would turn him into a real boy.

In Nana's bedroom, everything is even more beautiful, with mirrors and pink satin and gold. Except there is this one plain unframed black-and-white photograph that sits propped at the back of a group of framed photographs on a low table. I go in and look at this photograph. Nana told me it was taken on the day she and GranDad got engaged, when they believed.

"Believed in what?"

"Oh, just *believed*," she said.

The photograph shows four people reclining on rough-cut grass, mowed as a simple opening in a field, with grass tall and seeding against a white fence with a box-column newel post before which they're gathered together. Leafy trees and sky behind them halo the dark heads of a woman and three men, all in old-fashioned summer Sunday clothes, stiff collars and pinned-up hair loosened on a breezy afternoon. All four on the grass are touching, arms around one another, a smiling young Nana with her arms around both men at the back, one slim hand curving absentmindedly around the collar of one, but her face turning toward the other, as if saying something funny. He, in turn, has laid both forearms across the shoulders of the man with glasses in front. And the man with his forearms on the other man has a different appearance—darker, thick-haired, large-boned, smiling also. It's GranDad, the Italian. You see them there in that different world, so long ago, so young and slim, relaxed and happy and full of grace.

GranDad's room is next to Nana's, completely different, sleek, with elevated bed, dark woods, huge closets and mirrors, dressing room and bath modern with black tile, a desk, a fireplace, a painting of a naked woman, pale skin against dark drapes, and an artist at an easel. An entire wall is mirrored on one side of GranDad's room. When we sit in there, everyone keeps pretending not to be watching themselves, watching one another.

I walk through all the rooms. I open closets, where Nana keeps boxed handkerchiefs, toys, and boxes of

Arpège perfume for gifts. I look for the things that might later appear with tags saying "From Santa."

Party noises go on downstairs. No one has missed me yet. Oliver has disappeared also. How does he get away so fast? He knows how to be invisible, like me.

I open the door to the attic stairs. These stairs are scary, creaky, dark, climbing narrowly up to the huge attic, and it smells musty up there. I turn on the light and start up.

There's a commotion, footsteps, and then Oliver appears at the top, and with a stiff face turned away from me, he hurries down, rudely brushing past me and out the door.

I slip and almost fall down the stairs when he goes past. My knees feel funny. My throat hurts. My eyes sting. *Why does he act that way to me? Hasn't he always known me? Don't I know him? Why will he not even look at me? Why was he hiding up here all alone?* I can't catch my breath all the way on up into the attic, where I have to wait for this crying feeling to pass so that no one will have something to tease me about.

But I wasn't doing anything to him! I wasn't following him! Was I? I was not! I'd forgotten all about him! I had! I was just wandering around, and it seemed like something led me to where he was without my telling it to do so.

But what if it's true I was looking for him, not even thinking about doing it? What's so bad about that? All I want is for him to talk to me! I'm not one of the little kids! Why can't we be friends? Why can't he be nice? Why?

I still cannot get a deep breath. Whenever I see Oliver's smooth face, his soft dark eyes, like Mama's, even though he was adopted as a baby, it always seems to me that we know each other. *Doesn't he see it?* It seems to me that there was a time when we played together and were friends. But the truth is, the picture in my mind is the blowing curtains in the summer bedroom at Granny's house.

The attic is a long room, wood-floored, wooden eaves above, lined with wooden closets and shelves. I like the bareness of it, the smell of wood. I peer into the attic closets filled with winter clothes, and the mothball smell stops my tears.

I sit down next to a big dollhouse that was supposed to be mine but now is everybody's and nobody's, because Mama said they were so disappointed when I didn't seem to want it that much, and now I can never play with it anyway, with all the little cousins around grabbing things, breaking things, losing things, ruining everything. This always happens. Why do I have to be put in with them instead of with the much more interesting grown-ups?

It's true I never liked this dollhouse. It reminded me of a dollhouse that was in the office of this doctor Mama took me to one time to find out what it was that was wrong with me. She's always trying to figure out what's wrong with me. The doctor wanted me to play with this doll family he had while he watched me and asked questions about Mama and Daddy that I knew even then not to talk about with some strange man. Plus, there was the way he looked at me—too interested. Then he came out and whispered to Mama, as if I weren't standing right there hearing it. So this dollhouse sits day and night, no one playing with it, year after year, in the attic dust.

I do like to sit up here by myself and look through the musty old books. Some have Daddy's name or Uncle Ted's name written inside in child-writing. Many Oz books, *Arabian Nights,* Hardy Boys, Jerry Todd, and Poppy Ott books. Nana lets me borrow them to take home and read and then bring back. *Poppy Ott and the Freckled Goldfish* is my favorite, because it seems like the secret-club world of boys, and they talk the way Nathan talks.

There are dormer windows on both sides of the attic that look out through tree branches to the front and back yards so far below that they look like dollhouse yards, with dollhouse people walking around.

I look down and see GranDad and Uncle Ted standing next to the fish pond, talking. GranDad likes to fiddle with his fish pond, and Uncle Ted is talking to him while he does it. Then I see Daddy clump-CLUMPing out to stand with them. Uncle Ted turns and walks back toward the house. Daddy talks to GranDad, then turns and walks away also, but toward the garage. GranDad stands there looking down at his fish.

I go back down the attic stairs, then down the wide, curving front stairs. No one seems to notice my gliding quietly through the house, especially when we first arrived, the grown-ups greeting one another, getting drinks, wanting to talk and laugh together. No one's looking for me.

I go check where Daddy might be. I watch him stomp out of the room, where a group of men are talking about

Lyndon Johnson. Daddy's yelling, "Johnson and Rayburn are crooks!"

Papaw carries a letter from Lyndon Johnson in his breast pocket and shows it to people. Daddy cringes at this, jumps up, and leaves the room when he pulls it out.

I wander back to the center of activity, the porch that used to be screened in before Nana and GranDad were the first ones we knew to get central air conditioning, so now it's all glassed in and decorated fancy. And here they all are.

Nana sits on the side near the entrance in a wrought-iron chair with people around her. She sees me coming in and smiles.

"Come over here and let my friends see you," she says, then presents me to the blond lady who always carries a fancy paper umbrella she calls a "parasol," because she's allergic to the sun. Her husband has a thin mustache. Nana always says how this woman is trapped with having to be young all the time because she made the mistake of marrying a younger man, but how this woman is her good friend.

There are two children with their parents—a little boy with red hair and something wrong with his foot, and a tall blond girl named Ann, who's older and never says much to me or to anyone. They go to private schools.

I look around for Oliver. Then he comes in from the living room with Papaw and some other people, and then Daddy comes in, saying, "So when are we going to have this Easter egg hunt?"

Papaw goes *Ho-ho-ho-ho,* and Daddy dashes for the bar again.

I look at Papaw. I can't see anything that makes him so different except that he's noisy and wet and always seems to have his eye on me. They say Papaw's *a Jew,* but he's not foreign-looking or dark. He has kinky slicked-down brown-gray hair, small light eyes, and a jowly face covered with tiny pink veins.

Oliver is smooth-skinned, with dark hair and eyes, but no darker than those of Granny or Mama, who are not Jews. So what is it that makes Papaw and Oliver Jews anyway? They're always around with us at Christmas and at Easter, and the rest of it seems to be secret, something you're not supposed to ask.

I can't ask Mama anything now while she's chatting with Aunt Celeste. They stand facing each other at an angle, holding cigarettes and clinking drinks with their red-nailed jeweled fingers, laughing a lot, talking chummily yet guardedly together out on the patio with their beautiful clothes and their diamond-cut ankles, sleek birds circling, feathers out.

Aunt Celeste, with her shiny black pompadour, sharp blue eyes, red lipstick, and white pancake makeup, reminds me of the porcelain Japanese-lady lamps in Nana's guest room. She wears black and white, turquoise silk underneath, and a ring with a big purple stone and little turquoise stones around it on her small-boned, tanned hands, which don't match her face, holding a pink-paper cigarette. She talks in a deep, gravelly voice, and I could stare and study her for hours, but she looks down at me like the Wicked Witch in Snow White. She does not like me.

Mama wears her hair in the usual thick-braid crown, with her usual gold loop earrings and diamond rings, none of which matters at all beside that face that she has. And she wears a jade green ribbon-knit dress she made herself, carefully knitting all the thin ribbons into sections and then ironing the sections and sewing them together into, magically, a dress that clings and hangs like green silk chain mail, showing her to be far and away the most elegant of them all.

Mama's told me her stories about how she and Aunt Celeste play bridge every week with their friends, who've all known one another from long before air conditioning—from high school, from sororities and clubs for nice people, lucky people—and how they married brothers who went away to war, one coming home a decorated Air Force hero over France, the other coming home off balance, broken.

Nana stands up and then leads everyone outside for the Easter egg hunt. GranDad's already standing outside in his wide pleated slacks next to the fish pond. First, he comes hurrying over to the brick steps to pat our ankles and socks with fat pink-and-blue flannel pillow-puff squares to keep the chiggers off, the sulfur powder yellowing everyone's ankles. Then he goes back out and starts tapping his foot for his fancy goldfish to come and eat, calling the children to come and look at how he's trained his goldfish, but I'm the only one who goes over there to look.

The grass is golf green–smooth and tight. Clipped boxwood and low redbrick walls march around in perfect formation, marking this section from that, framing areas and levels of the yard, where row upon row of tall red Darwin tulips are nodding behind overflowing mounds of purple-and-white pansies that fill the formal borders. Nana says she's fed them so much bonemeal, you could pinch off pansies out of there for an hour and never see a gap. And it's true that there are bowls of pansies all around the house. Nana loves how their little faces look up at you.

The fish pond is at the back, with tall trees behind it. GranDad stands out there beside a gnarled Wisteria tree that drips purple blossoms onto a white wrought-iron bench and wafts its scent over the whole yard. Colored eggs peek out here and there. Every year, Nana and Elise decorate dozens of hard-boiled eggs the like of which you could spend your whole life of Easters trying to duplicate and never get it right—deep solids, rich whorls and squiggles on the multicolored ones, each egg a fantastic work of art, some with white wax designs or names written in Nana's slanting hand, three or four for each child.

The little kids chase each other across the lawn, Easter ruffles already torn, white cotton gloves lost, hats and barrettes askew, white socks and patent-leather Mary Jane shoes wet with grass clippings and sulfur dust, each clutching his or her fancy Easter basket, tripping, spilling out the jelly beans and Brach's chocolate cream eggs, which Margie snatches up, and then the screaming fighting and crying begins.

Orange-and-white goldfish swarm up for the fish food GranDad sprinkles on the water, some big ones up from the deep, bullying one another with their fat bodies, glassy eyes, dumb gulping mouths, a thrashing battle for food, for place.

GranDad laughs, saying, "It's good for them to compete."

Margie and Debbie, the cousins, are nearly the same age as my sister Annie, all three born toward the end of the war.

Margie, the elder cousin, a stocky, intelligent, wild-haired almost five-year-old dynamo of aggression in a pinafore and crooked wire-rimmed glasses she's worn since babyhood, teases, pokes, and provokes everyone, and no one stops her. Aunt Celeste does not believe in spanking, and Uncle Ted seems to think it's funny for her to disrupt and taunt everyone. You can see him whispering to her and pointing with a grin.

Uncle Ted strides across the lawn and speaks to Gran-Dad, who then announces that we are going to make our Easter egg hunt into a race, a contest for who can find the most eggs. Then Uncle Ted starts whispering again to Margie, who looks around, eager black eyes enormous behind the skewed glasses.

Debbie, the younger cousin, thin, shy, pale, doesn't say much, doesn't eat much, but hugs her basket and sucks her thumb, as if hoping just to be invisible and left alone. Annie sits with her but gets forced into the game.

I'm too old to be part of the race, and don't want to be part of it, either, which just shows once again how there is something wrong with me, because I, too, just want to watch and be left alone. I take my basket to the other side of the yard, where I can view the whole scene. I look across at Oliver, who stands with the grown-ups, being *oh so above it all.*

Now poor Annie has Daddy huddling with her, telling her she has to win with the most eggs, and exactly how she's going to do this. He doesn't seem to see how wrinkled Annie's forehead has become, how worried her small face.

Trudy's only a year old, too young for the race. She sits on the grass, happily crushing eggs in her pudgy hands, then trying to eat the colored shells. GranDad takes a picture of this.

Uncle Ted and Daddy and GranDad are excited about having an Easter egg race, all three joking around together, which you don't often see. Each scolds open violence, yet each father eagerly whispers tactics to his own. Annie looks as if the weight of the whole house has just been strapped upon her four-year-old shoulders.

And so the race begins. *On your mark, get set, GO!*

I walk around them and watch, pick up a few eggs for myself, and I'm so glad I don't have to compete.

The boy and the girl with Nana's friends are also not part of the race. They start out to be, but then step back, shy and quiet, both staying on the sidelines, picking up what eggs they can easily see. The girl watches us curiously. The boy clumps around, hunting eggs in his brown suit and a special shoe that's built up to make his legs and feet come out even. *Did he have polio?* I wonder. Because once in a while there's someone who's had polio.

The sisters-in-law, Mama and Aunt Celeste, as well as the invited friends, Granny and Papaw, other uncles and aunts, in their dresses and high heels and hats and gloves, have come out to stand on the terrace, holding their gin and tonics, their Bloody Marys, laughing and pointing at the amusing antics of the pastel-clad cousins chasing each other around the yard in a contest as vicious as that in any chicken yard.

All the cousins pile their baskets high with what would be enough eggs for a large orphanage, cracked eggs tipping out onto the lawn. *Finders keepers, losers weepers!* Margie and I are grabbing them up from each other. The baskets are too heavy with too many, too much. Baby Trudy picks up an egg and digs tiny fingers into the yolk, squishing it onto her dress, putting shells to her mouth before I come running over, speaking in imitation grown-up tones. All her eggs must be thrown away, but no one cares, there are so many.

I see Uncle Ted whispering to Margie again, and Annie looks so alone out there, so I go over and stand here and there around the yard, trying to point out eggs to her, but Margie watches me and snatches each one up before Annie can get to it.

We shout out, "No fair! No fair!" But it seems there are no rules in this game. Daddy tells me to stay out of it because I am older, but now I want to join in so we can beat Margie.

"Come on, Annie!" I'm yelling, but Margie bumps into Annie, causing eggs to spill, which Margie snatches up.

Margie is as fast as a little animal, and Annie, a year younger, is not having fun. She is crying and ready to stop, but Daddy and I keep yelling, "Don't give up, Annie!" We try to help her out until the baskets appear to be about the same.

Then Margie steals eggs from Debbie, who is still sucking her thumb and sitting behind a hedge. Annie cries out angrily and drops her eggs. Trudy crawls over, picks up an egg and squeezes with interest, watching the powdery yolk run between her fingers. The cheating is ignored.

The grown-ups look away, chatter away, seem not to want to make trouble or even to see any trouble, and Uncle Ted seems to think the whole thing is a hilarious joke he's going to enjoy for months to come. Aunt Celeste has her back turned and seems not to want to notice or care.

We try to get the distracted grown-ups to do a final egg count, but they've all lost interest now, looking away from us brats, embarrassed, starting to drift inside. Everyone just looks away from unpleasant behavior. No one's declared the winner, and there's no prize.

"I win! I win! I win!" shouts Margie, who obviously does have the most eggs now. She runs up close to me, sticking her face out, tempting me, inviting me to smack her.

And oh, how much I do want to smack her, how my whole arm aches to smack her good and hard! But I know the only way to defeat Margie would be all-out

hair-pulling, ear-biting, face-punching, rolling-over-
and-over-on-the-grass violence, and I have to act nice
with all these grown-ups around. I always have to be
the one to act *oh so nice, nice, nice*, all the time, even
when other people have not been forced and trained to
act *nice*. So I would get the blame, because I'm the eldest,
and those are Mama's rules.

Besides, if you cross Margie, she bites, and she bites
hard, and no one stops her.

Then GranDad, chuckling and Groucho-popping his
black eyes, goes running out to the garage, then returns
with a stack of gray cardboard boxes with holes in them.
He opens the boxes on the lawn, and out pour a dozen
live baby ducks dyed different colors, like the eggs, and
all the children scream with joy.

But Mama and Nana and Aunt Celeste are furious,
saying, "Oh no!" and "We told you not to do that!" and
"They'll all just die!"

The baby ducks spread across the yard in a swarm,
quack-peeping, jerking their tiny beaks into the thick
grass, looking for bugs. Margie starts chasing and
spreading them farther. A red one and then a green
one fall into the fish pond, then pop up and start to
swim in circles. Nana tells GranDad in her headache
voice to catch them, please, and to put them all back
into the boxes. GranDad runs after Margie across the
lawn. Trudy grabs up a blue duck to squeeze, but I'm fast
enough to get it from her, and she screams in outrage.

Annie cries, hiccupping, saying, "I hate Margie, I hate
her, I hate her!" Daddy, who's been standing by himself,

picks up a yellow duck and goes over to talk to her in this sweet way, giving her some jelly beans, and I watch and am jealous.

I see Mama and Aunt Celeste looking around, annoyed and disgusted. They aren't going to say anything. The two of them take their drinks and stroll back inside the house.

Each cousin tries to capture and possess one or two ducks, while also protecting her own piled-heavy Easter basket. GranDad's attempts to control the kids are ignored. The girl Ann and the boy with red hair stand on the side, watching all of us harridans wide-eyed.

I go back into the house to see what Mama's doing with the other grown-ups in there. I find her with the other women, all of them standing around with fresh drinks, walking back and forth in the large kitchen, talking about shopping and clothes and parties, gesturing with their cigarettes, their red nails, their diamond rings as they move from pantry to sink to countertop to stove, changing places around the room.

The little kids come running in and out with stories about who hit whom and who started it—a knee skinned, a chocolate rabbit smashed, a sash torn off. The women replace barrettes, look for the everyday napkins, try to joke around with Elise, who, grim-faced and sweating, but sometimes smiling, listens and nods and forks and turns the last of the sizzling and popping chicken wings, the livers, the necks, the hearts.

In another part of the house, the men, GranDad and Uncle Ted and Daddy and Papaw and some others, stand around drinking and smoking. Oliver sits in there with the men. I go in to see if they're ready to eat. They seem not to know what to talk about with one another. They look at the new Magnavox record player cabinet. They compare new cameras, talk about business, then cars. They have many cigarettes, many drinks. I go back out.

I hear Papaw's booming *HO-ho-ho-ho* laugh from in there. You can hear him all over the house. No one ever says anything or acts toward him in the same way they act when they say the word *Jew*, and I can't see anything different about him, except that he's always laughing loudly and somehow uncomfortably, always snorting, blowing his nose, clearing his throat, giving that little whistle when people are starting to argue or get mad, and it seems like somebody always gets mad—usually Daddy, talking loudly, shouting, then the *HO-ho-ho-ho*. Then the women come rushing in, shushing them, "It's a holiday, Dick. Dick, please!" and "Don't spoil it."

Soon Daddy's standing alone again on the porch, looking out at the yard. His hand on his glass holds two fingers out straight, off the wet surface, a cigarette between them. He drinks in rapid little sips, then gulps the last down with closed eyes. Then he's pacing through the house, pretending to be interested in things like books in the bookshelf, radio programs, his fingernails.

He clump-CLUMPs out to the kitchen, saying, "Are we gonna eat that chicken anytime this year, Elise?" grabbing drumsticks off the pile, until Elise shoos him out to the garage, where he lifts hoods and starts tinkering with the cars.

GranDad goes out to the garage and says, "Leave my car alone."

Daddy follows GranDad back in, saying, "Dad. I need to talk to you, Dad." GranDad doesn't answer him.

Mama whispers in the hallway with Nana, who oversees everything nervously, saying, "It's just a little headache. It keeps coming back." Uncle Ted goes up to them in the hall. I see Nana look at him very differently from the way she looks at Daddy.

Finally Elise and Ross step forth with the loaded silver trays, huge mounds of fried chicken, the juicy legs and thighs, the breasts, the crispy wings, the thick peppery chicken gravy, hot biscuits, deviled eggs, relishes, jellies, string beans with bacon, mashed potatoes full of parsley and butter and milk.

Everybody claps hands and cheers for Elise, who smiles tiredly but seems to enjoy this. She leans down and points out where she hid a wishbone for me, her face beaded with sweat.

Then there's the frantic jostling among all us grass-stained cousins to pile your plate with the most drumsticks and wings, and wishbones, of course, and then to get into the best places at the children's table in the breakfast room, which means not trapped in the corner, and not next to Margie, because she grabs the food right off your plate.

Oliver gets to sit at the grown-up table in the dining room. And he just walks in there as if he belongs with them, with no looks or even smirks at me, with no anything for me at all.

Mama and Aunt Celeste come in and tuck napkins around each child's neck, warning about manners, about teasing, whispering that Nana's nervous and has a headache and that we must not upset Nana. Mama gives me a glare. Aunt Celeste looks around distastefully at the grimy little monsters that we are, then both smooth their hair and dresses and go to eat with the grown-ups in the dining room with its gilt-framed fruit and flower paintings and the crystal bell for Nana to call Elise and Ross in to serve. They close the door.

Then we have our way with each other at the kids' table in the breakfast room. We eat as fast as we can, Margie and I seeming to be in an eating contest, while Debbie sits in the corner next to Annie, preferring her thumb, letting Margie take the food off her plate. Annie cries about wanting to sit with Mama and Daddy in the dining room, waving her fork, getting mashed potatoes in her hair. Trudy smears gravy and grape jelly around on her high-chair tray.

As I'm stripping my wishbone for later, hiding it in a napkin so no one will take it, we hear voices rising in the dining room, men arguing about Lone Star. I try to listen over the kids but can't catch all the words.

Daddy's voice has that twisted sound, angry, struggling not to cry. "I know what I'm talking about!" he says. Then Papaw's warning throat clearing and whistling, working up to a *Ho-ho-ho-ho.* Then I hear Uncle Ted's voice, reasonable-sounding. Then I hear Gran-Dad's voice above them all. A silence. Then the women's voices rising, all talking at once. Nana's is the final voice, as usual, disapproving, tired.

And then there's a commotion, something falling, a crash, Mama's voice crying out as if to make him stop with the force of just that one word: "Dick, Dick, Dick!" Nana's voice doing the same: "Dick! Dick!"

But Daddy can't stand it, whatever it is. My arms prickle with fear. We hear his clump-CLUMPing going out through the kitchen to the back bathroom, the door slamming. We hear Papaw in the dining room, clearing his throat over and over again, and *Ho-ho-ho-ho-ho-ho-ho.*

Oliver comes in, kind of sneers, as if to say, Uh-oh, it's the brats in here! Then he walks through on his way to the front bathroom. I spread grape jelly onto my biscuit.

The little kids start whispering, and I hear Daddy clump-CLUMPing around out in the kitchen, saying something to Elise, then heading out the back, the screen door slamming, and I hear a car start up out there, hear the tires squealing away. He's gone and left us here.

Mama comes in and cleans us up with a damp napkin, her face pouting and closed. Annie lifts her arms, wanting to be picked up, and then Trudy does the same, but Mama just wipes their faces. Aunt Celeste comes in and does the same with her children, squinting her eyes from smoke drifting up from the pastel blue cigarette bobbing in her red mouth. Then they go away again, making amusing remarks to each other. Time for second helpings.

Margie's watching my face with a grin. Why is she always watching me? She reaches over and snatches a biscuit off my plate. I try to get it from her across the table, grabbing her arm, then her hair. She yells out with this amazingly loud voice, and her mother comes rushing back in. My biscuit is in crumbs on the floor.

I stare at my plate while Aunt Celeste says that I'm too old for such things and should set an example. When she goes out, I kick Margie hard in the shin under the table, a satisfying direct hit. She yells again, with unnecessary loudness, it seems to me, but the strange thing is how much she seems to enjoy this. Grinning, she comes back at me.

I wish I could have left with Daddy, but now he's off somewhere again, alone and sad in the car. Where does he go?

Elise comes through the swinging door, bringing more chicken, serving each of us brats from our left, looking as though she doesn't intend to talk about anything, looking at me as if I know something about that, but I do not know a thing.

I get up from the table, put my wishbone in my pocket for later, and follow Elise back out to the kitchen, looking to see if Daddy's really gone, and Elise shares her own cleaned wishbone with me. I wish that Daddy will come back and be okay. But then Elise lets me win, which I know doesn't really count for getting your wish.

Nana's friends with the two children leave right after lunch, and while everyone's saying good-bye and getting ready to leave, and while the cousins are pounding up the stairs to the attic playroom, I sneak out to the porch and raid the overflowing baskets, already having noticed the ones I want to steal. I look for the beautiful ones, the unusual ones that I know the little kids won't even notice. I put some eggs back into Debbie's basket. Then I find four eggs that say *Margie* and I throw them out into the alley behind the pond, all the while knowing she won't notice or care, but it feels good doing it, even though I do know that this is more evidence that there's something wrong with me. Then I hide my own basket outside near the back door.

Oliver's standing in the doorway, looking at me when I come back in. He smirks and says, "Think you're invisible, don't you?"

And I say, "Sometimes." But he's already turning away.

Granny and Papaw leave now, and he goes with them. I watch them walking down the driveway, Oliver in front.

Daddy has still not come back with our car, so there's talk in the kitchen about who's going to drive us home. Or maybe we'll wait awhile, since there's no answer at our house and no one knows where Daddy went. Nana says she's going upstairs to lie down. Everyone's worried. When I come into the room, they stop talking and look at one another. I go out and sit on the steps to listen through the screen door, but nobody says anything about Daddy.

I find Mother in the kitchen, where the women walk around the room drinking, smoking, talking. Little kids come downstairs and run in and out with their rustling boxes of baby ducks.

GranDad comes into the kitchen and sits on a chair, stooped and tired, holding his camera up once in a while as if to snap a picture, but then not doing it, turning his heavy head back and forth, watching the women move around, listening to them. He seems to be listening intently. He seems to have a question in his mind.

Is he thinking of other women, other kitchens, when he was young maybe, kitchens peopled with poor Italian women in another place, another time? He has nothing to say to these women, and they seem to have nothing to say to him.

"Still so handsome." That's what everyone says about GranDad—"Such a good-looking man." He sits there with his thick hair, his angular nose and white teeth, his dark eyes watching his young daughters-in-law as if there's something he'd like to understand, but he never has much to say. He just sits listening, with his head hanging like a dog.

A few times he's talked to me while walking block after block after dinner at their house, telling me how he quit school in fourth grade because his own father was "too good to work." Then he'd get angry, saying "what bums poor people are," how you can't help them because they're "bums, who just want a free ride, and to drag you down to their level." Then he'd look at me with tears in his eyes and say, "You look exactly like my sister, Rose."

He doesn't join in the discussion about who'll take us home "way out there," since Daddy took our car, but he just stares up at the ceiling fan rotating steadily above, at the bars of late-day light slanting through the blinds over the sinks, at the arc of stripes flaring across the wall.

Finally, GranDad says quietly, "I'll take them home."

He says he'd enjoy the long drive on such a nice day, and when they talk about Daddy, he says, "Just leave him alone." Nana turns and looks at him like she does not agree with this.

On the way out to our house in GranDad's Cadillac, I sit in the front seat with him, and I look at the Cadillac crest on the dashboard with the little ducks on it.

Mama sits in the back with the babies, who both fall asleep, and nobody says a word the whole way out to the country, where our house is. I have our baby ducks and our Easter baskets full of eggs with me on a newspaper on the floor of the front seat. The ducks rustle and squeak in their box, and the car radio plays swinging band music, but no one sings. I keep looking back at Mama, who looks out the window sadly, as if thinking of something very far away.

GranDad doesn't say anything. He doesn't sing his funny songs or say anything at all the whole way out.

Hap and Hazard
and the End of the World

I hate it when Mama cries. Her face screws up and she looks at me with begging eyes, and then it seems like everything might be about to turn into something else, and I don't know what I will do if that happens.

Mama loves to bathe, brush, train, and play with the dogs more than just about anything. Her face looks so young when she gets down on the floor with them and starts telling me how babies are born. We try to count how many are in Hazard's—Hazzy's—swollen belly. Hap lies nearby, the daddy of these puppies— even though they're brother and sister cocker spaniels, which Mama says is okay for dogs. She looks so happy saying "Six or more, I'll bet," and Hazzy will need help, since it's her first time, and Mama says I can be there and watch when they're born!

Daddy comes bursting in the door and flinches when he sees us down on the floor. Mama and I flinch, too. We thought he was still back there taking one of his long naps that last all day. He looks down at the dogs and at us on the floor.

"You're not planning to let that dog accidentally give birth in the house, are you, Jane?"

"No, Dick, I was just about to put them out," she says

Sometimes it seems that Daddy likes dogs, too, *but not in the house*. He used to like to ride horses, but he's nervous and afraid of falling because of his war-injured feet and bad balance. He wants everything to keep away from him.

At a friend's house, their big dog jumped on him, long tongue slurping, and he fell reeling back onto the grass; then he clump-CLUMPed off to the car as fast as he could, and we all had to follow him, and then listen to his shouting all the way home that those people were "idiots" to have a dog not trained right. And anyone who'd own that big stupid breed of dog in the first place had to be a "jackass," somebody he could never ever have for a friend, or even speak to, "ever again."

I hate it when Daddy gets crazy. It's not all the time. Sometimes you can talk to him, ask him things. Sometimes I almost forget to be afraid of him. Sometimes if I say something funny, he gets this certain look in his eye, as if I hit the bull's-eye. It's a look that is like a small salute. But lately he's not doing it. Lately, he is always yelling about this or that.

Sometimes Mama goes out and sits with the dogs, and sometimes I hear her talking to them, telling them how she feels, but in words I usually can't pick out.

I hate it when Mama tells me how she wanted a different kind of life. She tells how when she was a kid like me, she used to visit Aunt Lee and Uncle Edward out in Brady, Texas, how Aunt Lee is Granny's sister, how they had all kinds of animals, how they had five tall sons, Mama's cousins, such sweet men.

She tells me about their farm while she's putting the carrots, the onions, the radishes, the tomatoes, and the strawberries into our "truck" garden out back. She tells me about her cousins when she's putting our clothes through the wringer, then hanging them out on the line one by one. She tells me of the wonderful people as she's feeding our dozen chickens and gathering our eggs, simple country people and yet so smart and creative out there in Brady, the heart of Texas.

When she puts me to bed at night, she tells me how they would read a Bible story and a *Saturday Evening Post* story every night, and how she always wanted to be just like them, have a life exactly like theirs. Then her tears dry up as she opens the Bible to the first chapter.

The Bible stories are interesting, about families, problems, fathers and brothers always fighting or killing one another, or sending one another away. Especially brothers always wanting to be the favorite. Long lists of families. God appears. The Devil and different angels appear to certain chosen ones of them. But the ones who are chosen don't seem to be all that good. They are just *chosen*, that's all, and we don't know why. They don't explain this in Sunday school, and Mama doesn't like questions. Also, some of those angels are not as nice as you would normally think angels are supposed to be.

It's hot summer now, and people say *drought*, week after week, no rain. We take naps, sleep in our underpants in front of fans; we get wet and sit in the shade; we drink water. We have mosquito and chigger bites old and crusty, bites new and swollen, poison ivy, and heat rashes.

Clouds of gnats stand in the shimmery air. The black dirt is as cracked as a scab. Our grass is brown, as if going back to desert because we're not allowed to water enough. The grown-ups talk about "Okies" and the "Dust Bowl" and each one has a story about it.

On the radio, they talk about frying eggs on sidewalks downtown, and Nathan and I want to try it, but there are no sidewalks out where we live, only a gravel and tar road out front. We stay outside and in what shade we can find most of the time.

Daddy stays at the office late because there is some air conditioning down there. He comes home and changes his shirt two or three times before bed. He never walks around in underwear. No one does that here.

Once in a while, we drive out past the cotton fields, past the mesquite and hackberry windbreaks, out Preston Road to the country club, where we swim all day. But we can't take Nathan anymore because of the way he acts, Mama says.

After dinner, I take the trash out. I stand looking at the moon, remembering how Daddy told me about it, and the billions of stars winking, sending me a message that someday I'll have my own life, not like this.

Clouds pile on one side of the sky. The air feels heavy. Then come dark clouds, thunder, lightning, and at last rain. Everyone jumps out of bed in the night and runs outside. We are all so happy about rain!

The next morning, everything seems alive again. I lift a pile of wet brush and find a green lizard, which skitters away, and I see a grass snake just slipping out of his old skin. I put the crinkly skin into my pocket. The sun comes out, clouds roll onto the other side of the sky, and Mama and May-May are moving washed diapers out to the clothesline, pinning them one by one to flap dry.

I call Nathan's name out near his clubhouse. There's no answer, but I hear voices out front, where there are deep ruts and puddles in the mud, gravel, and tar road in front of our house. Only the rare car passes.

Dams and lakes and rivers and canals can be made in the road, and there's a whole system built by the time I get there, Nathan and the Breards from across the street working on it, so I join in. We make little walls out of sticks and pebbles, and little boats out of leaves and paper and twigs, and float them there in the street. We make canals connecting the puddles. I take out the snake skin and trade it to Nathan for a promise that I can borrow his Captain Marvel comics for a week. He has a huge stack in his room.

The littler kids, the two Annies, and the dogs Hap and Hazard play and run around us. Hazzy can barely walk. She lays her big belly full of puppies on the grass by the side of the road, but Hap keeps running around and around us.

After a while, Daddy's car starts coming out. He stops at the end of our driveway, when all of a sudden a pickup truck comes around him from seemingly nowhere, honking its horn, going fast.

We jump aside for the truck to pass, mud splashing, but Hap is on the other side of the road. He tries to run across, but it's too late and the truck's front wheel hits him square. Both wheels run over him, and the truck just keeps going around the corner.

Hap squeals and squeals. He's broken, bleeding, the back part of him stuck flat into the tar pavement, the front part of him yipping, whining, pulling, fighting to escape.

Daddy struggles out of his car.

We run to the spot, yelling, then all standing helpless. Hap is halfway lying in the street, his back part wrecked, bloody, and stuck in the tar. He's trying to get up, but he can't. Hazzy's shaking all over, sniffing, licking him, yipping, whimpering.

Annie's running on her four-year-old legs up to the house for Mama, who's already running out across the lawn in her apron, saying, "*Oh no, oh no.*"

Then Mama's kneeling in the wet, hot, tarry road, begging Hap not to die, sobbing, "Come on baby, come on," and trying to unstick his legs, his belly, saying, "*Oh no, oh no, oh no, oh no.*"

Ricky Breard is saying how their dog Skippy got hit by a car once but now he's fine.

"It wasn't me, Jane; it wasn't me!" Daddy shouts.

Mama does not look at Daddy.

Daddy comes over, saying, "It's no use," but she pushes him away.

Hap stops struggling. His eyes are fading. Hazzy licks Mama and whimpers and whines and shakes all over. Mama weeps openly, shaking all over, as well, picking Hap up carefully, saying things I don't understand, holding him out in front of her, hurrying back to the house, and hiccupping like a little kid. I never saw her cry like that.

We follow in silent awe, Annie and Nathan and I. The other kids stand in the street. I look back at Daddy. Daddy turns and clump-CLUMPs toward the house as fast as he can.

In the house, Mama lays Hap on the back porch on a towel May-May brings and then calls the vet. Hazard howls outside the door. Mama cries into the phone. Annie and Nathan and I watch Hap make noises like a dog dreaming; then he stops. Hap is dead.

I hear Daddy in the bathroom, door locked, throwing up. Then he comes out, grabs his cane, and drives away.

We bury Hap in a Neiman's box next to the woods, Mama acting mad, not saying much, Nathan and May-May helping to dig the hole, May-May singing, all of us crying, Hazzy wagging her tail, licking our ankles as if pleading.

Nathan and I sit out there for most of the rest of the afternoon, something bad hanging over us. Then Nathan has to go home. I stay there with Hap, picturing him stuffed into that box, buried down there under all that dirt, stiff and matted now, alone.

I keep thinking of a dead pet turtle we buried once, how when Nathan and I dug it up later, only the shell was left. I draw a picture of the turtle shell in the dirt with a stick.

Then Hazzy starts digging, whining, digging with more and more excitement, and I can't make her stop. I run in to tell Mama, who's in there crying over a popping skillet of rice fritters. Mama turns off the stove, wipes her face with the dish towel, goes out and puts Hazzy into the pen, where she barks and whines and howls alone for the rest of the night.

Daddy comes back for dinner, acting like nothing's happened. Mama feeds Trudy early and puts her to bed, and Annie spends the night with the Breards, so it's the three of us at the table with creamed chipped beef on toast, which Daddy makes jokes about, saying how in the army they called it S.O.S., and Mama frowns about that, so Daddy starts getting in a bad mood, eating up all the rice fritters. When I ask for another one, he says I'm getting fat.

Daddy goes out to the toolshed after dinner, until Hazzy's barking makes him come in mad again. Mama goes out and talks to Hazzy, but when she comes back in, the howling's worse.

She puts me in the bathtub, where I carve the Ivory soap into the shape of a turtle as I listen to them fighting.

"If you'd just leave the dog alone out there, she'd stop."

"She's never been alone in her whole life, Dick."

"So what! She'll have to learn it now!"

"I just can't be that heartless about it."

"Really! You care more about those dogs than you do about me!"

Daddy slams out, roaring away again in his car. I wonder if Daddy will be killed in a car wreck, and I wonder if we will be sad.

I prop my Toni doll up on the table next to my bed, turn her head so that her blank eyes look over at me like a blind person might do.

Mama comes in, her face red and puffy. We say the "Now I Lay Me Down to Sleep" prayer, and we God-bless all the usual people, and tonight we God-bless Hap and Hazzy, as well. And we God-bless the puppies not yet born.

"Mama, do dogs go to Heaven?"

"I don't know. But I think they should," she says, kissing me on the cheek, then turns out the light and goes out. It surprises me the way she said this in such a real-sounding voice. Was she telling me that the truth is she doesn't really know anything about Heaven?

I hear her making phone calls as I lie there in the dark wishing I had someone to talk to, thinking about how Hap was alive one second and crushed the next, how everything changed so fast. I keep picturing the back part of his body stuck into the tar, how shockingly flat and *wrong* it was, mushy, twisted, blood seeping out. How he wanted to leave that ruined part of himself behind.

The next morning, Daddy's back again and in bed. Hazzy's barking again. We get up and Mama lets Hazzy out, and the dog runs straight to Hap's grave and starts rolling on it, then digging, then rolling, whimpering, digging some more.

Mama makes me go back and watch Annie and Trudy. She puts Hazzy in the pen, then makes Cream of

Wheat, and sits me down to feed Trudy. She drinks coffee, smokes a cigarette, makes phone calls, looks out the window, then goes outside again.

I feed Trudy, making sure most of it gets in, keeping her fingers out of it. Her little blue eyes look around and at me. I wonder what she sees looking up at us as if from the bottom of the pool, seeing the splashing undersides of things.

Daddy's up. I hear him clumping in the living room, in the hall, then back in their bedroom. I try to finish the Cream of Wheat before he clumps in here in his bathrobe, all cheerful, saying, "Don't you think your Mama would like it if I cook breakfast?" He paces up and down, clapping his hands, getting out the big black skillet, some bacon and eggs.

Mama comes in. "Why are you doing this, Dick?"

"I thought you might like some breakfast, Jane."

"You're a little late for breakfast."

"Well, how about lunch, then?"

"Oh, all right, go ahead, I guess."

Daddy looks at her for a long moment.

"Oh come on, Jane, it's not the end of the world, is it?"

She won't look at him.

"If you want to help me, why don't you come out back and help me dig up Hap. We need to make that hole deeper and rebury him."

"Jane! This is my day off. Isn't that what we have a yardman for?"

The skillet's smoking, bacon burning. "Uh-oh," he says.

"Well, why would you make a big mess in here for me to clean up on the maid's day off? Don't I ever get a day off?" She picks up the baby and walks out.

Smoke is filling the kitchen. Daddy takes the skillet outside all the way to the woods and throws it down, and then he stays out there. I can see him from the kitchen window and through the trees smoking cigarettes and stomping around, and then he disappears into the toolshed.

The week before this, I'd heard them fighting in their room, Mama saying, "But why would he do that?" Daddy slamming doors, pacing like a madman, then rushing through the house to the back door, Hap and Hazard scurrying away, Daddy yelling, "Why? Because he's a bastard, that's why! He's a goddamn bastard!"

Mama'd said he shouldn't talk that way, and then said, "Why would they?"

"Because I'm *the goat*, Jane, I'm the goddamned *goat*!"

"The *goat*? What does that mean, *the goat*?"

"Can't you ever just once try to see it my way?"

"I don't understand why you can't just get along."

"There's one hell of a lot you don't understand, Jane!"

Then he put his cane through the glass door on the back porch, Hap had peed on the door-mat, and Daddy had hit at him with his cane.

Now I go back to my room and listen to the radio. *Who knows what evil lurks in the hearts of men? The Shadow knows.* Lamont Cranston traveled to far-off lands, where he found the power to "cloud men's minds" so he could sneak around watching them, and they couldn't see him.

That sounds good to me. But I'd rather have the power to fly up away from them, just lift off like swimming, push high up out of their way, hover above them and watch. Then I wouldn't need any other powers.

The next morning, George comes and digs up Hap's box, which is already fraying, and sits it next to the hole as he digs deeper. Hazzy watches from the pen, yip-barking, biting the chain-link fence, trying to dig under it. Nathan's here to watch. George keeps stopping to wipe his face with a big red handkerchief. Dirt keeps falling back into the hole.

"I think that's deep as I can go right here, ma'am," he says.

George puts the box in, starts shoveling damp black dirt back in.

I ask Mama why Hazzy won't stop howling, and Mama says, "Because she thinks he's still there, and she has to stay loyal to him no matter what."

"But why?"

"Because she has to, that's all."

LATER, DADDY TAKES ME WITH HIM to a company ball game, where we see Uncle Ted talking to some friends, but he never speaks to us, even though we are right there. Daddy drinks from a flask and gets into a fight in the parking lot, and his driving scares me all the way home.

As we careen into the driveway, Mama comes rushing from the dog pens carrying something. She hurries in the back door, and Daddy and I go in after her.

"The puppies! The puppies are coming!" She's on the phone, begging somebody to please get off the party line.

"Maybe that dog will settle down once she's had those puppies," Daddy says, heading down the hall to their room.

"But it's too early! It's not time yet!" Then she's talking to the vet. I stand there until she looks at me and says, "Go to bed; you'll see them tomorrow. It's late."

I go to bed. Hazzy's not howling. Mama's rushing around in the kitchen, then goes out. I can't hear Daddy. The house is quiet, but the attic fan is turning, turning.

Finally. Early morning. Six puppies, tiny, hairless, pink, wet-rat things, not like the cuddly fat puppies I remember ever seeing. They're in a nest Mama has made of frayed towels and an army blanket, out in the tool-shed. The newborn smell is strong.

"You can't play with newborns," she says, "but they're big enough to live, and they'll grow soon."

Hazzy's trembling, licking the blind pink wormy things all over, until finally some start to nurse. Mama kneels down with a happy, tired look on her face. I like Mama's face with no makeup.

"I was up all night with them," she says.

"Can I get Nathan?"

"Not now."

On the school bus, I tell Nathan the puppies have come. The kids gather. "I want one!" "Can I have one?" Girls ask if they're cuddly and cute.

"Not yet, but they will be when they get bigger," I say, acting like I know all about it.

Later, I run out to look. They're not wet, but they're still blind and pink. And one is not moving, out on the edge. Mama takes it away and calls the vet. Now there are five.

Daddy comes home from work late, yelling in a garbled not-language. He goes to the wood bin. Mama and I stand in the kitchen, looking at each other, hearing him slam back out of the house again, but we don't hear the car. Mama picks up Trudy.

"Bring Annie," she says as she hurries us back to our bedroom. "I want you to stay in here with the babies." Then she goes.

I stand in the doorway, listening. I hear Daddy return to the house, bumping into things, talking like he's being strangled, Mama following him, saying, "Dick! Dick!"

Then it's quiet. I sneak down the hall, get a glimpse of Daddy with a gun in his hand.

"Dick, you just can't do that!"

"He's trying to kill ME, isn't he?"

I hear the car starting up. I hear Mama dialing, talking to Nana. Then I hear her making more calls.

Daddy bursts back into the house. I run and jump into bed, pulling the covers over my head, and Annie climbs under there with me. Trudy's already asleep in her crib. Then we hear nothing for a long time.

I wake to the sound of a car outside. The next thing, strange men are talking in the living room, Daddy shouting. Something falls; something else crashes.

Mama's shouting, "Dick, just go along! Don't make it worse!"

Daddy yells with a cry so terrible, I hold my breath.

More garbled noises, scuffling, bumping, loud bangs, crashing, a door slamming, then a car with a siren driving away.

I run down the hall into the living room. All the lights are on. Things are broken, chairs fallen, the bonsai tree with the little fishing Chinaman, broken, dirt across the floor.

Daddy's gone.

Mama stands in the middle of the room, her white body tense, her white face not crying. She's not going to tell me.

"What are you doing in here?" she shouts, "What did I tell you? Get back to your room right now!"

I'm not included. I'm not even liked. I lie in bed, looking at the dark.

But I am included with the puppies. The day after they take Daddy away, another puppy dies. Mama and I bury it next to Hap's grave.

The vet comes out to our house, looks at Hazzy, gives her a shot. He says something is wrong with the dog, with her milk or something. She has a fever. She can't nurse the babies. We have to take the puppies away and put poor Hazzy back out into the pen by herself, and she starts up again with an even more righteous howl.

Mama comes in my room in the dark early mornings with a flashlight, saying, "Come help me," and we go out to the toolshed to feed the puppies with eyedroppers and dime-store doll bottles, with hot-water bottles, with a ticking clock in a blanket.

She shows me how to hold a puppy and gently urge

his tiny lips to crack open and start pulling in the milk. She talks to the hairless pink thing and to me constantly, urging each puppy in turn to take something. Sometimes it works, but not for long. We can't tell if they're getting enough, and outside we hear Hazzy whimpering and howling.

Another puppy dies. Three left. We change the formula. We feed more often.

I follow Mama, do what she does, carry things, stand by, ready to help. Mama is unflagging, never late, never failing, a dutiful soldier in her schedule of feeding, winding the clock, refilling the rubber bottles with hot water, no matter what time of day or night. But even with all the things Mama does, every day they get weaker. You can tell when one is about to die because it will just give up, like it's too hard to eat or keep breathing. Another one dies, then another, until there's only one pup left.

It was always the strongest one, and Mama thinks we can keep it alive. We've never checked if it's male or female, but Mama gives it a name and calls to it, putting the tiny drops on its tiny pink lips, tries to gently pry the dropper into its mouth. Once in a while, some milk slips into its mouth. Once in a while, it moves its lips as if to start sucking, but it won't keep this up for long. It will not act like it wants to take the milk.

Mama spends the entire day stroking it, talking to it, begging. I sit in the corner in the shed, watching her try to put her own desire inside of that barely alive little thing, but finally its tiny mouth clamps shut. Finally it breathes once, twice, and then not at all.

Hazzy out there in the pen is howling, and Mama's face seems to fall apart. She yells at me to go back to the house, and she starts rushing around, cleaning up the toolshed, talking to herself, slamming things.

I go next door to tell Nathan. We sit in his yard for a long time, not talking. I watch ants and other bugs scooting around this way and that, tiny things, but alive. Why could that puppy not stay alive?

THE HOUSE IS QUIET NOW. Mama goes to her sewing room and cries and smokes and listens to *Sam Spade*. We take naps. Hazzy lies in the shade and won't eat.

Baby Trudy starts walking. May-May spoils her, sneaks her cookies after Mama says "No."

One night, I take the dog food out to Hazzy, but she doesn't come out. I find her in the doghouse licking on some tiny babies, and I smell the newborn smell. I run in and tell Mama, "Hazzy's *had puppies again!*" Mama comes running out with the flashlight, barely looks at them, says "Those are not puppies," then runs back into the house and calls the vet. The vet comes out the next day and says the babies are rabbits. Hazzy's found them, brought them one by one, five or six, hiding them in the doghouse, licking and trying to make them nurse, until now they're all dead. So Mama has to take them away from her and bury them. Then Hazzy howls again.

In a few days, the very same thing happens again. The dog finds some baby rabbits, brings them home, and tries to get them to nurse, until they all die.

I HATE IT WHEN MAMA TALKS ABOUT GOD. Usually, it's when she puts me to bed, after we say my prayers and we God-bless everybody. She has never talked about God when Daddy's been around. It seems that Daddy is not included in something between Mama and God, but it seems that she wants me to be included.

Since Daddy's been gone, every night when I'm in bed, she comes with the Bible in her hand. I try to find things out.

"But where is Daddy?"

"Daddy's in the hospital. Daddy's sick."

"Is he going to die?"

"No, no, he's not going to die. He just needs to be there for a while, and then we hope he'll be okay."

"Is it his feet?"

"No, it's not his feet."

I want to ask more things, but how can you ask all the things you want in a house so filled with disappointment? How can you believe any answers in such a house?

I want to ask "Why did they take him away like that?" But we're skipping over that and just going on to the next thing. Could anybody be taken away like that for being bad? I want to ask what she means by "sick," but I know she'll never tell me.

She starts reading the Bible. She tries not to cry, but it just comes over her, especially when she starts saying how this life and this world is so terrible and so bad, but how we're supposed to suffer, and sacrifice, just like Jesus had to suffer, so that everything can be better in the next life, when we go to beautiful Heaven with Jesus and with God.

She reaches over to touch me, but then something holds her back. Maybe she sees me pull away. I don't know why I pull away from her. I can see that her feelings are hurt.

I hate Mama's saying that this world is so terrible, as if God hates us. In Sunday school, they said that "God so loved the world."

I hate how Mama says we wish for the end of the world, how we look forward to earthquakes swallowing us up, thunder, lightning, people coming out of graves, people killing one another, killing themselves. Judgment Day! God and Jesus coming down to Earth to separate the sheep from the goats, raising up the sheep to be happy in Heaven, and the goats going down with the Devil to burn forever in black flaming Hell!

"But what is so bad about the goats?"

"Someday you'll understand."

"But why can't I understand now?" I don't see why the sheep can't just be with the goats. I don't see why the goats have to be the bad ones all the time.

Mama talks faster and louder when she says we hope for the end of the world to come soon. And as Mama gets to this part, about the whole world coming to an end, and everybody bad being punished, tortured, and burned in Hell forever, especially the goats, she stops crying.

That's the part I especially hate.

The Light Falling Across It Just So

Sometimes when Mama's busy having bridge club at our house, like now, when it's almost summer, because of our being the ones with air conditioning now, and Daddy won't be dropping in, since he is still gone to who knows where and for such a long time, then I go back into their dressing room closets to see if Daddy's things are still there. Sometimes I spend the whole afternoon just looking at my mama's and my daddy's things and smelling the powder and the cigarettes and the Shocking by Schiaparelli. Soundlessly, I open and close closets and drawers and look and look and then put everything back exactly so no one can ever tell I've been in there.

I hang around to watch when the bridge club ladies' day arrives, each one saying, "It's so hot!" as she walks in the door and greets my mama with a pretend kiss. First there's a dining-room sit-down lunch with tuna fish and iced tea. And then, after a silent smoking of cigarettes, and after they carry their chairs in to the already-set-up living room card table, and they talk babies and new houses and how it's somebody's own fault if she's losing her husband, then they sit down and discuss maybe playing for just a little bit of money this time. They cross their high heels up under their chairs, the nylons wrinkling in clear skin-colored folds around their ankles, all except for Aunt Dorothy, who wears loafers and glasses and keeps score, and whose husband, they say, was changed forever by the war. And then they get down to business.

Sometimes, I stay to see Aunt Celeste pick up the cards first, her red flashing fingernails shuffling and reshuffling them, her fingers dancers, the cards acrobats who've flown through the air a thousand times. They say she is real smart from some girls' school up east, but I think she doesn't like kids much, and that includes me. She always says to me, "What pretty pink cheeks," and then she sort of glares before she smartly slaps down one card after another, around and around, four little stacks of cards, her lips moving sideways around her cigarette, the smoke drifting white chiffon across her face.

The cards dealt, the ladies pick them up, raise their four little fans in front of their faces, and Aunt Polly says she isn't good enough to play this hand, and she lays it down and then picks a gardenia out of an arrangement nearby and sticks it in her hair. Then Aunt Celeste asks Mama if she's got any bourbon in the house, and says, "That's okay, I'll get it myself." And she gets up while the others are rearranging their hands.

Once, Aunt Polly made me paper dolls out of newspaper folded again and again while she was playing "dummy" in the game, and she whispered to me that "dummy" was her favorite part to play. The paper dolls were strung out, holding newsprint hands, except on the ends, where some were missing arms or legs—a long line of unbroken, attached-together dolls, hair and dresses alike, and she drew little faces on them, smiling all their lips in Crayola.

In my room, I thumbtacked them up, circle-eyed grinning faces the same, newsprint headlines running across their bodies and their just-alike dresses and their sometimes missing arms and legs, and I thought about when my daddy came and sang me a bedtime song about a man who wanted a paper doll that he could call his own.

The paper dolls I really like to play with are the dime-store cardboard ones my mama bought me, their tall glossy books filled with paper-doll dresses and suits and purses and jewels and things you cut out very carefully, and then you very carefully fold these little paper tabs over the shoulders and around the thin little waists and the tiny little wrists and ankles of the paper dolls. I can't decide whether I like my Myrna Loy paper doll best or my Betty Hutton one, so I play with them both together, as if they're friends. The thing about paper dolls is, that you can't walk them around or have them doing things all that much, because the clothes and hats and shoes that are attached by just these little folded tabs will all fall away and the paper dolls will be running around in their underpants, like in those dreams where you hope no one will notice, so you have to place the little dresses and jackets and hats and purses and gloves and shoes on them, very carefully folding the tabs perfectly into place, and then when they look just like dream-girl Miss Americas, you prop them up against something, because they can't stand on their own. Then you have to just look at them and look at them and concentrate on how pretty they are and on how lovely and perfect they are, and then you make up the game in your head and pretend that something is really happening. There are some girls who will play this with you in just the same way almost—it seems like—forever.

Boys usually won't play this with you for a very long time, but once, Nathan and I played with the paper dolls for almost a whole afternoon, on the day when I decided to make pink mink capes and hats to match for both Myrna Loy and Betty Hutton, and also for another paper doll I had then that was a Loretta Young.

It was well into the game on a hot summer bridge club day, with Aunt Celeste playing the hand in the living room and Nathan and I with the paper dolls all laid out under the dining room table, and Nathan saying he wanted to quit because this wasn't real, until I thought of making the paper dolls mink capes and hats to match by cutting up cotton pads and coloring them with watercolors. He said okay, but only if we could go back there in the dressing room closet and look at the real ones first, so we carried all the stuff with us down the hallway past the bridge club ladies, as though we were going back to my room to play.

They weren't noticing us anyway, and when we got back into the dressing room, we could hear the laughing and talking between hands about who got what and how they'd played it. We could even smell their cigarette smoke when we got back into the closet and were opening my daddy's drawers and looking through his key chains and cuff links and playing cards with naked women on them. He had a lot of stuff like that, and Nathan wanted to take some of it, but I stopped him by starting on my mama's drawers with the stockings and slips and the powder puffs and little red Maybelline boxes with the little gummy brushes in them. We were whispering the whole time, surrounded by the smells, dusty, perfumy, and dark, like the inside of the closet before I pulled the cord for light and drew aside the dresses to show the glowing plastic-covered pink mink cape and its hat to match that we were going to copy for the paper dolls still in our hands. Then, even though I was afraid somebody might come, I untied the cord, which I had never done before, on top of the plastic bag and pulled it slowly down, the pink mink emerging, glowing pale at the top, with softly swaying, alive-like hairs moving in the light, and we stood silent just looking at it, and I could hear Nathan breathing right next to my ear, so I pulled down the plastic a little more. And then right in the middle of this, Nathan grabbed up that Loretta Young paper doll, saying he was going to torture her to death, and then he ran through the house, with me chasing him and the bridge-club ladies exclaiming and Mama getting up to stop us, and he ran out into the yard, paper-doll clothes flying out behind him on all sides and me running and shouting behind, and he threw her into the street right under a car, so she got that hot, sticky black tar all over her front side. Then he said, "Oh, she needs a bath," and he threw her into the sprinkler, and then after that she had a wrecked-up face. And I was so mad, because he did seem to like her at first.

So then while Nathan was climbing over the white-painted three-plank fence and running away, yelling something over his shoulder, and my mama and Aunt Polly were tumbling out and down the back porch steps to see what was happening out there, I was trying to wipe the watery grass clippings off my Loretta Young paper doll's warping sad face. She would never look the same again. I started to cry, and then I yelled, "Nathan, I'm gonna get you!" and my mama said from out in the yard, "Well, we can always buy another one." That was after she'd yelled at Nathan that next time he could play over here right or not at all. She was always telling him that, but even though I could see that he did try, it never lasted for very long.

Aunt Polly came running all the way out to me in the yard and took that Loretta Young in her hand, smoothing and blotting and examining it, saying she'd bet it could be fixed up just fine. I, of course, said that I didn't want another one, but that I wanted that one. And no matter how nice and sweet Aunt Polly was, I knew I didn't want this one to have some new painted-on face, either.

Aunt Dorothy watched us coming back from the window, and then inside, the ladies went on back to the bridge table, where from the kitchen I could hear Aunt Celeste saying, "Are we playing bridge, or what?" On the kitchen floor I could see the Loretta Young had no chance now of ever being any dream-girl Miss America. Her whole face looked blotched and distorted, the eyes puffed and faded, the mouth crooked, her paper-doll body blighted with stains. She looked as though she'd been forsaken in some backyard for years, neglected, unloved. I stretched out on the linoleum floor beside her. Then Aunt Polly, who was dummy in the game again, came in and looked at both me and that Loretta Young. And then she said that we should have a nice funeral for Loretta Young and bury her out in the yard like they had done their cat that summer when it died of worms. Except, of course, it would be different, she said.

So then, even though I knew I wouldn't really be able to get my daddy to dig a hole for putting it in the ground, I let my Aunt Polly go on and find a shoe box while I laid out all the Loretta Young clothes that wouldn't work anyway for the Myrna Loy or the Betty Hutton—the skirts and sweaters and scarves and gloves and shoes and hats, all on the bed in little arrangements as they would have been worn in the Loretta Young dream-girl Miss America life, as it would have been if all this had never happened. Aunt Polly wanted to repaint the face for the funeral, like with the smiling Crayola lips, but I said no. Then even though I knew I was going to hide that boxed Loretta Young in my room in the bottom of my closet all covered up with shoes, so I could keep going in there and looking at her for years to come, I folded the tissue paper with Aunt Polly and then laid it and all the clothes into the box one by one alongside of the Loretta Young after we had put her in her favorite outfit. Then I laid in the cotton pads for the pink mink coat and hat to match, and Aunt Polly and I looked in the box at what we had done, and Aunt Polly said, "We are gathered together to say good-bye to a dear friend." And she carefully placed two pieces of honeysuckle on either side of the Loretta Young. Then she looked at me. I said, "She was the most beautiful and the nicest of them all." Then I arranged four pearl buttons I had stolen from Granny's dresser drawer in the four corners of the shoe box.

Then Aunt Polly said, "But bad things happened to this Loretta Young that weren't her own fault." Then she tossed up some M&Ms from the bridge club game so that they fell and bounced in the box like little confetti. Then I brought out my mama's bottle of Shocking by Schiaparelli, and we put sprinkles of it all over ourselves and each other and that Loretta Young. Then I said "Amen." Then we closed up the box without speaking or looking at each other, and Aunt Polly went back into the living room and back to the game while I carried that boxed Loretta Young back into my room. But before I hid it deep in the back of my closet, where no one would find it, I took a last look at the poor wrecked face with the light falling across it just so, and I very carefully drew new red-pencil smiling lips turning just a little bit up at the end. And then I dropped in, crushing them, some soft sweet white petals, just the same way Aunt Polly told me she once had driven a man crazy by eating her gardenia corsage petal by petal by petal by petal. . . . Amen.

Summer

When summer comes it is Nathan and me all the time, all the time, back and forth between our houses. We play together side by side sometimes all day every day until dark, not just in the yards but in the woods and in the creek beds and in the fields and in the huge silvered ghosts of abandoned chicken houses that stand in tall grass and broken glass behind another neighbor's "woods," and seem to glow from within, where we hide and giggle when they call, as the late-day sun beams through slow-swirling, drifting galaxies of dust motes forever resifting the echoes of every egg cracking and every pecking-order feud ever sounded in that space.

Here's Nathan and me playing in Mr. Moore's peach orchard in spite of having been told and really believing that Mr. Moore will come out with his hunting rifle and fire on little kids like us if he catches us stealing his peaches or even climbing through the fence. We never actually see Mr. Moore, but we believe we've seen him. I can picture the old man's face, angry eyes, overalls, a rifle in one hand, though I never actually lay eyes on Mr. Moore.

But the fear is in us as our legs go over the slats and as

we run, ducking down, making our wobbly beeline for the corner near the far edge, where we figure Mr. Moore can't see us stretched out under low branches on the cool dirt, and the fear is in us as we draw our dirty pictures in the dirt, as the fear is in us as we pick and dust and bite into the furry fresh peaches, and as the juice runs down our chins and elbows and makes Mr. Moore's dirt stick to our arms and legs, we are full of fear.

But even the fear of grown-ups and their million rules can't stop us from wanting to do the kinds of things that the punishments of grown-ups, who have their own problems, can not touch. Something in us has a life of its own day in and day out, and trying not to think about it is thinking about it, if you know what I mean.

Mama is always putting me to bed. In summer, I have to lie down for a two-hour nap when I am not the least bit sleepy and really much too old for such things. I lie on the glider on the screened-in porch, listening to blue jays bickering and to the voices of the afternoon radio shows coming in over the hum of the fan placed so as to blow across the length of my body as I lie there. I watch the red mud daubers building their odd little mud-dauber nests under the eaves, I make up stories about the Girl, who has a lot more nerve for adventures than I do. Sometimes Nathan comes and sits in the bushes, trying to talk me into sneaking down to the creek, saying they will never know, but I am too afraid of getting caught, so he goes off to have fun somewhere else.

Then I rock the glider screeching and banging back and forth and back and forth at an increasingly furious rate until May-May hollers at me to stop. So then there's nothing to do but you know what. Sometimes it seems like that is the only thing I have to keep me company.

No rain all July. Too many grasshoppers, scorpions, tarantulas, grass turning brown, and by the end of the month there is talk of water rationing and drought. Mama and May-May talked about polio, about ringworm, about rabies. On the radio, there's talk about a rabid dog somebody shot out near Josey Lane.

Nathan's mom sits us down and tells us to not catch wild animals, to report dogs who are strange-acting, Frothing at the mouth, biting at things. We listen in awe, then run to Bob Lynn's house, and he tells us that if you do get bitten, there are shots where a long needle is punched right into your stomach every single day! We run to the Breards' house to check this out, and they know all about it, as well.

"Mad dog! Mad dog!" We ran around yelling "Mad dog!" all month.

I also have to go to bed early at night, even in summer, when it is still light outside, and I hear other kids running around catching lightning bugs or playing out until they can't see the ball anymore. I argue, but still have to be there lying in bed half-nude in the heat, with nothing to do but listen to the sounds of the neighborhood and the house, where later during the long, hot nights each person rises, silent, feverish, to stand in the shower and then stand under the attic fan, wet sleepwalkers, each in turn stumbling back to bed.

Nathan comes and sits on a wide ledge outside my

window, his wiry body a hunched shadow against the blue light gradually turning dark. As the light goes down, the crickets come up, and we listen as each kid is called in. We whisper just above the crickets and fans and dogs barking, and in spite of the heat, I start shivering like something is about to happen. All I want in the world is for the two of us to run away to live in the woods, be night creatures with nobody's rules, wear paint and feathers and rove the countryside until dawn, when we'd withdraw to our secret burrow hideouts to sleep.

The fear is in us as one night we try to open the window so Nathan can hide under the sheets with me, all tickly and strange, but we can't get the screen off without making too much noise.

Mama comes in, and she is mad!

"What do you think you're doing?"

Nathan scrambles down and runs home.

The next night, I am lying in bed the same, and he appears at my window ledge again.

"Nathan!"

"I just came to say I can't do this anymore."

"But why not?"

"Momsi found out, and she says I can't."

"But just come when they don't know it."

"I can't. I have to be good."

"But why?"

"Because I'm being adopted."

Summer Legs

In a room that is not your room, in a house that is not your house, you lie at the edge of thought, at the edge of sleep.

Your tongue can't leave it alone, that place where a tooth came out, finally, after days of wobbling and hanging by a thread. Now your prowling tongue keeps going back to that itchy, pain-pleasant, dull, bloody sore spot in your mouth.

Moonlight falls through blowing curtains and through the room, across the sheets, your summer-child legs, your feet still dirty from the day. A fan rotates. Buzzing things buzz.

You lie half-dreaming of the long-fingered elf sandman dusting sand between your toes in the night. And you know that winged tooth fairy'll come in the window for your tooth, will slip the silver Mercury angel-head dime between pillow and sheet. You smile imagining it, believing it, drifting off with it.

Without a sound, a person comes and stands in the room, a boy shadow, who seems different in the dark from when you've seen him sitting around this house beautiful and bored, and no matter how much you may follow him and copy him, and taunt and tease him, he is always refusing to play with you or to even crack a smile.

But now here he is in the dark.

You can't see his face, but it can only be he who leans over you, across you, alongside you, where you lie suddenly alert to smooth warm boy arms and legs, boy cheek to yours.

So he does like you after all. And it's nice.

He speaks in a whisper, saying, "Lie still" and "Turn this way" or "Turn that way," and something warm and rubbery is rolling and rubbing in a friendly way down there against you. Nothing breaks into you, nothing bad happens, and the whole thing is nice as puppy bodies, an unexpected warmth of being together in a breezy summer night half dream.

The window. The moon. The curtains. The dark. The smooth arms and legs. Some time passing. There may have been sleeping. This is secret. You know this is perfectly secret. But now you seem to live with an awakened longing that looks for more of this, agitated, shy, but on the alert for what is no longer remembered as much more than a dream of heat.

The Heart of Texas

There's a map of Texas with a big red heart in the middle on a billboard as we drive into town. The billboard says BRADY, THE HEART OF TEXAS.

"Will Daddy be there when I get back home?" I shout over the hot wind roaring through the car.

"Maybe," Mama says, looking at the road, throwing her cigarette out the window, slowing, braking, turning, bumping over the rattling cattle guard at the gate, the dirt road leading left across blowing fields to the white-painted wood-frame farmhouse, the giant oak tree.

Aunt Lee comes out wiping hands on her apron to greet us.

"So you've come to see the country mouse," she says.

There's nothing mousy about Aunt Lee. Electric and comfy at once, she's got Indian-wide cheekbones, dark hair in a loose bun, and excited dark eyes that grab and hold you, eyes that love the world and love you. And love us. We all hug. She stands back, looks at me.

"Oh my goodness, you're growing too fast! We need to put a brick on your head!"

"I thought you'd fixed that cattle guard last year,"

says Mama. "I'll bet you hear that loose pipe banging for miles around."

Aunt Lee winks at me. "It warns me somebody's coming," she says, laughing, leading us into the kitchen. I smell pie.

Uncle Edward comes out from town for lunch and to see Mama before she leaves. He walks in the back door, joking, and Aunt Lee acts excited he's here, reaching way up to kiss him, joking about the pair of them being "Mutt and Jeff." He's tall and thin, with white hair and blue eyes in a face that looks like Founding Fathers hung on the walls in school.

Lunch is the main meal on the farm, and they call lunch "dinner." We sit down to pork chops, corn on the cob, turnip greens, warm rolls and butter, and the pie turns out to be peach cobbler, my favorite! Before we can eat, Uncle Edward says a long "grace" so fast that the only word I can catch is *sanctify;* then he winks at me, and we pass our plates around the table.

Nothing's wrong at their house. Everything's just fine. Mama's smiling. They're nice all the time at Aunt Lee's, talking, joking, making things fun. For some reason, I feel like laughing out loud.

After lunch, while they're having coffee, I fold my napkin and excuse myself, the way I've been taught, and I go outside to look around. They say I'm staying here for a month.

I find a horned toad in the side yard. I know horned toads. He plays dead and lets me scratch his flat belly. I let him go, and he skitters around the big tree. There're other oak trees around the house, but this one's the old-est, a giant of a tree. I can't put my arms even halfway around it, and the first crotch is too high up for me to climb. The ground's crunchy with acorns old and new all around underfoot, the branches full of nests. You can watch squirrels, scissortails, and mockingbirds busying in and out all day.

They call me in to say good-bye to Mama, "Be good, be nice, and do what Aunt Lee says," she tells me. Watching Mama's dusty Cadillac drive out the dirt road, across the cattle guard, onto the main road, and then speed away, I wonder what will happen at home while I'm away.

Have I been sent away? Why am I here right now? I don't want to miss seeing Daddy come home.

I walk around the big tree, remembering how last year the newly hatched mockingbird babies were falling all summer out of nests and onto the ground, peeping for res-cue. I tried so hard with shoe boxes and eyedroppers, and cried and prayed to Jesus, trying to get the prayers right, but I could never save them before their trembly pink heads would droop and die. Aunt Lee was right when she said you couldn't save them. And Jeff, the youngest son, still at home, Mama's cousin, was right when he said the cats would get them. He said the weak ones get pushed out of the nest by the stronger ones. I see a gray-striped cat now, waiting, crouched, across the yard.

Out in Brady, they kill and eat everything all the time anyway—pigs, calves, deer, rabbits, and especially chick-ens—and almost every day, things are born and things die, so they don't think that much about baby birds getting eaten by cats. Cats have to eat, too.

I go over the fence to the barnyard and walk farther out back. There are changes. The Mexican workers whose kids I used to play with are gone, as are the shacks and outhouses they used out there. The pigs are gone, too. Last year, there was a huge sow that was so fat, she could only lie in the mud, eat, and let her piglets nurse. The pink piglets were so cute, I wanted to take one home. Uncle Edward talked in a big voice, telling me to stay away from the pigpen because pigs were dangerous, and then he and Jeff told a story about a man they knew who fell into a pen and the pigs killed him and ate him! Then they both shook their heads. Then Uncle Edward said they were going to have them all butchered or sold and be finished with pigs.

Wild cats are all over the farm, mainly coming around the barn early for the cow milking. Jeff says they really do have nine lives, so my Kitty could die and come back as a girl cat to have babies, if he wanted to.

At home, they're not happy if I bring back animals. I remember the way they cooked my black lamb for dinner one night, Daddy laughing as if it were the funniest joke, his smirking face as he said, "What do you think we're having for dinner tonight?" and me looking away, not wanting to admit he was joking about what they had done to my poor pet, tied to the clothesline in the backyard for weeks, *Baaa, baaaaaa, baaaaaaaaaaa,* all day and all night, neighbors calling, complaining, after I'd brought him back from the farm, summer before last, after they'd decided out here to be finished with sheep.

The men had come up all sweaty from the fields on a late afternoon in June, straw and dirt and bits of wool sticking to glistening tanned arms cradling the sweet-legged baby lambs, tumbling the wobbly lambs onto the grass where I was sitting with Aunt Lee, snapping beans into her lap in the shade of the oak tree full of mocking-birds and quarrelsome blue jays that year.

The lambs had wobbled across the grass, bleating for their mothers, and Aunt Lee had smiled that smile she could pour on you like honey, her hands never stopping with the beans in her lap, *snap, snap, snap, snap, snap,* and she'd nodded toward me, saying, "Give the black one to the girl."

The black one, the black lamb, the black sheep—that's what I heard someone in Mama's bridge club say about Daddy one time. So is that kind of like being the goat?

So I'm here again now. The first night, I'm awake, with whining mosquitoes getting into the tented sheet with me until I'm finally too sleepy to care.

Things are happening at the farm every day. Every morning, I wake in the attic dark, hearing Aunt Lee call-ing Jeff to get up and milk that cow. I hear him getting up, getting dressed on the other side of the attic, going down the stairs. I hear the rooster crowing, birds chirp-ing, and I fall asleep again.

I wake up smelling bacon, and it's light out. I'm up here, where the whole bed fits into this oversized attic dormer window that looks out onto the big tree. On the inside there's a curtain across, so you can dress and undress and hide inside your own bed-size tree house room. It's my favorite place. I look down onto the tree full of nests and the yard where Aunt Lee's hanging towels on the line, as if she's been up for hours. She speaks without looking up at me.

"Don't you want to get up now? Breakfast is ready. Come down."

They milk the cow, feed the chickens, and gather the eggs first thing in the morning, and I do this with them some days. Sometimes Jeff wrings the neck of a young one to fry, or an old one past laying to roast, and I watch Aunt Lee clean it over the sink. She shows me the parts that make the eggs and tells me all about them. Aunt Lee loves to talk, and I love to listen. They have many more chickens than we had, most of them white and exactly the same, with one big bossy rooster, and three or four other type of chickens, small and speckled. And there are many chicks, yellow puffs darting and tumbling and pecking.

On the second day, I see the bull, brownish black and mean-looking, but penned up in a field. I think he must be watching and waiting to come after me the way a bull went after that boy in a movie I saw. It was a sad movie, but it had Uncle Remus, which I liked. But there was that bull, so I don't wear red out there.

On some days, Aunt Lee makes biscuits, and she gives me some dough to make tiny biscuits of my own. I set them out on a stone bench in the hot sun; then I wander through Aunt Lee's garden full of fancy lilies, snapdragons, sweet peas, "glads," "pinks," "flags" (She talks about her flowers a lot.), lavender, "Peace" roses with thick thorns, petals everywhere on the ground, towering hollyhocks and sunflowers at the back, also with tomatoes, onions, carrots, okra, beans, cucumber and squash vines, honeybees and bumblebees buzzing, hummingbirds hovering, butterflies fluttering, spiders, grasshoppers, lizards zipping away, once in a while a rabbit or a wild kitten or a field mouse to chase. I spend hours in Aunt Lee's garden, where the Girl can be a princess in a flowing dress, or a silvery fairy with dragonfly wings.

Flies are buzzing all over the scrawny wild kittens I already chased all morning, and they're all lying limp under the porch, where it's not so hot. Even then they're not so easy to catch as I thought they'd be after seeing them crazy-wild in the barn when I first got here at the farm, and I spotted that one yellow one I've gotten to where he'll almost come to me. When he does come to me, I'm going to do what the hired man said and cover him all over with bacon grease, which he will hate, and will run from in circles all over the farm, and the other wild kittens will wonder what is wrong with him, since they won't have to have grease on them, but the thing is, the grease will smother his fleas, then he'll lick it all off, and then he can come sleep on the bed in my room and have a name and be mine. And those other kittens will grow to rove the countryside, skinny-wild and youthless, diseased and hit by trucks, belonging to no one. Even when we see them, they will not be seen, like rats and squirrels, for any one of them seems like all the others, giving birth and dying young and never having names.

When I go near, they all run back up under the house, even that yellow one I have chosen to be the one that's going to be mine, and they look out at me with their little eyes. The one that's going to be mine has one blue eye and one green, both eyes looking out like they've never seen anything like me before.

A big dog runs into the yard one day acting crazy, with a neighbor boy chasing him. Uncle Edward and Jeff help him catch that dog and they all talk about how it's full of quills and it just can't seem to leave those porcupines alone, and they all laugh about dogs that mess with skunks, dogs that try to eat armadillos or terrapins or try to catch roadrunners or jackrabbits, and they try to get some quills out, but the dog gets away, the neighbor boy goes home, and everybody laughs about it during dinner, and we have fresh peach ice cream we made that afternoon, taking turns cranking the hand crank until your whole arm hurt.

After a big lunch-dinner of fried chicken and boiled potatoes, Aunt Lee throws a cloth over the whole table. Then later, she mashes the potatoes, makes a salad, takes off the cloth, and we eat the cold chicken left from lunch. Then they take the rest out to the pigs. Some days they have soup or corn flakes for dinner, and they call that "supper."

One day after about two weeks, I'm digging through a deep drawer where Aunt Lee said there were toys, and I find a small glazed skunk, shiny and perfect, black, with a white stripe. Aunt Lee said it was made by my mama, and that Mama'd wanted a pet skunk when she was a kid like me, which doesn't seem to fit with the Mama I know.

When Aunt Lee's not cooking or cleaning or working in the garden, she's crocheting something to be added to the many doilies on chairs and tabletops, about a million doilies sewed together into a spread on her bed. Also around the house are candy dishes like hens sitting on nests. You take the hen top off, and you might find peppermints in the nest.

There are also things around that were made by "the boys," who are all grown and gone now except for Jeff, whom Aunt Lee calls "Emasie," They tell the story of how Jeff came home after his first day of school saying "Why did you name me Emasie?" and declaring that from now on his name was Jeff. It's actually spelled Emisa. They all have funny names. One named Gaddis is a painter in Mexico and has long red hair; another, named Conrad, stayed in the Philippines after the war to live. Another one, named Campbell, has gone to New York.

I follow Jeff around the farm sometimes, and he's pretty nice to me and tells me stories. He's almost a grown-up now.

One time when I was here, they were bringing big machines up to the barn, and Uncle Edward called me to come climb up high in the loft to watch when the grain from the fields was poured in.

A whole day's heat was stored up where I sat. Golden light slanted onto the pouring, hissing mounds forming into hills of golden grain below me, filling the barn, the men shifting it, shoveling it, walking and sinking in it barefoot, bare-legged, with rolled-up pants, and bare-armed, bare-chested, shafts of sunlight shooting through swirls of gold dust rising, gleaming on grain, studding sweaty golden shoulders and arms. I had never seen men like this, working hard, breathing hard, muscles flexing, handkerchiefs on faces. They were the Men.

The heat and dust were overpowering, everything golden. I got dizzy watching, sneezing, dazzled by beauty. Uncle Edward kept saying to them, "Gently, gently," and later they said explosions in grain had been known to happen.

I want to look more at the Men and at Jeff in that barn full of grain and golden light. I hear him taking a shower with the door closed late in the day. I sit outside the bathroom door and listen, just wanting to look at him some more, not thinking of anything but just getting closer and looking. I hear the water turn off in there. I knock on the door and then open it, saying, "Jeff?"

"Get out of here!" he shouts in a mad voice. *Why is he SO mad?* Then he comes out, wrapped in a towel, hair wet, and stomps past me, and refusing to look at me. *What is so bad?*

OLD MEN SIT AROUND SMOKING AND TALKING on white-washed boardwalks in front of stores downtown in Brady. Aunt Lee speaks to them, then in the car she says she hopes she never gets that old. But I hope Aunt Lee lives forever, she is so nice to me.

They are all nice. They're the nicest people I've ever

seen, nicer even than the Breards, nicer than the Sunday school ladies, nicer than I could ever pretend to be for such a long time. They seem to be nice all the way down to their bones! They never show even a small crack of not being nice, day after day after day, until I'm looking for that crack. I'm searching for that crack, getting ready for it, wishing for it.

Aunt Lee takes me to church every Sunday, never to Sunday school, but to church, where she knows everyone and everyone knows her. I sit next to her, and we sing songs, which I like the most, especially the one that goes like this:

> *I come to the garden alone*
> *while the dew is still on the roses,*
> *and the voice I hear falling on my ear,*
> *the Son of God discloses.*

Aunt Lee sings in such a loud, deep voice that I scrunch down in my seat, afraid everyone is looking at us. I bury my face in the hymnal and try to sing as deeply as Aunt Lee sings, but I can't do it, and my high child voice seems puny next to hers.

> *And he walks with me, and he talks with me,*
> *and he tells me I am his own;*
> *and the joy we share as we tarry there,*
> *none other has ever known.*

Finally we close our hymnals, sit down in the pews, and the preacher starts to talk. Usually it's boring, but today we're right in the front row, and the preacher seems to be upset, waiting until everyone's looking at him.

He starts out talking about how Adam was tempted by the snake, who was really the Devil, of course. Then he talks about Cain and Abel. Then I guess I wasn't listening for a minute, because all of a sudden he's talking about Jesus in the desert being tempted by the Devil, and how the Devil is just waiting to tempt each and every one of us every day. Now he's talking louder and louder, until he's yelling in a mean voice that we are all sinners and that sinners are going to burn in Hell!

Now I can't take my eyes off him, because he starts looking at me. He says even a man who is rude to his wife just because he's had a bad day is in the claws of the Devil. He says that even children stealing cookies are full of the Devil. He says that there is not a one of us here who has not or who will not have a chance to shake hands with the Devil. He looks right at me and says, "And what will you do, when your turn comes?"

Why is he looking at me like that? He keeps on. I can't stop looking back, and he keeps on as if he's trying to make me cry! I try not to cry! *Does he know something about me? Did Aunt Lee tell him something about me, about us?* I'm afraid he might know how I am bad inside, mean to my sisters, and how sometimes I steal things.

Later, when we take naps, I lie on the dormer-window bed, looking down onto the big tree, looking into nests, listening to the buzzing, the dove calling, a dog barking, a cicada, the noises of the farm, and I think about home.

Daddy seems to be bad. He won't go to church with

Mama. He scares us and makes Mama cry. He won't act nice. He ruins everything. His own mother doesn't like him. He even said he's one of the goats. *Does this mean Daddy is going to Hell?* I wonder.

Maybe Daddy will die in the hospital and never come home. Maybe he's already died and they won't tell me, will never tell me, and I'll be wondering about all this for the rest of my life. I fall asleep. I have dreams.

You know that you do sleep because of the dreams you have—pushing off and flying high like swimming and then not being able to get back down to the tiny faraway people pointing and waving their arms. Then you're being chased by raging many-footed, long-toothed things that you cannot quite see or remember, through fields of tall somethings that are thick like water, tripping up your legs, your legs not working right. Your legs are stuck on backward. Something is wrong. Everything is wrong. A voice is yelling from far away and over to one side. Another voice is whispering next to your ear from behind. Small rocks are flying through the air. Smaller rocks like gravel pass right through your body. When you notice this, you stop to look around. The monster is gone, but the fields are inside out. The trees are upside down and waving like seaweed. The light is dark. You're falling away from the world. You're falling away from yourself. Something is tumbling away, lost.

I wake with a jolt, half-dreaming, half-screaming, shadows slipping along the floor like smoke, sliding under my bed. Something else floats on the ceiling in the corner with red Devil eyes, knowing that I'm bad, that I'm going to be punished, waiting to snatch my brain if I let myself lock eyes with it, if it sees fear.

I wake up. The attic is dark. Looking out the window, I see stars, and I make a wish, but there's no moon. I want to go home.

But when we come to the last week and I realize I'll go home soon, I decide I'd like to stay with Aunt Lee and live here. I tell them I could come back when I'm grown and build a little house out near the reservoir. Soon I'm begging them to let me come out and live here with them instead of at home with Mama and Daddy, and they seem to think this is a big joke. But this is not a joke.

One day, I talk back to Aunt Lee in a not-nice voice. She looks at me surprised, and she says, "Who are you? You're not my girl! You go away and bring me back my sweet girl!"

I slam out of the house and walk way out behind the chicken coops, where there's a toolshed. *You're not my girl! What does that mean? Are there different people in me?* I sit in there for a long time looking through stacks of old Sears catalogs and copies of *Reader's Digest*. Field mice come in and look at me. We sit very still, looking at each other.

I wonder what's happening at home. I wonder what Mama's doing now. I wonder if Daddy's come home yet.

The next day, Jeff is friendly again, and I ask him why don't they have goats on the farm.

"Goats are too much trouble. You can't control them."

Later, I'm sitting on the porch with Uncle Edward, and I ask him if I could somehow get a baby skunk to take home for a pet, because I heard somewhere that you could take the smelly parts out of them.

"Skunks carry rabies," he says, rocking back.

"But you could find one that didn't have rabies."

"No," he says, "Skunks carry rabies."

"But I've heard that some people have pet skunks."

"It's not a good idea. Skunks carry rabies."

"But they're not born with rabies!"

"But they carry rabies."

He says this every time, the very same thing, without any change, over and over again, as if that's the end of it. He won't argue or explain. And he doesn't look friendly at all. I never noticed Uncle Edward acting like this before. I just look at him. Finally I get up and walk away. And I keep walking.

On one side of the house are fields all grassy green and gold. You can see cows and calves out there and sometimes the bull. Rabbits or kittens or quail scoot in and out of the grass.

I walk to the other side of the house, kind of behind the house, over a fence, some distance away, toward the reservoir, where the ground becomes dry, cracked, and hard, with rocks, stickers, dried cow patties, thorny things, big red ants. I walk carefully, my feet burning, watching for scorpions and snakes, wishing I had worn shoes, but then thinking, *Oh well.*

I've been out here before. There're no trees, the sun high and hot. Tough grasses, cactus in scruffy clumps, larger ones growing out of dead, decaying ones. Some prickly pears spread out, live and dead parts, over areas the size of a car. One of these is home to hundreds of wobbly daddy longlegs, which all lean together in my direction as I pick my way past.

I stop to look at a nest of red ants. Some ants are almost a half an inch long, but I know these are slow to sting. There's a hole in the middle of the perfect circle they've raked out, and hundreds go in and out, carrying things. It's a big nest. I wish I could look down inside the nest to see what it's really like to be an ant. Careful not to stand on their circle or their path, I watch until I'm shooing away too many flies that have found me.

I walk again, trying to lose the flies. I see a jackrabbit watching me from a distance. He scoots away. A hornet buzzes around me a few times, then zooms off, speeding out of a wide turn like a tough little fighter plane.

I think about playing the Girl, but she's not that interesting right now. I think she's high up in her Wonder Woman airplane, watching me from the sky. I'm thirsty and hot. The sun beats down like it's personal.

When I get to the reservoir, I climb up to the mounded bare lip of it and sit down to look at the water, thinking it'll be cooler there, but it's not. The water's too low for me to reach, the reflected sun is blinding, and here come the flies.

I examine my feet, tough from summer, but no more beat-up than usual. I brush them off. Chigger bites around the ankles are itchy and hot. A worrying splinter has finally gone. The stuck-back-together, stubbed-off top of my right big toe is healing up, the Band-Aid so dirty, I throw it away. Nothing hurts that much, but my already-sunburned arms are stinging. I wave more flies away and look out across the shimmering-hot landscape. I can see the clump of trees up where the house is, so I'm not lost. But I am completely alone. No one knows I'm out here. Something could happen to me out here and no one would miss me until suppertime. I enjoy this thought.

Maybe I'm tired of being so nice all the time. Anyway, they're probably tired of having me here by now. A black-and-blue horsefly insists on my big toe.

A dust devil spins itself out next to a dead-looking crown of thorns bush. A breeze blows some tumbleweeds across, sending them skipping and bouncing until they run into something and pile up. Tall dark clouds on one side of the sky are rolling this way.

Over there I see a snake, a long sidewinder whipping itself along in my direction, moving so fast, I can't take my eyes away as it ripples and rolls itself across the cracked earth and past in a matter of seconds. I forget about the flies.

I am in the desert. If I want to listen for God's voice, I can see that this is the place. I'm like Moses crossing the desert, looking for a sign. I'm like Ishmael, hoping an angel will show me to the water. I'm Elijah, waiting for God to come and tell me I'm not alone. Even Jesus went to the desert looking for something, and things did come to Him. That's what they say.

I'm batting flies away, small flies, medium-size flies, and big glittery horseflies that insist on landing with a bite. A world of flies has found me and more are coming still. Shading my eyes, I look up and see almost a cloud of them, hovering above and around me, diving in, scattering out, then diving in again, as if I might be something good to eat.

I sit still and let them land on me. They crawl and tickle my arms and legs. I lie back and cover my eyes. At first, I can't stop twitching and shuddering when I feel those horseflies land, but finally I make myself lie perfectly still, letting them crawl all over me, letting them come.

The Girl is flying high above me, having her own life, looking down at me.

I try to think of God in Heaven looking down at me, with Jesus and all the angels, clouds, swirly things around the edges of the picture. *Here I am, God! Look down and see me, Jesus! This is how much I want you to appear to me, speak to me, or send an angel, Send something!* But nothing comes.

I close my eyes and let the sun burn into me. I welcome the flies. I wait. The flies tickle and bite me all over, my arms and legs, my face, my ears. It's like I'm dead. *Is this what it feels like to be dead?* I lie still, listening to their buzzings.

The imagining of angels doesn't seem real. I can't make the picture bright and clear like it used to be at night in bed. I am just here, lying on dirt, letting bugs crawl on me for no reason, being dead but not rising up. There's no rising up to be found out here at all.

Probably because I don't believe enough. A little voice in the back of my head keeps saying I'm only trying to pretend hard enough to make it real. But it's not real. I simply cannot go all the way to believing it's real. I'm faking, and something in me knows it. The Girl knows it.

Maybe I could die, lying out here like this. The flies want me to die, I can feel the force of them wanting me to die. I'm nothing but food to these flies, and they are ready to eat me.

I jump up! I dance up and down! I take handfuls of sandy dirt and rub it on my arms and legs and face. The flies scatter. I run down the side of the reservoir, look out at the bright sky, which is turning greenish, and I see dark clouds coming closer, stacked up and moving fast. I start walking back up to the house as fast as I can pick my way.

Why don't I believe? Other people do it. This must mean I am bad. But why do people act like something depends on it? What if you can't help thinking what's in your own mind to think?

I reach the house and I hear thunder. The sky's even more green and dark. I stand on the soft grass as fat, splashing drops hit my arms, hoping it will cool me down, wash me clean.

Aunt Lee sticks her head out of the back door, shouting, "Where have you been? I was looking for you! Come in the house right now; it's fixin' to storm!"

I hear the cattle guard's broken pipe twanging as Uncle Edward's truck barrels up the driveway, as she's pushing me into the house. He jumps out of the truck out there, yelling, "Tornado!" and I hear the truck door slam, and then *CRACK-POP-BAM,* the loudest sound— more than sound, with white light, too—I ever heard shocks the house, shakes everything. The next instant,

Aunt Lee's in the backyard yelling, crying, and I hear Uncle Edward's voice out there, too, and then both are coming in the back door, hugging each other, shaking, and Aunt Lee's talking a mile a minute.

There's a funny smell. I look out back. Lightning struck the tree right next to where Uncle Edward was standing. The trunk is split. We never saw the tornado, but lightning struck the corner of the roof, too, right there touching the tree. Lightning almost struck Uncle Edward, might have killed Uncle Edward. They keep talking about it, saying, "It wasn't your time" and "Well, we need the rain."

They don't know it, but I know that lightning wasn't after them at all. It was after me.

Bees

You can run across fields and through woods and up creeks and down roads, and you can run and run and run for miles and miles cross-country, and you could even run your whole life if you wanted to, but when you stopped for a minute to rest, or if you stopped for just a few seconds to catch your breath, no matter where your stopping might be, there the bees also would be, buzzing around your head, and buzzing around and around your ears, getting tangled in your hair, getting folded into your clothes, being trapped right next to you, buzzing and buzzing, and you can't get them out, and you can't get them away, and you can't even see their bullet bodies whizzing through the air, chasing you, and dogging you, and tracking you, because their little missile bodies and their kamikaze wills cannot be stopped, and you can't even knock them out of the air because they are so fast, and so knowing, and they will die to get you, they will hurl their whole angry, tough little bodies right into you, so the stinger impacts your skin like a slap. And then another slap, and another and another as each bee hits, and you are slapped and slapped, and you turn and turn, and you run and stumble, each slap socking into your skin, into your muscle, and into your stomach and into your brain, attacking and invading you with bee fury all through your insulted flesh.

So I am eight years old and I am on a big dumb brown-and-white paint horse that I have been given to look cute for a picture, and even though I can ride, and even though I am a good rider, I have been given this big stupid and stubborn horse because I am a child. Then everyone goes out on the trail, and this stupid horse wants to run right through big thick bushes, and Mama told me to be sure to keep the horse away from the river because big dumb paint horses just love to roll in water, and then we do go near the river, and when we are there near the river, I am so busy thinking about keeping this stupid stubborn horse from rolling in water that I don't see what's really happening, with the horse going through the thick bushes, the horse pushing through the dense, heavy bushes, the bees buzzing up out of the bushes and around its head, buzzing around the big dumb brown-and-white head of the stupid horse, the bees getting really mad, and the bees rising up and rising up out of the thick bushes like the head of a bee cobra, and then the horse shies and then the horse rears, and then I see that the horse is running for the river, and then I see a thick, low branch coming fast at me—a heavy-as-a-tree-trunk and too-low-to-duck big branch coming right at me fast—so I throw my leg over and I jump off the horse at a run, the way I saw a man do at the rodeo, and then I fall on the rocks and on the grass, and then I roll on the rocks and on the grass, and then the horse jumps around me and the horse runs away and then I am on the ground with the bees, buzzing around me, slamming their stingers right into me like fists, buzzing and buzzing, the bees' fury around me in a whirlwind of killing rage, so I run up the hill under the trees and I am slapping the air and I am screaming and I am turning and turning around and around and running and running, but it doesn't help, because nothing helps, and then some people ride up on their horses, but the bees have me to sting, and the people are older and the people are high in the air on their horses and my dumb paint has run away. And the people are laughing because the people see me red and running and crying and screaming, but people can't see the whirlwind and the stinging that is like fists, and the people just act as if they think that I am crazy, and that I am a funny puppet on a string out there far away from them, jumping and turning and made of wood and paper and of something else that they don't know, and jumping and turning and running and falling down and running again, and the people don't see the whirlwind and the people don't see the stinging, and one of the people yells out, "What's wrong?" but I can't answer and so I think that the people don't know why I am doing what I am doing and that the people think I am a crazy person and a funny person who does things for no reason, and then the bees start thinning out, and then one of people shouts out, "We're going to get help!" and then the people ride away on their tall horses—a sorrel and a bay and a palomino—the people canter gracefully away on their shiny and perfectly groomed horses, canter easily away over the hill. And after the people go away and all the bees that wanted to sting me have stung me, and then the bees will all die now, having given everything that was in themselves to me, and I even see some little bee bodies lying around on the grass and falling out of my clothes, having given all their fury and all their rage to me, then I just cry and cry and cry and walk and walk back toward the barn. And soon one of the people who laughed at me before comes back over the hill, leading my stupid horse, which is now all wet and tired, and the person helps me to get back on that dumb paint horse and I ride back with that person leading me, and I can't stop crying and imagining the bees and the rage of the bees and the people laughing and the people going for cocktails that evening and talking about amusing events of the day. And all the bee stings all over me sting and ache and throb, and the buzzing and the rage of the bees is in me now, and my whole body hurts now, and even my brain hurts now, and I know even now that something has changed inside me and will always be a certain way now that it didn't used to be. Something in me that was me got pushed aside by something else in me that seemed to come from somewhere else, and I know that bees are in me now, and that that is where they are going to stay now, that that is where the bees are now and are always going to be.

Cottonmouth–August 16, 1948

I remember the August Babe Ruth died.

We heard the news out back through radio static. The boys had a talk and made decisions. Some bigger boys brought a snake. They all came in from Texas sun to the shade of Bob Lynn's back yard.

They skinned a cottonmouth that day. We stood silent, watching the brightly colored organs spill out from the patterned skin, split open and nailed to a wooden table under the trees.

We stood around some more, and we looked at it.

Later, we walked home barefoot down the sun-hot gravel, past hedges, through clouds of gnats, and I was crying and crying.

And I didn't even know Babe Ruth.

Dapper Dan

Hazard is still suffering, Daddy is still gone, and it is almost time for school to start when a friend of Granny's in New York gives us a new dog. Granny's friend has to travel and can not keep the dog—a dog that my mama says belongs in whatever pantheon there may be of great dogs.

Dapper Dan is a pedigreed boxer raised in a New York City apartment, his sire a National Kennel Club champion with a fancy-sounding name. He's almost two years old when he comes to live with us, but he has never been outside off a leash, so he has to be kept in the house. Mama buys a book called *The Boxer,* which is full of things like correct tail docking, splayed feet, shoulder width, and set of head and ears. We all read it, and Mama and all of us fall in love with Dapper.

He's a dark brindle with a white chest, a blaze on the nose, and four white sock feet, perfectly well-trained, always thin, nervous, hypersensitive to everything in the house, and Dapper has eyes that understand all you are going through, and takes it all with a certain wit.

He's by Mama's side as she goes here and there throughout the house. She loves training such a smart

dog, and she shows him all that she wants a good watch-
dog to notice around the house—windows, doors. And
Dapper loves to play.

Sometimes when I am put to bed early at night, lying
there awake with nothing to do, the two of them pass by
my bedroom door and I whisper, "Dapper!"

He veers instantly, always ready, and bounds into my
room, jumps up on my bed, and we wrestle and play,
him grabbing a pigtail in his mouth, the two of us rolling around in a little frenzy, and then he bounces out
again with a doggy grin and a little dance, as if to say,
We're bad! We're bad!

Hazzy has stopped digging on Hap's grave, but she
still takes her naps right on top of it, and she's never
happy with being alone out there in the yard. Even
though Mama does everything to make her warm and
comfortable out there, she howls for a while every night,
but she is still not allowed in the house.

With Dapper suddenly here, and Hazzy knowing we
have this other dog in the house, it is just about breaking
her heart once again. She hangs around the doors whining, and Mama cries, but still will not let her in.

One day, Mama starts talking to our plumber, Mr.
Allball, about it. Mr. Allball has been around our house
a lot, at first for the septic tank, and then later for the
city-connected plumbing. He's a large tousled man
Mama and Daddy and all of us really like. He has several
dogs and lives farther out in the country. He says Hazzy
might settle down in a new place with other dogs where

she can have a new life, and it might be worth a try if he takes her for a while.

Mama's worried about this, but she agrees, so we say good-bye to her. And later Mr. Allball says she has had more puppies, so everything does work out fine for Hazzy.

DADDY COMES HOME RIGHT BEFORE school starts. Just one day all of a sudden, there he is, sitting out on the screened-in porch off the living room in his bathrobe, looking sad. No one tells me anything. He does not go to work, but sits on the glider every afternoon for a while, his cane propped against a wall, his face turned away.

Dapper lies down on the floor next to him, watching him with sad eyes. If Daddy changes position, Dapper jumps to his feet, wary, knowing something is wrong. If Daddy gets upset or does anything too sudden, Dapper throws up on the rug, and next the whole house gets upset.

I escape to next door, where I find Nathan with his visiting cousin. We talk about school starting, having to wear shoes every day again, having no time for adventures, and what the next grade will be like.

But soon Nathan just wants to talk to his cousin about which would be worse—to be hanged or to be killed in the electric chair. I think the electric chair would be worse, but then they just want to argue about guns and knives and things, so I borrow an *Alley-Oop* comic book and leave.

Daddy is still in the same spot. I hang around in the

living room, looking at books, walking back and forth a few times, wondering if he knows I am there, but he never makes any indication. I never saw him so inward and low. He seems smaller.

I wander casually out to the porch, hoping he'll talk to me, but he stays quiet. Finally he glances over, looks at my eyes as if openly checking something, which is surprising. Then he looks out again, as if he needs to get back to something out the window, something he's been watching.

At the other window, I look out and see Mama in the front yard with Dapper on a short leash.

Back and forth they walk, Mama and Dapper, with her calling for him to heel, to sit, to stand in show-dog stance, then praising with treats, as if Dapper didn't already know all this. But he's happy enough to go along with his humans.

Daddy turns suddenly and asks if I am grateful for all I've been given. Then he and I just look at each other. I don't know what to say.

Then, still talking loud from outdoors, I say, "Daddy, what's the worst way to die?" My words seem to leap across the screened porch, making too much noise.

"Falling," he says immediately, almost whispering. I didn't expect that.

"But why is that the worst way?"

I notice his eyes are red. Daddy has been crying!

I walk closer slowly, sit on an ottoman, careful not to touch or even look too closely at the scarred-ankle feet propped there.

I can barely hear his voice when he answers.

"But what if you didn't land?"

"What? But what about gravity? You have to land!" I laugh.

"Yeah," He says, "Gravity."

"What if you jumped in the dark, thinking it was just a ditch, but then you didn't land, and you didn't land, and you still didn't land, until your heart was up in your mouth, until . . ."

"Did that happen?"

"In North Africa."

"But why did you jump?"

"We were in the desert after dark in a semicircle. It was a blackout, German planes out there. I was told to run across and tell some idiot to put out his campfire."

"I felt the ground slip, rocks sliding. I thought it was a ditch I could jump, but when I didn't land, and I didn't land, I knew I was dead."

"But . . ."

"I don't know how long I was out. When I woke up, I saw nothing, heard nothing, felt nothing, just black. Then I really knew I was dead. After a while of that, I heard Doyle calling, rocks falling. *Zoom, back to life!* I was afraid he'd fall on me! My mouth yelled out without my even thinking about it."

"But how did you get out?"

"They had to get me out. It took a while. I was in shock. I didn't feel much at first. Everything was broken. It was a rock quarry. The hell was lying on that cot in the desert 'til they could ship me back. When I looked down and saw what was left of my feet, my legs. . . . Boy that morphine was good."

"But didn't they know the rock thing was there?"

"Someone must have known. I don't know. It was my mistake."

"I remember seeing you in the hospital."

"The best guys I'd ever known were in that hospital. The jokes, the pranks. That was what we did. Nobody sat around whining like in the movies they make. You couldn't feel sorry for yourself when you saw the guy next to you."

Then he turns his face away and doesn't talk for a long time.

"There was this one guy at Valley Forge, both arms and both legs blown off. Well, you had to do what you had to do. Nobody understands that. Dad can't understand that."

Then Daddy talks about his father, GranDad, tilting his head back on the glider pillow, his eyes flickering at something only he could see. His eyes are wet.

"You didn't see him when he was young."

Gradually, Daddy gets better. He starts puttering with cars and with clay and wood carvings and drawing cartoons. He smokes cigarettes. He shows me how he can blow smoke rings.

School starts. We get central air conditioning in the whole house. Then we get one of the new television sets, but almost everything on it makes Daddy mad. He gets especially upset about Kraft cheese—the commercials on television, and the cheese itself. When Mama buys it he starts yelling, "Do not buy it! It is not cheese!"

He gets mad at the telephone party line. He gets mad at the neighbors because their chickens wander over and eat our strawberries. Gradually, Daddy gets mad at more and more things, until he is almost his old self, and he starts getting dressed and going out in the car again.

One Sunday, Daddy says Dapper has to be taken outside and let off the leash, so we all go out in the yard to watch. Mama has doubts about this, but Daddy says "Do it," so she leads Dapper out. I see Nathan and his mom watching from the next yard. We all stand frozen as she unhooks the leash. Dapper stands frozen, too.

Dapper looks at Mama, looks at Daddy, looks from one to the other of us again with his eyes, asking about this. It was as if he'd always known what unhooking that leash might mean but never allowed himself to think this might happen. He begins trembling, a tremor that starts in his shoulders and spreads, until it seems almost that more than one dog is standing there before us in a mighty shivery shaking.

Mama hurries across the yard and calls to him, clapping her hands. He takes a few steps, shaking so hard he can barely walk. He looks back at us.

"Go, Dapper, go!" We all start shouting to him, "Yes! Go!" He takes a few more steps. We keep yelling and clapping. He walks. He trots haltingly. He keeps looking and we keep yelling. I see Nathan at the fence over there yelling, too.

Then suddenly, Dapper seems to realize he can run, he

needs to run, is made to run, and the running starts jolting through him, taking hold of him, as he bounds from a trot to a canter into a full-out gallop, going faster and stronger as we are cheering and cheering for him. You can almost see the gears shifting up and up in him, his muscular boxer body stretching and pounding, twisting and *cavorting* across our yard, jumping the fence, turning in air, leaping hedges. He is looking over at us, sharing it with us, tongue flying out of his happy boxer big mouth of joy. I am jumping up and down, wanting to run like that, too. He pounds up to each of us in turn, wagging, jumping, licking, and we are jumping and clapping all together, seeing his doggy sense of humor, and we are a running and laughing family for once as well with this dog who is in every molecule a dog set free.

Then Daddy turns to me, puts a hand on my shoulder, and says, "Now then."

This is our dog: Dapper Dan.

Kid Show

Nathan's cousin Phil visits again, and the two of them come to my bathroom window as I'm about to undress to take a bath. They try to talk me into letting them watch, but I say no. I start considering it, but Mama knows what's going on, because after my bath she comes in as usual to paint calamine lotion on my poison ivy and chigger bites and Mercurochrome on my scratches and skinned knees, and I have to dance around naked, painted red and white all over, until it dries. It's tingly and cold as I jump and twirl under the attic fan, and just as Daddy comes around the corner and up the hall, I run toward him, shouting, "Daddy, Daddy, Look! I'm an Indian!" thinking this is a great joke.

Mama runs down the hall and slaps me hard.

"Don't you ever let a boy see you naked!" she hisses. Daddy disappears. So I know all this must be bad.

This is about the same time my little sister starts stripping the sheets off her bed, the slipcovers off the sofa pillows, and all the clothes off of her dolls, my dolls, and herself out in the front yard. It kept Mama busy for a while, last summer. Now she's doing it again.

Nathan is always asking me to take off my underpants

and show him what my girl's thing looks like. He wants to see what I have down there, since he knows I don't have a thing like his thing. He wants to talk about this all the time, and he starts acting like maybe we won't be friends anymore if I won't do it. I don't know why, because I am curious, too, but I always say no, even though Nathan gets mad and says I am just like any other girl. And I know what the boys think of girls. Girls are tattletales and teacher's pets. They don't want to play fair or fight fair—they wimp out and blame somebody, or they cry and go home. I know what they think.

When we talk about the movies, Nathan says that maybe the kissing scenes have to be done with people who are already married, and what do I think about that?

I don't know what to say. I don't like the way he's acting. Then he asks why he and I don't ever kiss like that. I say I don't know why. Then I say that the boy is supposed to make it happen. But then Nathan says no, it's the girl who's supposed to make it happen. I don't think so, but I secretly know I do not really want to kiss Nathan like that. Why can't we just keep being pals the way we are? But Nathan starts being very quiet.

The boys all talk about their "weenies," and things like that, with an enormous amount of giggling. Sometimes they say, "No girls allowed!" and Nathan goes along with the others together in his clubhouse.

One day I wait outside and call them "Dumb eggs!" when they come out—one of those half-accidental utterances—and they laugh at me, but then later all the boys say it, too, "Dumb egg! You're just a Dumb egg! Dumb egg" becomes the insult of choice and goes around our neighborhood for a couple of years.

One day, I go next door and find Nathan out by his clubhouse, and Bob Lynn is there, all the way across the yard, purple-faced with deep and righteous rage, and with his brother's BB gun pointed at Nathan. He starts firing it over and over, hitting the ground in front of Nathan's feet, and with a look on his face such that you know before anybody yelled at you that you had better *get away*!

We are all well trained in the safety rules of BB guns, yet Nathan does not seem to be shocked or outraged at this behavior. He seems aware of danger, yelling at Bob to stop, but also seems unsurprised and not fighting back.

You can tell by the furious crying face and behavior of the normally responsible and sober Bob Lynn, that something serious has happened, and the two of them will no longer be the friends they have been. The shock is that Bob is so willing to be what we all know well is "in the wrong."

He fires and fires and cries, and then just turns and walks home. And Nathan will never tell me what it's about, but I just accept that in the way I accept everything about Nathan.

The next day, Nathan and I sit on the porch, watching a dust storm blow across, the wind and stinging dust, the sun high and white as a hole at the top of the brown tepee of the sky.

"I've seen it before," Nathan says.

Then Nathan remembers other places he has lived, other mothers and daddies and houses he's had at other times, because he was six years old by the time he came here, and by now he is almost eight. Usually, he won't talk about it, but on this day he does. The next day he is going to start building a treehouse in the woods behind his clubhouse, and he starts saying how he's seen another kid build one when he lived with some people who had a ranch in East Texas, and how he'd worked on it with that kid, but then that kid had gotten mad at him about something and had gotten him into trouble for trying to ride one of the calves, which turned out to be a prize calf, and it went crazy and hurt itself after that and had to be shot.

And then those people sent Nathan back to the orphanage. Every place he went, he would do something to get sent back.

"Which place did you like best?"

"That one with the ranch and this one," he says, "about the same, I guess."

But Nathan never tells me what his real name was.

"But why not?" I beg, "I cross my heart and hope to die, stick a thousand needles in my eye, I won't tell."

"The Calders wouldn't like it," he says.

"But is it a secret?"

"It might hurt their feelings."

After that, the drought breaks. Dark clouds bump each other along the upper air, fat raindrops tap-dancing down the streets, marching into culverts and thirsty creeks, steam rising from the hot tar road.

Nathan and I make a run for it from the culvert, where we were crawdad fishing with safety pins and bacon. We make a dash for it past the tumbleweeds driven bouncing against the fences, past the faces at window and porch screens gazing out gratefully at the longed-for summer rain.

By the time we get close to Nathan's house, we're so wet and giddy, we decide to stay out and play in the rain, then go back and catch more crawdads. All arguments are forgotten. The happy toads and soaked pink earthworms are coming out. But they're clang-clanging the back-door bell, which meant, *Come home! Come home! Come home right now!*

On Saturdays, we go to the Kid Show at the Inwood Theater. It costs twenty-five cents and we'll be there eating popcorn and candy and running up and down with other kids until we get picked up at dinnertime. There are cartoons, serials, newsreels, and a feature film, and we sit behind teenagers to watch them make out with their dates, which is not easy, because the older ones sit up in the back row. We move around, seeing which ones are best. Finally, we get behind this one couple, a girl with bleached bangs and a guy with a ducktail. He moans and groans and tries to get into the seat with the girl, and she moans and groans and squeals, "No, Bobby-Ray, no!" It is very exciting.

"Nathan, do you think I'm pretty?" I ask.

But then Nathan goes running up into the balcony and starts dropping things on them and on me, and we wind up getting thrown out of the theater. The manager says he has "had it with this sort of thing." He calls Nathan's mom, and when she comes to pick us up, she is really mad. She won't speak to Nathan all the way home.

We sit in the backseat, and all the way home, Nathan rocks himself back and forth and back and forth, and he puts his face out into the wind just like a dog.

After that, I don't see Nathan out in his yard or at his clubhouse for a long time, and none of the other kids are seeing him, either. I go to the Calders' front door and peer through the screen a few times, but never do see him. Mrs. Calder comes out and says Nathan is being punished and cannot come out to play. The next day, she says the same thing. I'm afraid to ask how long it will be, afraid he's not even in there, afraid they've already sent him back, and I will never see him again.

I never ask Mama, because she doesn't like Nathan anyway, and she starts saying things to me about how I should invite some of the little girls in my class over to play, or how I need to make more new friends. But instead, I get interested in the books in the bookshelf, where Daddy showed me how to use *The Book of Knowledge*. Then Mama starts complaining that I always have my "nose in a book."

And Daddy starts sitting in the living room in his bathrobe all the time again. No one will tell me anything. There's no one I can ask about anything.

Snow White

My dime-store Snow White costume is carefully folded in an overnight bag for Halloween at Granny's house this year. Mama and Daddy are going out. Daddy doesn't like Granny's house, so Mama's dropping me off there.

There's always something going on at Granny's house. Aunts and uncles and cousins drop in or stay over at Granny's house, having just driven in from some flat, dusty small town, miles of two-lane blacktop away— Granny's sisters, Granny's friends having drinks, neighbors playing cards, and sometimes even Papaw's other family, who wear funny dark clothes and have beards, and who are never there at the same time as everyone else. We hardly ever see them.

I run in and hear Granny talking on the phone on the porch about different horses, calling them by name, as if the horses were friends of hers. She's sitting with a blond woman, and when Mama comes out to the porch, the blond woman gets up and goes out, leaving her drink unfinished and her lipsticked cigarette burning in the ashtray. A radio is on, blaring horse-racing results.

Granny looks at me. "You're getting so tall! We're

gonna have to put a brick on your head if you don't watch out!"

Mama says it looks like the two of them were sitting on the back porch drinking and throwing money away all afternoon.

Granny says, "I'm not hurting anyone!" and walks away into another part of the house. We hear her singing, "I don't want to play with you . . . you're just a little tittle-tattle-tale," then moving on to the one about "You won't see me anymore, sliding down your rain barrel," then the next of many old school-yard songs she sings in her deep trembly voice, often looking right at me, as if telling me something I should already know.

But I am not a tittle-tattle-tale, never have been one, knowing already from neighborhood kids, from Mama, and from everything else that a tattletale is the lowest thing you could be, so why does she sing that song to me? I didn't tattle when Bob Lynn shot his BB gun at Nathan from across the yard, a thing breathtaking with wrongness, we all three knew, and were awed at his being so enraged that he was willing to do something so wrong. But that was between the two of them, the three of us.

I didn't tattle when the Breard boys tied me to a tree and stole my Raggedy Ann, or when George tried to show me his thing, or when Granny let me get into bed with her, or anything else. All that was between me and them.

But what if something was so bad, worse than a *compound fracture,* that it had to be told? Would a person have to keep that secret even if it went on eating a hole up inside of them and warping their entire life, even affecting the lives of other people in their family over all the years? Would a person be a traitorous *tattletale* if they let that thing with all its damage out of themselves and into the world to do more damage? Are there things that won't go on into forever being untold?

And what if the things are told? Is that the end of it? Or might that be just a new beginning of a whole other cycle of telling and retelling and damage to this one and that one—and then this one and that one have to go on spreading the damage, until it's a thing that never ends, but having been started who knows how long ago, decades, centuries—it just goes on and on and it seems we humans are helpless to stop it. And you yourself are helpless to stop doing your part of one way or another passing the evil of that thing on and on?

Mama leaves, saying, "And don't you let her get into bed with you!" as she gets into her car.

"Okay, Dear, okay," Granny says as she goes back in. I sit on the front steps, watching Mama's Cadillac drive away up Beverly Drive, hearing Nona's radio through the kitchen window playing *Amos 'n' Andy,* then she and Granny are talking and cooking and laughing in there while Granny plays solitaire on the kitchen table.

Papaw takes me on an errand down to the *Dallas Morning News,* where he works. We enter through the basement and watch his cartoonist friend speed-draw cartoons for the next day's paper, and I think of Daddy's cartoons, which he draws fast like that. Papaw loves the newspaper, and he especially wants to show me the huge inky machines that turn out the papers, so I can see it all happening. All the way back, I ask Papaw over and over again how I can get to be a cartoonist for the paper, too, but he just keeps shifting in his seat, clearing his throat, and going, *Ho-ho-ho-ho, ho-ho-ho-ho-ho-ho-ho!*

When we get back, I'm excited about tagging along with Oliver and his friends for Halloween, but they don't want to take a little kid like me off to their party somewhere for bigger kids to have fun among themselves.

I watch Oliver from across the kitchen. He's as tall as a grown-up now, graceful, gentle-seeming, with thick wavy hair. His dark eyes seem to have a sweetness in them, and yet a distance.

One of his friends has small and watchful eyes, and his initials are the same as mine. I try to get this friend to talk to me, but he's hurrying out the door and won't look at me. I hear them all say they're coming back later to change clothes. Then I have this great idea of a way to show them that I am bigger and smarter than they think I am. I know how to be one of the boys.

I go back to Granny's desk for paper, and I make a cartoon drawing the way Nathan would do it, a long thing and a short V-thing with a line up the middle. It's just the kind of thing the boys in my neighborhood always giggle at. Then, laughing to myself at my clever prank, I fold this piece of paper, put Oliver's name on it, and leave it at the back door, where I know he'll come back later, pick it up, unfold it, and see my little pencil cartoon joke. He will see that I am wise to boy talk. I think this is a good joke.

Then I forget all about that. I run up the stairs, take out my Snow White costume, get Granny's nail scissors and cut out the eyes and the mouth of the dime-store painted cheesecloth and paste mask so I can see better, and so later I can put candy into the mouth without it getting frayed and gooey, or at least not so much.

I dance around the room, pretending to be Snow White in the dark woods, imagining the "Who is the prettiest?" magic mirror, the Wicked Witch, the Seven Dwarfs, the apple, the curse, and especially the long sleep waiting for the prince to come to see the beautiful girl asleep in the forest. I like the part with the kiss at the end, when the princess wakes up.

I go downstairs and find Granny made up as a witch. The sofa bolsters sit up in costumes and wigs, rubber masks looking crookedly over at me, at the door a giant jack-o'-lantern Cleveland carved with a gap-toothed grin just like his own, and wicker baskets of sugarcane sections and homemade candy apples all ready for the trick-or-treater kids.

Granny's her funniest self, singing, whistling, joking around with me and with Nona in a way that's not what a person usually expects from a grown-up, even a grown-up you might turn around and see down on the floor at the checkout stand in the grocery store, looking for something down there. Then leaving, she would cackle and whisper in your ear that she liked to look up that checkout woman's dress to see her panties and her fat legs under there.

Everyone in the family rolls their eyes when they talk about Granny. But everyone does laugh a lot at her house.

The moon is low and glowing orange through the trees,

night falling as I go out by myself to trick-or-treat. Papaw follows me, as Granny told him to do, but then he wants to go back to the house. He finds a group he knows, tells me to follow them, to stay with them, then leaves me alone to tag along with these strange people. I follow first this group, then another group, but I don't know them. I'm not part of them. I'm not part of anyone now. At first, I am scared, but soon I like it.

Soon I am running through shadows stretching deep and dark between houses, pretending to be part of each group, following people I don't know, up and down the street, *Trick or Treat! Trick or Treat!*

I tie up the skirt of my costume so I can be more quick and invisible in the dark. It's a game of being on my own, not even being the Girl, but being me, a wild thing, magical and bad, wishing to belong but enjoying not belonging, in and out of bushes around the lit-up houses lining the long cathedral of giant elm trees with branches arching and meeting high above Beverly Drive, treetops lit from beneath all up and down the blocks, scampering ghosts and goblins slipping across connecting streets from house to house, the carved pumpkins, flickering candles, dopey smiles, evil grins.

People give out homemade cookies and fudge, store-bought candy and sticky popcorn balls. People invite you in to see their kittens, want to give you a kitten to take home. But you cannot take a kitten because Granny does not like animals at her house—she says animals are nasty.

Here in Highland Park the houses are closer together, and the kids are tamer than out where our house is, where we trot across moonlit stubble fields like a nervous pack of dogs, the boys carrying stuff for soaping screens, egging cars, papering houses if no candy's left out. *Treats for us or a trick for you!*

When the trick-or-treaters thin out and mostly go home, I walk up and down the street, feeling it can't be over yet, that something exciting has to happen, that something more is out there waiting to happen, but porch lights go out one by one, and the street goes dark. A group of older kids cross the next block over, where a streetlight glows, making their shadows stretch out long and wicked as they walk along. They don't see me. No one sees me, and no one calls me in.

I'm Snow White alone among clutching branches in the deep woods, branches curving into claws reaching out to snatch me. I see a witch's face in the leaves; then I see a demon's face looking as if it knows me and knows my fortune. Many faces seem to come around me, watching, following, knowing something bad about me, getting too close to me, until I jump back onto home base at Granny's lit porch and look back. But then all I can see are moths and flies foolishly flapping around the hot bulb.

Looking up to overarching branches, now shadowy, I see another face near where the streetlamp shines on the leaves, evil around the eyes, evil around the mouth, even evil around the nose and ears, but something in this demon's eyes seems to be my friend. I look and look, can't take my eyes away from its gleaming eyes, as if something is about to become clear to me.

This has been the best Halloween ever, new freedom,

new power, new omens of life being exciting and *mine* to hold in my own hands, to take to heart. *It's going to be MY life. Mine.*

That constant ongoing inquiry at the back of my mind about what's it going to be like to grow up, what's life going to be like as it becomes really *mine*—a question at the back of my child mind that seems to undergird and surround everything: *What will it be like? How will it be?*

The overarching elm trees, the dancing and comical-scary flitting and dancing ghosts and goblins, the soft Texas-October cool breezes, the adventure of being alone out there among the shadows, the low orange moon—it's all a fantastic adventure and I am strong and good in it.

I hear the voices of Granny and Papaw in the living room, where they're listening to the radio. She still has her makeup on, her drink in her hand. It seems Granny's wicked witch act was the hit of the neighborhood and all the kids came here more than once.

I go up the stairs. It's late, but I'm not tired. My clothes feel gritty. I take everything off. I scrub my face and arms and legs with a wet washrag and put on my nightgown without bathing. Time to go to bed, but I'm wide-awake, and all the grown-ups are busy somewhere else.

I grab the wrinkled, velvety, fraying paper bag, dump my candy loot onto the floor, divide it into piles, then start eating the caramels first, the dark ones and the light ones, unwrapping the sticky cellophane, until every-thing seems sticky. I take a handful to the bedside table and sit on the turned-back bedspread, chewing them and wishing Nathan were here to enjoy this with me. I hear the crickets outside, the sound of the radio downstairs.

Knock knock knock knock knock.

Oliver bursts through the bedroom door, stands there looking at me. There's something wrong with his face.

He steps in and closes the door quietly behind him. He stands looking right at me, speaking right to me for a change, but his voice is angry, his eyes are dark, and he's holding a piece of paper, the same piece of paper I drew on earlier.

I had forgotten all about that. I must have wanted to tease him into having to deal with me. Now he's here, holding the paper out, shaking it at me.

"Did you do this?" His anger seems over-done, like it couldn't be real. This might be a little game.

"Yeah, I guess so." I start to laugh.

"This is so dirty! This is so low! This is the most disgusting thing I've ever seen!" he goes on. "How could you have even drawn this, much less given it to me? You are disgusting, you are just plain bad."

He crumples it up and puts it in his pocket.

He seems serious. I know it's bad, but surely it's not all that bad. I did not expect this. I'm caught. We're alone in this room together, something is about to happen, and I'm caught.

"I'm going to show this to your mother and to everyone, show them how bad and disgusting you are. Unless you do exactly whatever I say."

This does not scare me. It's the sort of thing kids say.

He's coming toward me diagonally across the room.

The moment freezes as I see him coming toward me and coming toward me across the room diagonally again and coming across the room again, and again, at this point where I could still put a stop to this, because something seems funny about this.

I could still say no, but he is coming across the room and I do not say no, again, and for a very long time, as if that part of events becomes stuck at this point where I could still say no but do not say no, and he is still and again coming across the room and I could do something, but I do not do something.

I know I do not want Mama to see that drawing. She gets so upset over things like that.

"Okay," I mutter, wondering what it is I'm going to have to do. I don't think much of it.

But the real truth is that I am curious. And the real truth is that I do want something to happen between us, but I don't know what. I'm sitting on the bed, afraid to move. We're in some kind of a danger zone. Everything is standing on end.

He's there on the other side of the other bed when he says, "Do whatever I say," again, and his eyes, angry like I've never seen on him, bear down on me. I'm frozen in place, caught. *Do whatever I say.* And then he's sitting on the neatly maid-turned-down bed on my side, and I'm saying, "Okay."

I say *Okay*, and I grin as I move back on the bed for him, and I try to catch his eye as I'm grinning, trying to make a game of this, trying to make something shared out of this. Now something is happening between us. And

I'm grinning as I'm thinking this might be a joke or this might be something of a bond between us or this might be fun.

But he will not let me catch his eye. He will not let me share with him what is happening or whatever the game is now.

He tells me to pull up my nightgown, to lie down on the bed with my knees up, with my knees facing toward the lamp, which he turns to shine on me down there. I don't like it, but I do it, since I did say "Okay." He kneels above me with the light behind him, and he looks at me, but not at my eyes.

I do not like this. This is not fun. I could still say, no. But I've already said, "Okay." I hesitate. I try to catch his eye.

He does not look back. His face is blank as he looks at that secret place of mine down there. It's the way he's looking at it, not with anger, but as if he's looking at something cut open, disgusting, dirty, inhuman, strange, and now no longer alive. His eyes are spoiling my secret place down there. My core of something deeply *mine* is being burned away.

There's something ugly around his mouth, even though his eyes are blank. All of a sudden, I see clearly that he's not just pretending not to like me, he has no feelings for me at all. He doesn't even hate me. I'm just a thing to him. I'm nothing to him. I'm nothing.

I'm frozen, watching his face until my own face feels like it's sliding away. I squeeze my eyes shut. He's turned the lamp shade so that the light is bright on me down there, yet it seems my head is in the far-off dark, and not safe. He unzips his pants and puts himself against me. Then he puts his thing into me! *This is not supposed to happen!* I turn my head away.

Why don't I why don't I why don't I say NO! No! no no no no no no no no absolutely NOT! Get away from me, you evil creep! But I just turn my darkness-covered head away more almost as if I could turn it all the way around and press my face deep inside the mattress. And that *NO!* goes inside of me, seeps into me and all through me, dulling and killing things inside there. Putting some kind of a curse on me. It seems like a blank spot occurs for a few minutes, and I go away from myself, both into the bed and also drifting to the ceiling, away, toward the far side of the room, while something is dying. *Why didn't I do something? Why didn't I put a stop to this?*

There's something gooey and bloody on the sheet after he goes out. I don't know what that is, but it is shameful. I put a towel over it and I just sit on the bed for a long time. I don't even want my Halloween candy. Halloween is far away now. I lay my head on the bed, not sleeping, but blank.

He said something, leaving, some kind of threat, but I do not know what. I didn't really hear it or I cannot remember it. My mind slides away from it. The way this turned against me—I cannot make it real, cannot name it, do not want to admit it.

The next morning, I see Oliver in the house, but he

won't look at me, and around his mouth is disgust. I try to act like it was okay, like it didn't bother me at all, didn't matter, that it's not important, that nothing's wrong. I can't admit anything. I have to pretend everything. So it's going to be like this, pretending I'm having a regular life from now on, pretending I'm something, when really I'm just a big nothing.

Everything starts getting flatter, like it's all a photograph or a drawing of a life. I don't want to touch myself anymore. I think about it, but it's not mine anymore. I don't even want to look at myself anymore, or too much at other people. They might know. Telling would make it more real in some way I might not like. They might say it was my own fault, part of a dance, and a game that was partly mine, a game that I lost.

Soon everything back there seems to have been done underwater, like in those dreams where you need to run fast, or you need to slap somebody hard, but you can't get up enough force against the cold weight of dead ocean around you.

I eat up the rest of my hoarded Halloween candy, and after that I keep stealing and eating more and more candy, cookies, ice cream. I have headaches and dreams. In third grade, I get glasses, and I'm tired all the time. The fun has gone out of things. But I pretend nothing is wrong. Pretending Nothing Is Wrong becomes a big part of my life, but it's a substitute for what it was like before.

There is a change in the universe. There are no more witches and goblins out there. There is no Blue Fairy. The world is plain and flat now, more gray, the mystery and brilliance gone out of it. And all of the darkness is inside of me.

Because I've been kicked out and locked out of the good and happy world. I've been cursed, and it is my own fault. I'm going to have to be a part of all that is alone and sad.

The stairwell clock was striking—*bong, bong, bong, bong, bong.* The striking went on in a forever of time passing away, being lost. I did not count the strokes or notice the time. I heard the sun and the moon chasing each other around faster and faster in there, but getting nowhere.

Chicken Shack

It wasn't in the chicken shack with the sunlit dust motes swirling through the air that it happened, but that's where we are going to put it.

It was actually behind a bush in the yard, and in broad afternoon daylight in summer, with normal kids playing normally out in a normal suburban yard on a sunny day, but these kids, like all kids, were always playing games of who is the best King of the Mountain, and who can do what, and who are the best friends and who are the enemies, who is bigger and older and who is too little and can't play—who is who and what is what and all the normal stuff of mean-kid games out in the yard.

But if one kid starts pushing for something and won't let up and another kid is starting to get jealous of a third kid, who is always the cute one and the funny one, the one who knows how to slip into any breach, taking things away from you, knows how to kiss up, and the one who is and is always going to be the favorite, then something is out of balance, the way things have a tendency to get out of balance, especially if there are more than one or two, then things go awry.

At least in some cases, this could represent a theory,

or an explanation, or even an excuse of sorts of sorts of sorts if you will if only you will.

So if two who have been two for a while start to be destabilized by the entrance of a third, then that first one will be, as a matter of reflex, looking to reestablish the two or else to spin away as only one again. And be alone.

But you play your part in the dance; you turn and bow and twirl and circle, not knowing to what effect, the way all life gets twirled and curtsied away and all the others do their bits on the eddies already in motion—and others from them and on and on—things you would not have imagined take place and the eddies even come back to you, until you want to stop doing the dance or anything at all, lest the effects cause too much to fall apart in unexpected ways.

You might later decide not to be pulled into things that might wind up being something you did not want to find yourself having passed on, so it might be better to stay away. And you never know what other people might do.

But yes, you did pass it on. Not so bad, only looking at her, but her little eyes looking up at you in the yard are still in your head, and then still looking at you as she pulled up her little white cotton pants and walked away and Nathan walked away with a funny look after you yourself walked away first and shouted, *"NOW YOU KNOW!"*

But even though all this happened in the course of a plain summer day, you have to put it in the chicken shack, because the dusty, gorgeous chicken shack holds the secret glowing, something more than child's play that can't be undone or shifted or spun into a better place just because when you walked away from the scene and from the two who were trying to team up against you, having pulled your own play, having caused everything to change into something else, as if to make it not all your own fault, you did shout out to the both of them, *"NOW YOU KNOW!"*

Hunchback Girl

Once in a while Mama and Daddy would argue about going to church at least on this one day.

"That preacher is a jerk!" Daddy said one Sunday.

"How can you say such a thing?" Mama said.

"Jane, everybody's selling something," Daddy said.

Mama started to cry. Daddy roared away in his car. Then Mama took us to Sunday school and went to church alone, with this look on her face about something secret and sad. The babies were put with some ladies at Sunday school, in a roomful of babies.

I like Sunday school. There are no requirements like regular school. No one watches me. I could even steal something, but there's nothing to steal. I like to wander the big halls by myself, sometimes for the entire hour, just looking at everything. There're no bells ringing and no tests, which means I can just listen to the stories. I go into a classroom, follow along, do as I'm told, and talk to no one. They tell stories, sing songs, talk about Jesus, say prayers. When Christmas is coming, they never talk about Santa Claus. They talk about Mary and Joseph and the Holy Ghost and the donkey, Bethlehem, the star, no room at the inn, angels, shepherds, the baby in a manger, the Three Wise Men, and we sing songs while one of the Sunday school ladies plays the piano.

After the singing, we sit around a table and the teacher will read us a story from the Bible, then ask what we think the story means. Usually, the only one who has anything to say about it is a hunchbacked girl who comes in some-times, and who seems to know all the Bible stories and the answers to all the questions about Cain and Abel, about the other brothers, Jacob and Esau, about Joseph and the coat of many colors, and how Joseph's jealous brothers sold him into slavery because his father liked him best.

It seems that God likes to have favorites and is always telling people that he favors this one or that one. God is in there talking with them all the time, telling them to kill this one or that one. And then there's the Devil, who used to be God's favorite but now is always jealous of the human favorites, really mad, and tries to ruin things for everyone.

But God told Abraham to kill his own little boy! And Abraham and the little boy just believed and went along with this! And that was somehow a good thing! But then God stopped Abraham, saying that he didn't have to kill the boy after all, but now he would be God's favorite "chosen one" and would now have everything as far as his eye could see.

Maybe I am not so eager for God to talk to me after all.

Maybe Daddy doesn't want God talking about who's the favorite either.

Usually, the teacher says the stories mean something about "believing in God," or about "sacrifice," or "being good," which makes me think it must be true that I am actually not very good at all. And maybe I don't want to be as good as all that.

Lately, the teachers have been telling us about Easter, about Jesus and the twelve disciples, the Last Supper, lots of miracles, the stone rolling away, doubting Thomas. I don't get it.

Once in a while, the older one of the teachers says something interesting. She doesn't speak up much, but smiles to herself and seems nice. This week, she said something I find myself thinking about and trying to imagine.

She said how every person feels the same way you do inside their head. Even though they may look different, dress different, act different, they look out of their eyes the same as you do. They want what they want, the same way you do. And if you look at any other person in a certain way, you will be able to realize that even though they appear to be different, they are actually just the same as you. She said how this is really the main thing that Jesus wanted us to know.

But she's the only one who says that.

Then they tell again how they put poor Jesus on the cross, and how Jesus was "The Lamb of God," but then later, of course, "He rose from the dead."

The Sunday school lady has been telling us about the mean Romans laughing at poor bleeding Jesus, his crown of thorns, and the nails right through his hands and feet!

Then suddenly, the one-sided, limping hunchbacked girl comes in the door, late. She usually comes in late. There's this long silence. The teacher and all the kids at our table turn to stare, then turn all eyes away from the way she walks in, from the way she carefully sits sideways on a chair at our table.

She sits on one side and then hangs the longer leg down in a way that I can never look at long enough to figure out the twist, and the way the whole thing works. But she has definitely figured out ways of doing things.

Then that hunchbacked girl speaks up. She always speaks up. While she's speaking up, it's okay to look at her, so I take this opportunity to study her face, which is kind of pretty in a thin, pale ivory, yellowish, blue-shadowed way. Around her green eyes you can see a pulse beat. She seems old but could be any age, hair long and thin, also ivory-pale.

She speaks up and answers a question about something in the Bible that we were talking about, but I don't hear it, because all I hear is the sound of her voice, so certain about something so long ago that no one remembers it; they only hear and read about it, and just all believe what they hear.

I know it's embarrassing to keep on, but I cannot stop watching her. I do not know how to get to know her. I know she goes to private school, but I see her here and other places around town from time to time.

She talks in this deep, flat voice and looks right at the teacher, as if they are two grown-ups together, even though she's only my age. Then when she looks at me, she keeps talking in the same way, as if to say, We're dealing with the real thing here. We are pretending nothing. As if to say she doesn't care who you are or what you think.

And she doesn't seem to care that people are looking at her all the time.

It's the same way Nathan talked that first time I saw him, and it's the same way that little girl in the movie talked when she said there was no Santa Claus. Could this hunchback girl believe in Santa Claus? I'd bet not.

I'd like to find out what she knows about it. But I'm a little bit afraid of her. Everyone seems afraid of her, but she is afraid of no one. The way she talks is as if she knows she's one of God's favorites. How does she know that? How did she get to be the way she is?

I sat behind her one day during the singing and was able to look and look at her twisted body and the way she was sitting on her chair, with one long thin leg hanging down, but I still could not figure out the twist. I've heard other kids call her a "freak." I wonder if she hurts like Daddy hurts, all the time.

One day, I tried to scrunch myself up on one side and walk the way that girl walks, not sure if I was doing it right, but I wanted to do a lot more of it, for some reason, not to be clock-struck crooked and hunchbacked like that forever, and not having to walk the way that girl has to walk—the naked struggle of the one-sided, broken lope she moves with across a room, through the halls, down the sidewalk, just out there in the bright sunlit world with everybody seeing it so plain! Especially not that! But just for an hour or a day, maybe, just to feel what it's like on the inside of that girl's crooked body, like a suit I could still take off if I wanted to.

She can never take it off—that twisted suit of iron she

has to wear for the rest of her life, a life changed by that one thing, and everyone can look right at her and see it.

Could it have been polio? Because once in a while somebody gets polio, and people worry about polio and talk about polio. Or an accident? Does she think it was somehow her own fault?

At Sunday school, women still tell over and over the Bible stories about jealous brothers and crazy fathers who are God's favorites, always fighting about being God's favorites, and stories about people being talked to and punished and even killed by these angels that suddenly appear and do things you would never have expected.

I wonder if that hunchback girl knows the reason for this. I wonder what it's like at her house. I wonder if she has friends and who are her friends? I wish I could get to know her and ask her some things. Because I have a feeling that hunchback girl might know everything.

Caveman

It's almost time for Christmas again when I see Daddy sitting by the fireplace in his chair, reading the paper. I go in to sit by the fire with him.

It's a big hot fire, logs piled up, flames licking up around the logs, looking to me like people sitting around a table hotly talking and gesturing, each in his place around the table, exactly as if the flames were all of us sitting around Nana's dining room table at Thanksgiving, when Daddy and Uncle Ted kept arguing about something that seemed to start from nowhere and get bigger fast, and all the women kept trying to shush them. But they would not shush.

There was this moment of a long silence right after Daddy'd said something like "We're just as smart as they are, and without all the horseshit. It's having the will to do it."

Which was right after Uncle Ted had said something like "But they have the best engineers in the country up there, and all you have is your old tank mechanic army pal who never even went to college."

In that moment of silence, everyone stopped talking and looked at Nana, especially Mama, who looked like something was hurting her feelings and maybe Nana could fix it.

Daddy was looking around and turning red.

Then Nana said, "Oh, Dick, you're always getting on some crazy idea. Maybe you're not as smart as you think you are."

Daddy looked like he'd been slapped in the face.

Uncle Ted smiled, saying, "Those guys know what they are doing up there."

"That is just plain stupid," said Daddy.

"Oh, Dick . . ." Mama said.

Then everybody talked at once; "Settle down now!" and "You don't have to get ugly!" and "Who do you think you are talking like that?"

Then Daddy said, "What do you think, Dad?"

Then there was an even longer silence, in which everybody turned to look at GranDad at the other end of the table, to see what GranDad would say.

GranDad kept looking down and talking about the roast beef being rare enough, while everyone kept waiting for him. I looked around at each one. Each one was looking at Daddy and at GranDad.

Then Uncle Ted and Aunt Celeste looked at each other.

Then GranDad glanced at Nana.

Then Nana said, "Is this necessary?"

Finally, GranDad said what it was he had to say. He went ahead and said, "Well, that's probably true. If it could be done, they would have already done it by now."

Then Uncle Ted smiled and sat back.

And then Daddy looked like he might cry, and he

jumped up, grabbed his cane, knocked over his chair, and clump-CLUMPed away from the table, stomping off into another room far away in the big house as fast as he could, everyone shouting after him, "Dick, Dick, Dick, Dick, don't be that way!"

My arms and legs prickled with fear of Daddy and with fear for Daddy when all this happened. I wished I understood all this. I kept thinking, *Compound fracture!*

But then, and here's the thing: *Surprise!* Daddy came back! He turned around out there and walked right back into the dining room, where we were all sitting and looking up at him, and he stood and looked back at each one of us, even at Nana and GranDad, and he smiled!

And he said, "Well, it doesn't matter, because I already know what I'm going to do."

And then he went back out onto the back porch for a smoke as Ross and Elise cleared the table for dessert. Pumpkin pie!

I LOOK OVER AT HIM, and now he's also staring into the fire.

"Daddy," I say, "will you read me the funnies?"

But he just hands me the comics section, and I lie on the floor to look at it. I can read most of Li'l Abner and of Alley-Oop. I ask Daddy why Alley-Oop dresses like that and looks like that and carries a club and has a dinosaur for a friend.

Daddy says, "Because Alley Oop is a caveman. A caveman had no house, no car, no anything like we have. Even no books to tell him things. No one knew anything. A caveman had to start from scratch, make it all up for himself. He wasn't as lucky as we are, having so much that's been given to us. Just look around, kid, at all that's been given to us. Many generations created all that has been given to us. We should remember to be grateful. It wasn't always there. A caveman had to make up everything in his world for the very first time."

Then Daddy goes to the bookcase and brings out volume one of *The Book of Knowledge,* which he says is for me to use anytime I want, and he sits right next to me, puts his arm around me, his face close to mine, until I smell the lotion on his slicked-back hair, his alcohol and tobacco breath, his voice low and close, and he shows me how to use the index, the table of contents, the different volumes, everything. He shows me how to look things up—dinosaurs, and cavemen. I can read almost all the words now.

Then he goes back to his paper and to himself, and I sit on the floor at Daddy's feet and read books.

FOR DINNER, WE HAVE SALMON CROQUETTES and mixed vegetables and, after that, pistachio ice cream, my favorite. And no one fights at the table the whole time.

After dinner, I go out in the backyard and look up at the full moon. It's funny about the moon, how you can look and look at it, thinking, *Is that a full moon?* or *Is it a full moon now?*

But when it actually is a full moon, there are no questions. You just know it.

There it is, looking directly at me, and I am looking directly at it—there is nothing between the two of us—the moon up there so far away, and small lone creature me, just standing out here on the Earth's surface.

The air is chilly. It's almost Christmas again on our green little Earth, and we are whirling through the cold machine of the universe tick-tocking around regardless of our feelings about it.

I'm alone out here, but I don't feel sad. Looking that distant thing in the face, I begin to sense the Girl coming back to say how I have to be brave—brave enough to stand out here alone and just look at what all this truly is, and to dare to live a human caveman life in the face of it.

Skaters

All the way downtown to the Adolphus Hotel in the car, Mama and Daddy argue about how he has to make up with Uncle Ted.

And Daddy keeps saying, "How can I?"

Christmas is coming again. When it's only two weeks away, GranDad takes our whole family downtown to the Adolphus for a fancy dinner and a show. It's in a big room with lots of red, black, and gold. There are white tablecloths. Red velvet curtains are hanging here and there.

We sit in the center of the room at long tables right in front of the small stage. Everyone is dressed up. I get to sit with the grown-ups this time. Oliver sits with the grown-ups, too, and I try to pretend he's not there.

When we arrive, I see Daddy and Uncle Ted speak, but they don't look at each other or sit together or talk. Mama and Aunt Celeste go to powder their noses. I sit next to Granny and Papaw.

Waiters whisk around with trays of drinks, and I have a Shirley Temple, like all the other kids.

The band plays and grown-ups get up and dance. Granny wants me to dance with her, but Papaw grabs me, and Annie jumps up and gets to dance with Granny.

A blond woman sings while people talk and eat. I hear GranDad saying to Daddy, "You'll have to go out on your own."

Aunt Meg and Uncle R.E. get up to dance. Aunt Celeste and Uncle Ted get up to dance. They all know how to whirl around cleverly and with studied grace. Daddy starts dancing with Mama but then leaves after the first dance and goes out to the lobby, where you can see him walking around, staying away from everyone.

Mama goes and talks to Daddy. She looks unhappy. He stays out in the lobby and smokes.

Waiters hurry in all at once, carrying trays, also in a dance of their own, swooping the plates in front of each person, many plates, many courses, piles of food, shrimp cocktails and prime rib on dishes with gold rims, blood on the plate. Daddy comes in and sits at the table with us.

Everyone has bland little smiles on their faces. Nana doesn't feel well. But she and Granny watch their grand-children and laugh at the funny things children do. Mama and Aunt Celeste seem to have things to talk about. The cousins fight, and I'm glad I don't have to sit with them. After the first course, Granny comes over, sloshing her drink in her perfectly manicured hand, and tells me how her cousin in vaudeville told her she could be a big star if she would move up to New York, but she never could do it. Papaw starts whistling his warning whistle behind us. He's always doing that, issuing warnings with that certain whistle. Mama rolls her eyes when she hears it, and keeps talking to Aunt Celeste. Mama's smiling, but it's not a happy smile. How can she look happy when she looked so unhappy in the car all the way downtown?

When it's time for dessert, GranDad goes around to all the cousins, saying, "Watch this! Watch this!" Then, amazingly, a small stage rolls out like a drawer from beneath the bandstand, and this is covered with sparkling ice.

The next thing you know, out come six young women in short skirts, cowboy hats, short cowboy boots attached to ice skates, lots of tassels and fringe, and they skate dazzlingly around and around on the small ice stage in tight formation, while everyone claps and laughs and is so surprised at the way they can do that. All of the skaters are young and pretty and have big smiles, as if there are no problems at all, and they've decided to be happy and have fun for the dance.

The skaters link arms and high-kick. They hold one another's waists and skate around in a line, then in circles, spraying icy mist into the audience. They jump and dip and twirl together, exchanging positions, some dropping out, then coming back, going in and out alternately and together, the way all things are revolving around and affecting each other, doing first one trick and then another, one dance and then another. Everyone is dazzled by their formation and grace. We all have wide eyes, openmouthed smiles of amazement. I cannot take my eyes off of the way these skaters are doing such an excellent job of being beautiful and smart and amazing in this small square space and time they have been given.

When the skaters take their bows and file away, and

the little drawer of ice rolls back to hide again beneath the bandstand, and the band starts up again, small but big-band dance band–style, Daddy stands away from the table, smoking a cigarette.

Elegant Aunt Celeste goes over to talk to the cousins. Beautiful Mama's sitting alone, and it seems to me there's a sadness behind the smile on her face. She seems small. I move over and sit in an empty chair beside her.

"Mama?" I say.

"Yes," she says, and her voice is flat.

"Mama, there's not really a Santa Claus, is there?"

"No," she says. "There's not."

Then I reach over and put my arm around Mama.

And she lets me do it.

The Bullfrog

They came with Shasta daisies in masses, so the flag-stone patio would be more "natural" in the photo-graphs, they said. From my color-coordinated Early American bedroom, banished, pouting, crying, dream-ing runaway dreams, after being spanked for refusing to clean the blue protozoa-shaped swimming pool, I could hear my father hurl his ginger ale across the kitchen, shouting that *House Beautiful* could goddamn well pho-tograph it the way it was, instead of the way some fag New York photographer thought it ought to look! And next my mother would, of course, come upstairs, mad at me for getting my father upset in the first place, like he really was after that last spanking, since I was about as big as a grown-up by this time, which was why I was being banished for not apologizing, for reacting to being ordered to do things in such a tone, as if I were some low slime barely making it across the Earth's surface, and just to do his swimming-pool, fancy-house bidding.

And you know what? I was glad he was upset.

Not that cleaning the swimming pool wasn't a job that I sort of liked—slowly, slowly skimming the leaves and then slowly, even more slowly, sweeping the underwater,

black-segmented, tightly wound-up doodlebugs, swirling them just right to swim-dance in whirlpool circles
around and around, down and down into the deep blue,
into the gently pulling-down drain—seemingly, at least,
of their own accord.

From my bedroom picture window, I could look across
the rolling St. Augustine grass, where they were bringing the daisies, and bringing the daisies, and arrang-
ing the daisies here and there, and my father was out
there pacing up and down, showing them at least where
to place the "goddamn daisies." And I could see all the
goings-on out there, just like a movie—the swimming
pool embedded in the lawn like a big sparkling jewel
in a navel, and my father and all the men hurrying and
scurrying back and forth, the short sleeves of their summer white sports shirts sticking out like little wings, and
the photographer and my mother pointing and talking
up on the patio, shading their eyes and sometimes pat-
ting the heads of the squirming matching brindle box-
ers pushing against their legs, red tongues lolling out of
their black-as-tar-baby, foo dog–grinning mouths.

The truth is that I wanted to be out there teasing, running with the dogs, or seeing how far to lean over the pool,
moving the skimmer in slow motion to trap one more
leaf, fencing around and around, until the whole water
surface seemed to vanish into floating sparkles, dazzling
the eye that looked now into the mysterious undulating shadow blue pool floor, along which I'd then slowly
scoot the long-handled brush, firmly feeling along every
curving surface, insinuating gradually so as not to stir

up the whole pool at once, but persuading, inducing bits of leaves and dirt, a few snails, and hundreds and hundreds of doodlebugs to rise up, whirling and swirling in dozens of undulations from each brushstroke, circle after circle down into the deeper blue at the inevitable drain at the deepest center at the deepest part of the pool—down where my sisters and I played mermaids, transformed underwater into lithe fish creatures, never surfacing, our seaweed hair writhing—not covered by the rubber caps we really had to wear to keep the overtreated (our eyes red all summer) pool from being dirty and disgusting, and like some low somebodies might have in their pool. But then sometimes we would all three be Esther Williamses, endlessly pursued by Latin men, only having to hold in our stomachs real hard, take on and off those bathing caps, and backstroke and sidestoke up and down the pool a lot, just as in the movies they would take us to see—even before we had to move to this fancy house—on Thursdays, the maid's day off, after having gone either to the country club for the family buffet or to El Chico's for lessons in restaurant manners, and for secret flirtings with a particular black-eyed waiter.

But even though I wanted to be out there, saying "Oh well" and cleaning the pool anyway, how could I give in now to Daddy's world's-worst-gloater victory smirks? I knew he'd look at me as if to say, "So, you finally saw it my way." Or else: "And these are all the reasons why I am right." Or even: "I'm acting humble, but I win again and can barely keep a straight face about it."

So I stayed in my room, watching through the picture

window, the daisy placement–frenzy movie, hearing the "Now that's what I call music" big-band sounds piped all over—even outside and even in my room—until I put on my own 45 records and had to keep turning them up louder and louder. And then I saw him out there, hearing it, and getting that eager, *Aha!,* furious look, wheeling around to charge the house and then my room, yelling about "trashy nigger music"—music like the kind of kids that would have the nerve to drive up in a car to my father's fancy house, yelling, "Hey, Let's go swimming!" would play.

But I knew that if I did hang around with those kids, he might just go crazy again, the way I had seen and heard him go crazy before, with drinking and breaking things, and going out with guns in the night, and then even being forced and tied and carried away with a crash and a cry that I cannot forget, and with Mama saying, "What are you doing up?" as if something was my fault. And then Daddy coming back after months, and being bathrobe-sad in the house for more months. So I was really a chicken about having those kids as my friends, worrying whether they'd drink beer or get hair or grass in the pool—so it was hopeless probably. And then he'd say, "How could you be friends with those people?" and, "How could you listen to what isn't even music?" and, "If you don't change your tune, you'll find yourself on your own out on the street someday!"

So then my mother would come in again for a talking-to, asking, "Why can't you just humor him instead of, just like him, always having to stir up some kind of big upset?"

"Why can't we just be happy?" she would say, looking at me. And I'd glare at the floor and hide under my pillow my secret paperback called *Tomboy,* with the bulging yellow sweater on the cover, who always gets in trouble with the leader of the gang, who's always threatening to tie people up and burn them with cigarettes, and who's secretly her boyfriend, but neither one of them knows it. I wouldn't say much, and Mama would say that maybe I could think about it while they were out for the evening.

But I knew I wouldn't think about it, but would wait until they had gone to their dinner party at some other house ready to be photographed for *House Beautiful.* I'd be baby-sitting and waiting until dark—with all the Shasta daisies white ghosts of flowers in the dark—to go out and turn on the pool light, to find there a giant golden spotted bullfrog come up from the creek where he used to swim flat out for miles, but now he was trapped in the glowing, undulating, bluer-than-blue pool, powerful legs pumping and stretching to coast the blue width and length, pushing off from one side and then the other, from one end and then the other, stirring the whole pool and all the leaves and doodlebugs into whirlpools on all sides as he repeatedly, frantically, swam, back and forth and up and down, with no place to get a leg up, banging back and forth—that bullfrog, leapfrog, frog in the throat—pushing off the deep end, then the shallow, then the deep, then the shallow, ranging the shape and size of the pool, being the shape and size of the pool, forgetting that there was ever anything else but the shape and size of the pool.

Acknowledgments

My thanks go to Dawn Raffel, Erika Goldman, Kris Elliott King, Rick Whitaker, Lisa Wohl, Sheila Kohler, Victoria Redel, Campbell Geeslin, Nancy Allen, Richard Omar, June Roth, Maria Gabriele Baker, Molly Elliott, Gordon Lish, and others who have read whole or parts of this material, given encouragement and feedback, and listened to my whining over many years. I am forever in their debt.

BELLEVUE LITERARY PRESS is devoted to publishing literary fiction and nonfiction at the intersection of the arts and sciences because we believe that science and the humanities are natural companions for understanding the human experience. With each book we publish, our goal is to foster a rich, interdisciplinary dialogue that will forge new tools for thinking and engaging with the world.

To support our press and its mission, and for our full catalogue of published titles, please visit us at blpress.org.

BELLEVUE LITERARY PRESS
New York